the MiRROR
of
fiRe and dReaMinG

Award-winning author and poet, Chitra Banerjee Divakaruni is widely known for her novels, *Sister of My Heart, The Mistress of Spices, The Vine of Desire* and *Queen of Dreams.* Translated into 11 languages, including Dutch, Hebrew and Japanese, her other writings include two prize-winning short story collections, two volumes of poetry, and her novels for young children. Among the awards and citations she has are the O. Henry Prize, two Pushcart Prizes, and the American Book Award. Born in India, she currently lives in Texas where she teaches creative writing at the University of Houston.

the MIRROR
of
fire and dreaming

THE BROTHERHOOD OF THE CONCH: BOOK II

CHITRA BANERJEE DIVAKARUNI

IndiaInk
ROLI BOOKS

*India*Ink

First published by Roaring Brook Press, USA, 2005

First published in India in 2007
*India*Ink
An imprint of
Roli Books Pvt. Ltd.
M-75, G.K. II Market
New Delhi 110 048
Phones: ++91 (011) 2921 2271, 2921 2782
2921 0886, Fax: ++91 (011) 2921 7185
E-mail: roli@vsnl.com; Website: rolibooks.com
Also at
Bangalore, Mumbai, Varanasi, Agra, Kolkata, Jaipur

Cover Design: Suchita Agarwal
Page Layout: Narendra Shahi

ISBN: 81-86939-34-2

Price: Rs 295/-

Typeset in AGaramond by Roli Books Pvt. Ltd. and
printed at Anubha Printers, Noida (U.P.)

Contents

one

Anand's Troubles

It was a beautiful day in the Silver Valley. The warm air, carrying the scent of a flower Anand did not know, felt like springtime on his skin. But he had only to glance at the icy peaks that surrounded the valley, glinting coldly in the clear mountain air, to remember that cruel winter shrouded the world outside. He looked down at his sun-warmed arms, thinking, *this must be what magic is!* Was it really going to be part of his life now? The thought made him feel a little dizzy.

When he had awakened early this morning, for a moment he hadn't known where he was. Then he'd looked around him in the dawn-light beginning to seep through the window, a pale, misty pink, and seen the boys sleeping on their pallets. With a quickened heartbeat, he had remembered. He was in Purav, the sleeping hall located at the eastern edge of the village where the Brotherhood lived. Master Abhaydatta had brought him there last night.

'You'll be living here with the other new apprentices,' the old healer had said. 'You'll spend much of your day with them, doing chores and taking lessons.' He'd gently pushed the reluctant Anand toward one of the unoccupied pallets. 'Settle in. Tomorrow's a big day for you, the day you start your study of magic.'

Now, dressed in their yellow tunics, the apprentices followed Giridatta, the healer in charge of this morning's lessons, along a narrow path that ran between two fields of bright green rice plants. Beyond these were fields of a darker green. Anand guessed that vegetables were grown here. Further away, he could see the mango and guava orchards, the green of the trees speckled with orange and golden fruit. And further yet, though he couldn't see them, he knew there were gardens where herbs and flowers with special properties were grown. Apprentices were only allowed there – and other places of power – when accompanied by a master healer.

'Let's make use of this fine weather and hold our class outdoors, shall we?' Giridatta had said as he strode down the path, staff in hand, his shaved head glinting in sunlight, his white robes swishing energetically. The remark had surprised Anand. Ever since he'd arrived in the Silver Valley a week ago, the weather had been bright and mild, and he had surmised that the weather-masters always kept it this way.

The apprentices joked and laughed as they hurried to keep up with Giridatta. From remarks they let fall, Anand understood that he was one of their favourite teachers, younger and less strict than some of the other healers. He did not mind if they had a bit of fun before the lessons began. Anand listened to their chatter attentively. He was intrigued by the things they talked about: the spell they learned yesterday, in Mohandatta's class, to make the body weightless, or the sending-off ceremony for a senior apprentice who was going to Tibet to live with another community of healers who specialized in the telling of past lives.

He longed to feel part of the group, but he was too shy to elbow his way into a conversation. And while the apprentices were not unfriendly and answered whenever he asked a question, they rarely talked to him of their own accord. Perhaps, Anand thought, they were awed by the fact that he was Keeper of the Conch, the most powerful and sacred object in the valley, from which the healers drew their power. He didn't blame them. He himself felt giddy with awe and disbelief when he thought of it – and of the adventures that had landed him in this place, so different from the dingy shack in the Kolkata slums where he once lived that it seemed impossible that the two could belong to the same world.

These adventures seemed too amazing to be true – how he had agreed to help the healer Abhaydatta return the stolen conch to its rightful location, how Nisha the sweeper girl had joined their quest, how they had been pursued by the enraged sorcerer Surabhanu, who used all his black arts to try and regain the conch. How in a cave in the mountains Abhaydatta had fallen, leaving Anand with the responsibility of carrying the conch to safety. Some nights, Anand still had nightmares about the obstacles he and Nisha had to face as they made their way towards the Silver Valley – the bitter, freezing cold; the gibbering apes, Surabhanu's servants, who had captured them; the guardian in the river that had almost drowned them; the avalanche of rocks that had broken Nisha's leg in a narrow mountain pass; the giant red snake with its seductive, hissing voice. He would awake sweating with fear, his leg tingling as though it had been grasped by a tentacle a moment ago. Even now, walking in warm sunlight, the memories sent a shiver through him.

But it's all over now, he said firmly to himself, tucking his unruly black hair behind his ears and straightening his yellow tunic, his fingers lingering for a moment on the small embroidered conch on his chest that marked him as the Keeper. *The conch is back where it should be in the Crystal Hall, Abhaydatta's himself again, and Nisha and I have been accepted into the society of healers.*

A current of excitement surged through him at the thought. All his life he had believed in magic, had felt its tantalizing presence just beyond his grasp. He'd had to keep this belief hidden deep in his heart because no one he knew – not even his mother whom he loved so dearly and missed so profoundly – would have understood it. Now magic surrounded him at every step!

'Anand!' he heard Giridatta call. 'We're waiting for you.'

With a start Anand realized that the rest of the boys were already seated in a circle around the healer, in the shadow of a krishna chura tree filled with flame-red blossoms. A couple of the boys glanced at him and snickered. His face hot, Anand sat down quickly, wishing he could be invisible. But as Giridatta began the lesson, fascination overcame his embarrassment.

'Today we'll learn about pain,' Giridatta was saying. 'As healers we believe in removing pain, whenever possible, from those who come to us. But that's not what I'm talking about. Others will teach you those arts.

'I'm talking about your own pain, and how you must deal with it. It's something your enemies can use to bend you to their wills, or to force you into the wrong choices. When pain overcomes us, mental clarity is lost, and we're unable to use even the simplest magical skills we've learned. Therefore, as healers you must learn to control pain, both physical and mental. We'll start today with physical pain, as it is less complicated.'

Giridatta asked the boys to hold out their right hands in front of them. 'You all know the importance of will power in enduring pain. But will power can take you only so far. In today's class, you'll learn a different technique.' He raised his own hand and Anand felt a moment of searing heat, as though he'd held his palm over a flame.

'You felt that, didn't you?' said Giridatta. 'I'm going to bring it back again, and when I do, I want you to go inside and see the pain. That's the first step to conquering it.'

The burning was back in Anand's hand. He gave a gasp and looked around at his fellow-students. Some had their eyes tightly shut. Some were gazing down, biting their lips. He didn't know what the healer meant by *going inside*, or *seeing* the pain. Though he felt the pain throbbing in his arm he saw nothing except what was around him.

Suddenly one of the boys cried out, 'I see it. It's like a red wave about to crash over me.'

'Mine is blue,' another boy gasped, 'like fog.'

Others described their pain as a rain of needles, or a fire blazing around them.

'Good,' Giridatta nodded. 'Now each of you must send out a mental force to counter that pain. If your pain is like a wave, you could, for example, construct a dam to block it, or a ship so you could ride over it. To put out a fire, you might call up a waterfall or river. Does everyone understand?'

The boys nodded. Their faces were still clenched, but Anand could see that their attention was drawn inward, and that this had removed them from their pain. How did they do it? Try as he might, he couldn't visualize his pain, let alone move away from it. It burned up and down his arm, intensifying until he couldn't bear it any longer. His skin felt as though it had turned into a mass of blisters. A groan burst from his lips.

'Anand, focus your attention inside yourself!' Giridatta called out. His brow was creased – Anand couldn't tell if it was because he was puzzled, or because he was annoyed. 'Try to travel inwards, into the vast space of the heart. That's where you'll find your pain.' But the pain slammed into Anand, wrenching his body to the ground. He couldn't focus on anything else.

Giridatta waved his hand and the pain disappeared. Anand hung his head, ashamed at having failed the very first task his teacher had set him. But Giridatta merely said, in a patient voice, 'You mustn't focus on the pain. By doing so, you give it additional power. Don't blame yourself for what you couldn't do. It takes practice to be able to see what is invisible to the physical eye. The other boys have been working on their skills for many weeks now, and it's only your first day.'

Anand held his breath, hoping Giridatta would say something more, perhaps something like, *Don't worry. The skill will certainly come to you as well.* But Giridatta moved on to another student and began to question him on his technique.

※⑳☙⁓

As Anand stood in line in the lunch hall, Nisha ran up to him, her face glowing with energy. In her short hair and yellow tunic, she looked almost the same as the other apprentices, though she had the unique distinction of being the only girl who had ever been allowed into the Brotherhood.

'You won't believe what a wonderful morning I've had!' she exclaimed. 'Our group went with Master Ayurdatta, the herbalist.

He took us into a secret garden – it's an amazing place. I don't even know where exactly it's located. To get to it, we had to be blindfolded. Then we all stood in a line holding hands, and Ayurdatta took the first apprentice by the hand and led him along a hidden pathway. After some time, he told us to take off our blindfolds – and we were inside the most beautiful garden! It was in a clearing inside a forest. There were trees all around, growing so thick we couldn't even see the path we'd used to get there. You won't believe how many kinds of plants grow there, and what you can do with them! Everything from curing illnesses of the body to cleansing a sick mind to protecting against evil spells. Today, Ayurdatta described the ten kinds of roots that are used to make Dashmul tea, a basic energy potion. Then he asked us to find them in the garden. I'm the only apprentice who was able to recognize every single root! Master Ayurdatta says I have a natural talent for herbalism, and that I might have to be moved to a more advanced group of students!' She gave a little jump of pleasure, then requested the server to please fill her plate with a double helping of everything. 'I'm starved,' she added. 'Aren't you? And doesn't the food smell delicious?'

The food did, indeed, smell delicious, and there was a great variety of it. Fragrant, steaming rice, soft wheat chapatis fresh from the tawa, still puffed up, rich stews of lentils in jewel colours, eggplant simmered in a spicy yogurt sauce, tiny potatoes fried whole and crisp, and tangy, emerald-green chutney made with mint and coriander. There was a whole tableful of desserts, too, from milky-white sandesh to pale green burfis made from pistachios to the orange squiggles of jalebis that spurted syrup when bitten into.

In the eating area, they sat on woven mats and placed their plates on long, low wooden tables. A bell rang for a moment of silent thanksgiving; then lunch began. The room filled with talk and laughter. From what Anand could overhear, it sounded as though everyone except him had had a great morning.

'You should eat up,' Nisha said, chewing diligently. 'I've been told that every meal isn't so lavish. A healer must be able to adapt to all kinds of situations with equal ease, so there'll be days when we eat only rice and dal, and other days when no meals are served and we have to forage in the fields and make do with what we can find.'

But Anand pushed around the food on his plate without enthusiasm. Nisha's account of her morning had depressed him further. Her success made him feel even more useless. He was afraid that any moment she'd notice his silence and ask him how his first lesson had gone. And then he'd have to confess that he'd been the worst student in the class, the dumbest one, the one who couldn't even understand what his teacher was talking about when he said, *go inside*.

Luckily, Nisha was too excited to be her usual keen-eyed self. She chattered on about her living quarters. She'd been put in a small house at the edge of the compound with a wise-woman who'd been brought up from the village to live with her. 'I have a room with a western window that looks out on the three-pronged peak! It smells beautiful – Mother Amita has put a bowl of sandalwood powder by my pallet. Remember how I used to sleep in a little box of a space under that street-shop in Kolkata? I can't believe I actually have a room of my own now! Isn't life marvellous?'

The bell rang, saving Anand from having to come up with a suitable reply. Nisha ran off to join her group, while he followed his fellow-apprentices to the vegetable field where they spent the afternoon weeding and watering. It was hard work, but Anand took comfort in the fact that here at least was something he was able to do. By the end of the afternoon, his muscles ached from carrying buckets of water from the well to the vegetable beds, but he was calmer, and ready to face his next teacher.

This was Vayudatta, the master in charge of the wind watchers. A short man of enormous girth, with a white beard that fell to the waist, he met the apprentices at the foot of the tower where the watchers spent much of their day – and night, too. Vayudatta explained as he instructed the boys to climb up to the third level.

'You're the new apprentice, aren't you?' he said to Anand, observing him keenly from under his bushy white eyebrows. Anand thought he was going to ask him a question, but after a moment Vayudatta only said, 'Watch out. It's always windy here.'

The tower was a curious structure, an uneven cylindrical shape that seemed to be made of polished wood, but when Anand got close to it, he realized it was actually a giant tree with a smooth, shiny trunk. The tree must have been very old, because its trunk was massive. Thirty boys, hands clasped, would not have been able to encompass it. A man-made staircase wound along the outside of the tree, which seemed to Anand to reach all the way up into the sky. The staircase looked rather flimsy and had only a narrow railing, which Anand gripped nervously as he climbed. With every step he took, the wind moaned around him, snatching at his tunic. The tree-tower had a number of platforms, woven from vines and branches. They were each on a different level and faced a different direction. On each a healer sat cross-legged, holding a thick book in his lap. From time to time, he would write something in the book.

'He's writing down what the winds are telling him,' explained Vayudatta as they climbed past a platform. 'There are many winds, as you know, and they come from different directions, bearing us news of the world. Later, the healers on the different platforms will compile their information and check it for contradictions – for often winds are shifty and mischievous, and it's easy to mishear them. Then they'll bring it to the council so that we may know what's going on outside, and what, if anything, we need to do about it.'

He led the apprentices out onto the third platform they came across. The young man who had been sitting there, writing in his palm leaf notebook, rose to his feet. Vayudatta clapped him on the shoulder. 'Still here, Raj-bhanu? Wasn't your watch over an hour ago?'

'It was, Master Vayudatta,' the young man said, bowing respectfully. 'But the winds are so fascinating, and they tell me so many tales about faraway places. Sometimes I can't bear to tear myself away from them.'

Vayudatta smiled indulgently. It was clear that he, too, loved the winds and was at ease among them high in the air, with his robes flapping like a great bird's wings. 'It looks as though you will soon be joining the ranks of the master wind-watchers, Raj-bhanu!' he told the young man, who smiled with pleasure. 'That'll be splendid!

There aren't enough of us.' To the boys, he explained, 'Most apprentices find our job too tedious and too demanding. It requires you to be alert at all times, even though you may have to wait for weeks before the winds bring you news of any importance. Come, sit down and we'll get started.'

The other apprentices moved sure-footedly across the platform, but Anand found himself hesitating as he stepped on the springy woven surface. He was afraid that his feet might go right through the loose webbing. As a result, the only spot left for him was uncomfortably close to the edge of the platform. There was no railing here, nothing to grab if he lost his balance and fell. He ventured a downward glance. The ground looked very far away. He lowered himself gingerly, putting out a nervous hand to clasp one of the vines that made up the floor. To his shock, it slithered under his hand – like a snake, he thought – and a green tendril shot out and wound itself around his wrist. He gave an involuntary yelp, causing the boy next to him to turn and stare.

Vayudatta smiled. 'Don't be alarmed, Anand. The watchtower tree senses your fear. It's trying to reassure you that it will not let you fall.'

But the thought of a live tree that could think and move and grab him made Anand feel anything but reassured. As soon as he could, he surreptitiously pulled his hand from the vine's grasp and then felt guilty for doing so.

'There are eight major winds and eighty-eight minor ones,' Vayudatta explained to him. 'As you study with me, you'll learn their names and characteristics, and how healers might make use of their powers. If you have a special aptitude in this area, like Raj-bhanu, who is one of our senior apprentices, you may train to become a wind-watcher. In addition to gathering news from the winds, master wind-watchers can control the force and direction of winds and use them to send messages. There are other things they do about which I cannot speak to you – they are secret. Each master develops a relationship with a special wind that brings him information and guidance. Sometimes the wind helps a healer to see things that are happening far away. But these take years of training

– and good fortune as well. Today we'll merely practice listening to the winds. We'll also try to see them.' He turned to the other apprentices. 'Who remembers what I said earlier about that?'

A boy raised his hand. 'Each wind has a colour which helps us determine its nature and how far it may be trusted. A warm coloured wind, in a shade of red or yellow, for example, is straightforward and will bring news that is clear. A wind shaded green or dark blue will tell the news as a riddle, and leave us to decipher its true meaning.'

Vayudatta nodded. 'Who can chant the spell to call the winds?'

A different boy stood up. In a high, sing-song voice, he recited,

From east and west, south and north,
Marut, wind spirit, I call you forth
From sky and earth, far and near,
Bring me the news I need to hear.

'You may start now,' the healer said.

The boys moved to the different areas of the platform of vines and sat very still, gazing out to the horizon. Some of them took out small notebooks from their tunics and began jotting down words. As though in response, the flurry of winds around the platform increased. Anand, too, stared out, but all he could see was what was happening in the valley below: healers conducting classes on the porches of buildings, server-apprentices stirring pots over the big, outdoor cook-fires behind the eating hall, cows grazing in the pastures, all diminished to miniature toys. It was interesting, but he knew this was not what he was supposed to be doing. But what exactly *was* he supposed to do? Wasn't Vayudatta going to give him instructions? Anand's heart sank as he wondered if all his classes were going to be like this, with the teachers expecting him to intuitively understand and wordlessly follow what they were saying. For the first time, doubt gnawed at him. *What if I don't have the gifts these other apprentices have? What if I don't belong here?*

He jumped as he felt something on his shoulder. But it was only Raj-bhanu, touching him with a gentle hand. 'Don't look at things,' the senior apprentice whispered. 'Unfocus your eyes and gaze on the air.'

Anand tried to do as he instructed, but he wasn't certain he was doing it correctly. Around him, boys were calling out what they saw.

'The wind I see is yellow and stately and comes from the south,' one apprentice said. 'Perhaps it's the Moloy wind – I'm not sure. It tells me that spring is on its way, that the lotuses on the Swarna Sarovar have started to bloom, and that herds of yaks are moving up from the valley where they wintered onto the mountain slopes.'

'I see a green wind, a minor one whose name I don't know,' another said. 'It whispered to me that there was a village fire in the southwest before it flitted away, but I don't think that is entirely true.' He looked towards Vayudatta for confirmation.

Vayudatta smiled. 'You're right to be doubtful. That was one of the mischievous gandharva winds. What it actually said is that there is a fair today in a southwestern village. I do believe it meant the village of Motipur. They often hold a camel fair around this time.'

Other boys spoke up about their experiences. Anand tried to shut their voices out. *Air, air,* he said to himself. *Gaze at air.* But he didn't know how to do it. He saw only the blue sky with fleecy clouds, and a few soaring hawks. He shut his eyes in despair. Soon Vayudatta would call on him, and he would have to confess, in front of the entire group, that he had failed once again.

Then he saw it against his closed eyelids. It appeared to be gray at first, but as it grew closer he saw it was black. Tornado-like, it spun toward him from the southeast, and as it came it whispered two words again and again. It was huge now, hanging above the watchtower tree. Any moment it would suck him into its black mouth.

Anand gasped and, with an effort, wrenched his eyes open. He was lying flat on his back at the very edge of the platform, and everyone was staring at him. He sneaked a look at the sky. It was a clear and benign blue.

'What happened?' he asked Vayudatta, who was helping him up.

'I was about to ask you the same thing,' the healer said. He looked concerned. 'You suddenly began moaning and pitched over.

You were trying to say something over and over, but none of us could understand you.'

The words came back to Anand. *Evil stirs.* That's what the black wind had said. But surely that couldn't be. Surely he had heard it wrong.

'Did you see something?' Vayudatta asked.

'I saw a wind, but only after I'd shut my eyes. It was black …'

He saw a quick glance pass between the healer and the senior apprentice.

'A black wind? Are you sure?' Vayudatta asked, his voice sharp. 'Did it speak to you?'

Anand hesitated. Around him the winds had died down and the sun, low in the sky, bathed the landscape in its gentle rays. In this peaceful setting the words he'd heard seemed even more of an anomaly, a mistake made by his untrained ears. But finally, because everyone was waiting, he reluctantly mumbled them.

'Evil stirs?' Vayudatta's bushy eyebrows met in a frown that made him look unexpectedly fierce. 'I haven't heard a wind-message of that kind in decades, not since …' He broke off and shook his head.

'We all know how easy it is to mishear such things,' Raj-bhanu interjected swiftly. 'Maybe it was something else the wind said. I remember making similar errors when I first began interpreting …'

'Maybe the wind had come through the valley of trees and was reporting what it saw there,' an apprentice ventured. 'Maybe it said *regal firs.*'

'Maybe it was addressing us as *noble sirs,*' someone else quipped.

'No, no,' said a third boy. 'I know what it said! It must have come from Motipur, where the camels have been brought for the fair. You know how quarrelsome camels can be. A bunch of them must have got into a fight. That's what the wind was telling us about. *Camel wars!*'

Everyone laughed. Anand tried to join them, but he did not feel much like laughing. He'd made a fool of himself again.

'That's enough for today,' Vayudatta said. 'You'd best be off to the Crystal Hall for evening assembly!' But as Anand followed the other apprentices down the ladder, he glanced back and saw that the healer was deep in conversation with Raj-bhanu. Their faces were grave in the failing light.

※◎※

The Crystal Hall was almost full by the time Anand's group reached it, and Anand had to sit all the way in the back. On another day, this would have disappointed him, as he loved to watch the conch glowing in its shrine at the very centre of the hall. But after the disasters of today's lessons, he wanted above all to avoid the conch. The conch had the ability to look into Anand's mind, and right now Anand didn't want to share his doubts and humiliations with it. What if it came to the conclusion that Anand's fears were correct, that he had no magical talent and thus didn't belong in the Silver Valley? Would it expose him as a fake and cause him to be sent away? Anand's heart clenched at the thought. He hunched lower on his mat. Perhaps if the conch didn't actually see him, it wouldn't think of him.

At dinner he saw Nisha waving excitedly to him from a table, but he pretended not to have noticed her. He couldn't bear to listen to her stories of success, or to share his own failures with her. He sat instead at one corner of a table filled with second year apprentices who chatted among themselves, paying him no attention. As soon as he could, he left and went to his sleeping hall, where he lay down on his pallet and pulled the sheet over his head. *Tomorrow will be better*, he said to himself as convincingly as he could. Tomorrow's lesson would be taught by Abhaydatta in the Hall of Seeing, Abhaydatta whom Anand knew and loved, whom Anand had helped. Surely he would teach Anand in the right way, explaining, helping, and leading him along, so that Anand could learn what he needed in order to remain in the Valley. *Rest, rest,* he ordered himself. *You must be alert so that you can perform well at tomorrow's lesson.* But for a long time he tossed and turned, and when he finally did fall asleep his dreams were filled with malevolent, whispering winds.

two

In the Hall of Seeing

The cold awoke Anand very early, even before the morning-call had sounded. Shivering, he opened the chest that sat at the foot of his bed and pulled out a rough-woven wool blanket and huddled under it, marvelling at how the weather had changed. The weather-masters must have decided that today was to be a challenge, something to toughen up the students in their care. Through the window, the sky was a stony gray, hung with the dark coils of rain-clouds. Anand wondered if there would be a storm. Did his chest contain a waterproof cloak, or was he supposed to put up stoically with a soaking? What if he fell ill as a result? But what he was really worrying about, underneath these flitting thoughts, was how the lesson with Abhaydatta would go, and what would happen if he failed once again.

Then it was time to start the day. Along with the other apprentices, he pulled on the heaviest kaftan and leggings that he could find, and put on a furred cap. At the bottom of the chest he did, indeed, discover a waterproof cloak, which he wrapped around himself thankfully as he made his way to breakfast. The freezing wind knifed at his face, making his eyes water. He was looking forward to a hot cup of aromatic tea, the kind they'd served yesterday, and maybe a spicy paratha stuffed with a potato filling, but when he got to the dining hall, there were only lukewarm bowls of rice-porridge and a basket holding shrivelled green apples. He let out a groan, then bit it off, startled, as the boy behind him jabbed him in the back.

'Quiet,' the boy, whose name Anand didn't know, hissed. 'Part of our training is to accept cheerfully whatever comes to us. If you get irritated, you'll be given even more difficult situations — and since you're in our group, so will we.' The boy picked up his bowl of porridge and gave Anand a knowing look. 'And it's no good pretending to be happy while you're upset inside,' he added. 'The healers can tell.'

Chewing on his apple, which was every bit as sour as he had expected, an abashed Anand mused over this. How did people accept unpleasant things cheerfully? And how could they make themselves happy when they were feeling irritated, or miserable and nervous, as he was right now? Such mental dexterity seemed as difficult to achieve as controlling physical pain or translating the wind's words, and he was afraid he'd be equally unskilled at it.

⁂

The Hall of Seeing, a low, round structure built out of intertwined trees, comforted Anand with its familiarity as he stood before it, for he had been here with Abhaydatta before. But when he followed his fellow apprentices inside, stepping through the doorway that was formed by two silver-barked trees that arched to meet overhead, a wave of bitter-sweet longing washed over him. This was the place where he'd last seen his family, shimmering against its magical walls. This was where he'd made his agonizing, fateful decision: to not return to his parents and his sister Meera; to remain, instead, in the valley so that he could develop his gifts and help the world. He'd asked Abhaydatta to use his skills to modify his family's memory so that they would no longer be sad at his absence, and Abhaydatta had done as he requested, wiping Anand from their minds.

But now, he thought, *it seems like I did it all for nothing. Because I don't seem to have any gifts. Did I make the wrong choice?*

'Anand!' Abhaydatta's voice broke into his doubts. 'Here you are!' The old healer stood in front of him with an especially welcoming smile, as though he could feel his hesitation. In the glow from the circular walls – blank at the moment – his white robe and beard glimmered gently, and his eyes were deep and kind. Looking into them, Anand felt a little better.

'Come,' Abhaydatta said, and laying a hand on Anand's shoulder, he led him to an unoccupied section of the wall. There were thick jute mats on the floor, and Anand sat down on one. Around him, other apprentices had already taken their places and were gazing with great attention on the wall-space in front of them, though Anand couldn't see anything there.

When Anand sat down, though, the segment of wall directly in front of him changed colour, turning from marigold-yellow to a pale violet, as though it had sensed his presence. But how could a wall do that?

'As some of you know already,' Abhaydatta said, 'though we live in this beautiful and untroubled valley high in the Himalayas, as healers we are deeply concerned with the rest of the world. We do our best to keep abreast of the news of the world, though we rarely interfere in it. We let natural calamities such as floods or earthquakes run their course. We realize that from time to time a civilization must come to an end – perhaps through a bloody war, or the rampage of disease. The world has her rhythms, both peaceful and violent. We know we must not upset her balance as she sways between pain and joy. We try, where possible, to bring comfort to those who suffer, but we intervene actively only when evil stirs.'

Anand tensed. Had he heard correctly? Had Abhaydatta just repeated the exact words the black wind had whispered to him yesterday? *Evil stirs.* Was this a coincidence, or was there a deeper meaning behind it? Perhaps he should tell Abhaydatta about what happened at the wind-tower? But what if Abhaydatta, too, thought he'd misheard? Worse, what if the healer concluded that Anand was making something up to hide the fact that he had no magical gifts? He decided to remain silent.

'In order to know what is happening in the world,' Abhaydatta said, 'healers must possess several kinds of powers. You know already of our brothers who listen to the winds. There are also brothers who read patterns in water or in the sky, and those who commune with other healers in distant places. Here, today, we will practise the skill of far-seeing. The healers who become adept at this are able, at will, to call up scenes from every corner of the world, even if they know nothing about the place they are visualizing. Such a gift is rare. At this time, we have in the Silver Valley, only three such masters. However, through effort and practice most of you will be able to learn enough of this skill to visualize places of which you have some knowledge, or places that you have been to, and see what is going on there.

'Today we will focus on something relatively easy, the Silver Valley itself, and try to see what is happening in its different parts. I want each of you to choose an area of the valley you know well. It will help if it is a place that you love or are attracted to, for emotions can create a powerful energy bond. Banish all other thoughts from your mind and visualize this place with all your attention. Sharpen your awareness until it is keener than the keenest knife. When you have created a clear mental picture of this place, hold your hands up to the wall, taking care to ensure that you do not touch it. Close your eyes, breathe deeply, and concentrate. If you do the exercise right, the place will appear on the wall in front of you, and you will be able to see exactly what is going on there. At the end of the class, each student will describe what he saw.'

The apprentices nodded, and several closed their eyes and slowed their breathing. Anand could tell they were calling up scenes onto their sections of wall. He could see the walls rippling with colour, although he could not see what was there. It seemed that only the person visualizing the scene was able to see it.

Anand decided to focus on the mango orchard he'd visited when he had newly arrived in the valley. He felt an uncomplicated fondness as he thought of it – it had been a peaceful place, filled with the laughter and camaraderie of the apprentices who worked together harmoniously as though they were one family – no, as though they were part of one body. Anand longed to feel that way, too, but would he ever manage it? He darted a glance at the boys around him. They were strangers to him, and he did not feel anything for them. The thought depressed him; he no longer wished to focus on the orchard.

The Crystal Hall would be a better choice. He had loved its beauty and elegance from the very first time he entered it: the ceiling that soared up like a song, the dome that was transparent so that at night stars shone through it; the hundred crystal pillars that changed colour with the day's passing, turning from gold at sunrise and white at noon to burnished orange in the evening; the small shrine in the centre that glowed with the power of the conch. Yes, that was really why he wanted to call up the Crystal Hall – he missed the conch and longed to see it again, even as he stayed away from it for fear of what it might discover about him.

He closed his eyes and held up his palms as Abhaydatta had instructed. Concentrating, he thought he felt heat radiating from the wall in front of him, but when he opened his eyes, the wall was blank and dark. Again he tried. Again, blankness. All around him, apprentices were calling up images, smiling or frowning intently as they focused on the scenes that appeared. In desperation he closed his eyes and held his breath. *Something! Let me connect with something!*

Then an idea came into his head, making his heart pound. He knew it was forbidden, but that made it all the more powerful. Perhaps he could call up his home on the wall, for just a few moments? He'd done it once before, with Abhaydatta's help. Maybe he could do it by himself this time? Hadn't the healer himself said that emotions created powerful bonds? The longing to see his parents and his sister, even though they no longer remembered him, leaped inside him like a lion. He loosened his hold on it and felt it take control. It pulled him through a dark, airless passage until his trapped breath burned inside him like embers. And then he was inside a room.

But it was not the room where he'd seen his family last. Nor was it the Crystal Hall, or any part of the Silver Valley. He was inside a hut – an old, damp mud-daubed structure, from the little that he could see. A fire had been lit in the centre of the earthen floor, inside a circle of oval stones. It threw long, flickering shadows onto the walls. The room was bare, and for a moment Anand thought it was empty.

Then he saw the woman. She was sitting in front of the fire, half veiled in a white cotton sari, chanting and rocking. When she raised her face, he saw that she was old but still beautiful. There were lines of worry between her eyebrows and tracks of tears on her cheeks. She glanced this way and that as if she could sense a presence, but it was clear that she wasn't able to see Anand. She stretched out her hand, feeling around her as one might in the dark. Her hand came close – and then it went right through Anand's body, as though he were a ghost. Frightened, he shut his eyes, trying to will himself back into the Hall of Seeing, wishing he hadn't disobeyed Abhaydatta. But when he opened his eyes, he was still in the hut, and the woman was speaking to him.

'Thank the Light that you are here,' she said, 'whoever you are. I've been trying to send out a message for so long, but each time it recoils upon me. I think he's put a net around me, around this village. My people disappear into the forest, and when they come back, they are changed. Often they don't remember who they are. Often they are cruel to their loved ones, or gaze around them vacantly. It has been this way ever since he arrived in our village and promised people money to go with him into the forest and dig for treasure. My own powers grow less every day, even as his increase. Help us! You must help us before it is too late ...'

'Who are you?' Anand cried. 'Who's the man you're talking about? And what's the name of your village?'

She must have heard him, because she was saying something. Her lips moved, but he couldn't hear the words. Did the net that she'd mentioned keep her words from him? She was fading, or perhaps it was he who was moving away. He reached out to hold

The Mirror of Fire and Dreaming

onto her so that he could ask her to repeat whatever she was trying to tell him, but an invisible force slammed into him, throwing him back. An image flashed against his eyes, then exploded, filling his head with pain. The woman disappeared. A blast of heat hit Anand's face, and he fell over into blackness.

≈≈◦≈≈

When he came to, he was in the Hall of Seeing, lying on the floor some distance from where he'd been sitting. He looked up into the faces of his fellow apprentices, crowded around him, curious and apprehensive.

'What happened?' Anand stammered.

'You suddenly toppled forward onto the wall,' one of the boys said. 'There was a flash of light and a loud noise, and then you went flying across the room.'

'What on earth did you call up on your seeing-space?' another asked.

Before Anand could think of a reply, he heard Abhaydatta's voice. 'Make way,' the healer said as he pushed past the apprentices. His face grim, he leaned and felt Anand's forehead, then stared at Anand's face till the boy looked away uneasily.

Abhaydatta turned to the other apprentices. 'The lesson is done for today,' he said, dismissing them with a gesture. They milled about for a bit, reluctant to leave. Anand could tell they were longing to ask the healer what had happened, but finally they obeyed. In the silence left behind, Abhaydatta said, 'Tell me.' His voice sounded harsh and forbidding to Anand's ears.

Anand sat up shakily. 'I saw a woman,' he said. 'She asked for help.'

Abhaydatta's brows drew together, and he seemed about to ask Anand how he came upon this woman when he was supposed to be visualizing a part of the Silver Valley. Anand's mouth grew dry. He knew he'd done something very wrong in trying to call up his family after having chosen to give them up. If Abhaydatta found out about that, surely Anand would be sent away from the Brotherhood in disgrace.

| 20 |

Fortunately, the healer was more concerned with his vision. 'Describe the woman,' he said, 'and everything else you saw.'

Thankfully, Anand complied. When he finished, the healer paced up and down the room, looking concerned. 'A village from which people are disappearing,' he said, 'and coming back changed in some disturbing way. This is troubling, indeed. Did she name the place?'

'I think she was trying to tell me that when she faded away. Then something exploded.'

'An explosion,' the healer mused. 'That is most strange, and worrisome, too. It indicates a contra-power – an evil one – so strong that its effects can reach even into this protected valley. Few entities in the entire magical realm have such a capability! But think again. Did you see anything else before the explosion occurred? A mental image, perhaps, that the woman was trying to pass on to you?'

'Yes, there was something ...' Anand tried hard to recall what he'd glimpsed before pain had filled his head. 'A lake that gleamed golden, and a forest. On the trees, large round leaves, thick and sturdy and dark green. I've seen those leaves somewhere ...'

'Where, Anand? Try to remember. You are the only link we have to this woman who badly needs our help.'

Anand forced his mind go back into his old life, painful though it was. *He was walking on a city street with his mother and sister, all three of them laughing as they ate fried onion pakoras from ...* 'Street vendors in Kolkata make little cups out of the leaves to hold their snacks,' he said.

'Shal leaves,' Abhaydatta said. 'They grow in many parts of the country, but particularly in the state of Bengal. The hut you described is typical of that region, too. But Bengal consists of hundreds of villages. We need to know more if we are to locate the woman and bring her aid before it is too late. I must call a council meeting. Perhaps the master geographer can help us solve this riddle.' He sighed and looked at Anand. 'I cannot understand why we didn't get her messages before this. Even yesterday one of our master seers scanned the walls for news of the world, and saw nothing. And if indeed there is a net around her, how did she manage to slip out of it – or was it you who slipped in?' He shook his head. 'Ah, mysteries. In the magical realm, no matter how much we know, there are always questions we cannot answer. But you'd best leave now – aren't there duties you have to perform? Someone told me that the shrine of the conch wasn't cleaned yesterday.'

Guiltily, Anand hurried to the door. But he was stopped at the entrance by the healer's voice.

'Anand,' the old man said, his face at once sympathetic yet stern. 'It is natural to long for what we are not supposed to have. But if we don't learn to control such desires, they may well destroy us.'

three

The Council Makes a Decision

Carrying a heavy bucket of soapy water and a handful of cleaning rags, Anand staggered into the Crystal Hall. He'd been afraid that the hall might be empty, but he was relieved to find a group of healers sitting around the shrine, meditating. With so many people around, the conch wouldn't be able to hold a conversation with him. I'll do my cleaning quickly and leave, he thought. And if I can just keep my mind away from what happened yesterday and today, the conch won't know how badly things have been going for me.

But he'd hardly dipped a rag into the bucket when a voice boomed inside his head. *So!* It said. *Been having too much fun to come and see your old friend, eh?*

Anand jumped, almost spilling soapy water on a meditating master healer. Preoccupied with his troubles, he'd forgotten that the conch could communicate with him without words. Until now, he'd seen it as a great benefit. Now, he wasn't so sure.

Sorry, he mumbled.

The conch coughed accusingly. *You should be. I'm so dusty I can hardly breathe.*

This was an exaggeration, since the conch was sealed inside the crystal shrine. Additionally, Anand suspected that it didn't need to breathe. Still, he knew he was in the wrong. No matter how many troubles he had, he shouldn't have neglected the conch. As its Keeper, that was his foremost duty – and in that, too, he had failed.

Biting his lip, he busied himself with cleaning the shrine.

That's your problem, the conch said. *You want to handle all your difficulties on your own. Did you ever think it might help if you discussed how you were feeling with someone?*

Startled, Anand raised his eyes to the conch. How much did it know?

I know as much as I wish to, said the conch. *And in your case, that is a great deal indeed. Foolish boy, do you think you're the only apprentice who feels confusion and doubt in the first few weeks, who misses his family and wonders if he made the right decision?*

But I've done everything wrong, Anand said. *All the other apprentices seem to be so good at what they're doing – even Nisha, and she hasn't been here any longer than I have.*

Each person's gift surfaces at its own pace, the conch said. *You cannot rush it. Be patient. Don't you know the story of Binata and the magical egg she broke open too soon, so the baby inside it was crippled for life?*

Anand nodded, abashed, but the conch shimmered encouragingly, with a soft, mother-of-pearl glow. *And you haven't done* everything *wrong. Didn't you hear the warning wind yesterday, and see the medicine-woman this morning?*

You know about the woman also? Anand asked, incredulous. *But how? It only just happened.* A thought struck him. *If you know this much, then you must also know who she is, and where she lives.*

The conch was pointedly silent, and Anand remembered what it had told him earlier: It was only allowed to help humans when they had exhausted every possibility of helping themselves.

All right, he said. *But at least you can tell me what you think the council is going to do about all this.*

He thought the conch would refuse to speak again. But to his surprise, it said, *They will send Abhaydatta to help her, because he is a master of remembrance and forgetting.*

Anand's nerves jangled with excitement. *He can't go alone,* he said. *He'll need an apprentice. He'll need me, like last time. And maybe Nisha.* What a wonderful opportunity this would be, to get away from all these lessons where he performed so poorly and do something worthwhile, something that he was good at – and in the company of the two people he liked most of all.

But the conch said nothing.

And you, too, of course, Anand added hastily. *If they'll let you go, that is.*

Still the conch said nothing.

Anxiety struck Anand. *He will want me, won't he?*

I hear the dinner bell, the conch said. *Go now, and remember what I said about being patient. Everything will become clear soon enough.*

<hr>

As soon as he entered the dining hall, Anand sensed a difference. The room wasn't cheerful and noisy in its usual way but heavy with the sense of something momentous about to happen. He noticed all the healers seated at a long table at the other end of the hall, and that too was different. The healers usually took their night meal in the chief healer's quarters, so that they could discuss the events of the day. All around Anand, apprentices were whispering excitedly. But every time Anand passed a table, the boys seated at it would fall silent and stare at him. His companions at the Hall of Seeing had obviously been talking about the morning's goings-on. The attention made him uncomfortable. He couldn't tell if the apprentices were eyeing him admiringly, or with suspicion. Luckily, while he was waiting in line, he caught sight of Nisha at a distant table.

'Now what have you been up to?' she asked. 'I heard that you conjured up a demon who flung you across the Hall of Seeing, and that your brains have been addled ever since!'

Anand was about to tell Nisha what had really happened when the bell rang three times. It was clearly a signal for silence, for all conversation around them ceased. Anand noticed the Chief Healer, Somdatta, standing on a dais in the front of the hall.

'There is trouble in the world,' he said. 'Someone has reached us with a call for help. The nature of the call indicates that dark magic is at work. As you know, we of the Brotherhood must respond to such a call.' He spoke in a soft voice, yet Anand could feel the authority radiating from him. Beneath that was concern and something else – was it uncertainty? But how could someone as wise and powerful as the chief healer be uncertain? Anand glanced at Nisha to see if she, too, sensed this, but she didn't seem to notice anything out of the ordinary.

Somdatta continued, 'The council has decided, after much thought, that because of his special powers, Master Abhaydatta would be the best person to lead this mission. I must apologize to him for sending him on another dangerous journey so soon after he returned from his previous one.'

Abhaydatta stood up, bowing formally. 'I am happy to be of service,' he said.

'We will not, however, send you alone,' said the chief healer. 'We would have preferred to send another master healer with you, but it is important that you travel undetected. The presence of two masters would change the power balance in the village where you are going. It will alert the enemy. Thus we may only allow you an apprentice.'

Anand felt dizzy with excitement and fear. It was now or never! He stood up and raised his hand.

The chief healer's brows drew together at this unexpected interruption. 'What is it you wish to say, boy?'

'Please, Master ... uh ...' In his nervousness Anand found that he'd forgotten the chief healer's name. 'Please, sir,' he stammered on, his voice wobbly with embarrassment, 'I would like to go with Master Abhaydatta on this journey.'

Whispers broke out all across the room. A few people stared in amazement. Others laughed. Anand's face burned, but he forced himself to keep standing.

'It is brave of you,' the chief healer said, his brow clearing. 'We appreciate the spirit behind the offer. However, we need someone who is more experienced, with greater skills than you have yet gathered ...'

'Please, sir, I helped him last time, and I knew even less then ...'

'That was a different situation,' the chief healer said. 'Abhaydatta was cut off from the Brotherhood at that time and could not contact us to send him help.' He held up his hand to silence Anand. 'We have already chosen him an apprentice, one of our best – '

'But ...' Anand persisted.

'Quiet, Anand!' It was Abhaydatta, and he spoke more sternly to Anand than he had ever before. 'One does not argue with the chief healer.'

Anand sat down, wishing he could sink through the floor. Abhaydatta had never spoken so severely to him, not even when Anand's mistakes had jeopardized his life.

'The council has decided that Raj-bhanu will accompany Master Abhaydatta,' the chief healer announced. Raj-bhanu, who was at a table in front with the senior apprentices, stood up. A wild wave of applause broke over the room, but Anand couldn't bring himself to clap.

'This is a great and unexpected honour,' Raj-bhanu said, sounding a trifle dazed. 'I will do my absolute best to help you, Master Abhaydatta, even to the point of death.'

Abhaydatta smiled. Jealousy seared Anand at the sweetness of that smile which was not directed at him. 'I know you will,' the healer replied. 'Meet me after dinner at the Hall of Seeing, so we may prepare for our departure tomorrow.'

The healers sat down, and people turned their attention to dinner.

'Food's really good tonight,' he heard one of the apprentices at his table say. 'Didn't expect that, after the gruel we got at lunchtime. Did you try that palak paneer?'

'It's delicious!' Nisha said, her mouth full. She'd taken an enormous helping of the creamy spinach curry on her plate. 'Want some?' she asked Anand, who was sitting silently, head bent. When he didn't respond, she nudged him. 'Come on! Don't take it personally. Abhaydatta has to take the apprentice who can help him the most.'

I can help him the most, Anand thought, choking back his tears. He and the master healer shared a history. He thought of how they'd travelled together from Kolkata all the way to the mountains, Nisha and him disguised as Abhaydatta's grandchildren to throw off pursuers. How Abhaydatta had fed them and taken care of them as though he really were their grandfather, how he'd entrusted Anand with the most precious object in his life, the conch. How Anand had held Abhaydatta's limp, injured body in his arms and wept after the healer had battled with Surabhanu. Anand had been willing to give up even the Silver Valley for the old healer's sake. What skill did Rajbhanu possess that could equal that?

'There'll be many more opportunities,' Nisha tried to console him. 'I bet in a couple of years you'll know enough for Abhaydatta to take you with him anywhere he needs to go. Meanwhile, there's so much to learn here – and it's all so exciting …'

But Anand had stopped listening.

❧

Anand awoke with a start in the dark sleeping hall. Someone was shaking his shoulder gently. He bolted upright, his sleep gone.

'Hush,' he heard Abhaydatta whisper. 'It is almost time for me to leave. I wanted to see you before I went, to say goodbye. Come outside.'

Outside the hall, a pale, slivered moon hung above a parijat tree. No one else was around.

'I know you are sad at not being able to go with me,' the healer said. 'You are most dear to me, so I want you to understand why I cannot take you.'

'I thought we were a fellowship,' Anand blurted out. 'You and me and Nisha and the conch – didn't you say so?'

'We are. But it is not yet time for you to leave the Silver Valley,' Abhaydatta said. 'You need to grow stronger.'

'But I want to help – '

'You've helped me already. Your vision allowed the council to figure out the name of the village I have to travel to: Sona Dighi, golden lake. However, I will give you something so that you may help me further. Hold out your hand.'

Anand did as he was told. The healer took a strand of pearls from a small silken pouch and placed it in Anand's palm.

'These are special pearls,' he said. 'I want you to check them each day. As long as they remain shiny, you'll know that I'm well. But if they grow dull or dark, it'll mean that I'm in danger. You must go straight to the chief healer then. He will know what to do.' The healer put an arm around Anand and gave him a quick hug. 'Go back to bed now.'

Waking in the morning, Anand wondered if he'd dreamed the entire encounter. But when he reached under his pillow, there was the pouch! His heart beating, he sneaked a quick look. The pearls gleamed, pure and white.

At breakfast the chief healer announced that Abhaydatta had left during the night. 'He should already be in the village, as he and Raj-bhanu used one of our portals to convey them to their destination,' he added.

Sadness rose once more in Anand's mind, but it wasn't as sharp as before. Ever so often, as he walked from one lesson to another, he touched the pouch, which was safely tucked into his pocket. A small smile made its way to his lips as he remembered Abhaydatta's words: *You are most dear to me.* Whenever no one was around, he checked on the pearls to make sure they had not changed colour. In spite of the council's decision, Abhaydatta had made him part of his mission. Anand was determined not to let him down.

four

The Vision in the Waterfall

Anand's elation at being the watcher of the pearls faded over the next few weeks. Whenever he checked on them, the pearls, shining innocently, looked exactly the same. He began to wonder if Abhaydatta had made up the part about them changing colour. Had he just given them to Anand so he wouldn't feel excluded? He grew less vigilant about checking on them, and though he still carried the pouch with him, sometimes an entire day would go by before he remembered to take the pearls out.

At least he was doing better at his lessons. He could catch faint glimpses of the winds now, though they hadn't told him anything significant since his viewing of the black wind. The winds that appeared to him were innocuous – pale yellow or pink for the most part – and spoke of nothing more exciting than the birth of a calf in a nearby village, or a fishing expedition to a mountain lake. But Anand was so thankful that he could see *something* that he didn't mind.

He was also learning the language of beasts. The healer in charge of tongues had started the apprentices off with the brotherhood's cows, placid animals who were patient with the boys' stutterings. Anand could now converse, though jerkily, with goats and mules as well, and had, in the last couple of weeks, learned more about the different types of grass available in the valley than he'd quite wanted to know. The apprentices had to take lessons in human languages as well, for their work might require them to converse with people of many races. Anand's group – boys who, like him, had grown up speaking Bengali – was started off with Swahili. To his delight he discovered that he was one of the better students in this class.

He accompanied Nisha to the herbalist, and though he wasn't half as quick as her, he learned to make several potions, such as the lost-object-finding potion, the truth-telling potion and the death-dissembling potion. He learned the rudiments of telekinesis, which included making a book hover in the air and opening and closing doors and windows from a distance. He ventured back to the Hall of Seeing with a different master, and this time he was able to call up the Crystal Hall without too much difficulty. He had not yet mastered the more complex skills – the casting of a freezing spell to render one's enemy immobile, the creation of a sheath of mind-energy to protect oneself, the fading chant that allowed one to become invisible in the presence of danger, or reading the future in the patterns of the clouds. But for the moment he was satisfied by the fact that each day he could do something new.

Maybe I do belong here, he thought. *And maybe by the time Abhaydatta returns, I'll learn enough for him to pick me as his apprentice for his next adventure.*

He began to feel less lonely as well, though he missed Abhaydatta all the time. Still, there was Nisha to eat meals with and discuss the events of the day, and Govinda, the guide from his early days, who was happy to answer his many questions about the valley. He made friends with three of the newer apprentices as well: Shankaran and Mangalam, twin brothers who had come to the valley from the southernmost tip of India, and Ali, a dark-skinned boy with frizzy hair, who had come from a country in Africa – for the Brotherhood consisted not just of Indians but people of many races.

They belonged to many religions, too. In addition to Hindus such as Anand, there were Christians and Muslims and Buddhists, as well as apprentices belonging to religions Anand hadn't even heard of. All who were interested in helping their fellow humans were welcomed into the Brotherhood. Sometimes in the dining hall, Anand would listen with fascination to a group of people speaking in their native tongue. He noticed, however, that only a few of the healers who taught them were foreigners. This, Govinda explained, was because once the healers finished their training, they were encouraged to return to their own country to help the people there. This also enabled the Brotherhood to create a community all over the world that they could call on when needed.

Every week the apprentices had two afternoons off. Anand and his friends liked to spend theirs exploring the valley. There were so many places in it that they had not yet seen! Anand had noticed something mysterious about the valley: it seemed to expand and contract at will, and though the central area where the brotherhood lived, worked and studied remained the same, its peripheries often appeared to shift. On one morning, Anand might see a hillock to the west of his sleeping hall. The next day, looking out of the same window, he might find the hillock gone, its place taken by a copse of trees. There was, therefore, always an element of adventure in their wanderings.

This afternoon Anand, Shankaran, Mangalam and Ali decided to explore the northern part of the valley, where, they had been told, there was a beautiful river with white sand banks that sparkled like diamond dust. They walked for a couple of hours without seeing it. Then, just as they were about to give up and go back, they heard the sound of rushing water. They rounded a corner and there was the river, as beautiful as it was reputed to be. The boys drank deeply from its cool, sweet waters and lay down on the fine sand that bordered it. Then, since the day had turned hot, they decided to go for a swim. Stripping down to their undergarments, they jumped in the water, yelling with pleasure, though Anand, who could not swim, stayed close to the bank. There was much to enjoy here, too, for multicoloured polished stones lined the river-bottom and tiny glittering fish played around his legs. One fish in particular caught his eye. It was larger than the others and its scales were a bluish-silver. Unlike the others, it was swimming upriver, with elegant, purposeful flicks of its tail. Anand decided to follow it and see where it was going.

He must have walked for quite a while along the shallows without realizing it, for when the fish suddenly disappeared behind a large rock, he lifted his head to find himself in a different part of the river. He could no longer hear his friends. Here the river forked and to the left, its gentle melody turned into a roar. Intrigued, Anand decided to take the left fork. When he rounded a corner, he saw ahead of him a sheer rock face, with a waterfall cascading over it. The sun caught the droplets of water as they fell, creating a shimmering rainbow. Anand was strangely attracted to the waterfall. Cautiously, he ventured closer, and was surprised to find the river quite shallow here. The waterfall was like a splendid silver curtain, and he felt a great desire to touch it. As he went closer, he caught a movement behind the curtain. It seemed there was a little ledge behind the waterfall – and someone was standing there. Or were there two silhouettes? For a moment, Anand was frightened. But he knew the Silver Valley was wound about with powerful spells. Surely no one intending the Brotherhood harm could enter it! Overcome with curiosity, he held his breath and ran through the waterfall to the other side.

Immediately, he was in a different world, dim and dry and completely silent. Even the floor felt different beneath his feet. It was as though he wasn't standing on stone but cracked earth. When he stepped forward, dead leaves and twigs crackled underneath, startling him. He put out his hand to hold on to the cave wall, but his fingers touched what felt like the rough bark of a tree. There was a winding path in front of him, overhung by thick, leafy branches. At the end of the path, Anand could see the ruins of an ancient wall. Near it, a figure lay face down. A man in a hood leaned over him, trying to revive him. Anand couldn't see the man's face, but something about him was familiar. As he watched, the man threw back his hood to look behind him. Following his glance, Anand saw a puzzling blue glow coming from deep in the forest. The scene had grown darker, as though night was falling, but Anand could see the man's face now. It was Abhaydatta! Once again, more urgently now, he tried to rouse his companion – Anand guessed it was Raj-bhanu. But Raj-bhanu didn't respond. Was he dead?

'Master Abhaydatta,' Anand called. 'Where are you? What's happening?'

The healer did not look up but, as though his words had shattered a screen, the scene in front of Anand broke into pieces and disappeared. Anand found himself wedged into a small, damp cave behind the waterfall, his heart heavy with misgiving but certain of one thing: Abhaydatta was in danger.

He stumbled out of the cave and waded as fast as he could in the direction where he'd left his companions. He walked for a long time, the blazing sun disorienting him. Then, just as he'd begun to fear that he'd taken a wrong turn somewhere, he saw them sitting on the bank, eating some wild lychees they'd picked from a nearby tree. They waved to him to join them, but he ran instead to where he'd left his clothes and rummaged in the pocket of his pants for the pouch that held the pearls.

It wasn't there.

His heart skipped a beat. *I must have dropped it!* he thought. He fell on his knees, searching through sand and rock, but there was nothing. He gabbled the finding spell that he had learned recently, but in his panic he must have got the words mixed up, for the pearls did not appear.

'What's the matter?' Ravi asked.

'I've lost a pouch,' Anand gasped. 'I can't tell you what's inside, but I have to find it. It's very important.'

The boys looked curious, but they didn't ask any further questions. Trained in the ways of magic, they understood secrets and were respectful of them. All the way back, they helped Anand look for the pouch, but though they searched diligently, and recited the finding spell several times, they were unsuccessful. Obviously, magical objects like the pearls did not respond to ordinary spells. Back in his sleeping hall, Anand turned his pallet upside down, hoping he'd left the pearls there without realizing it. But there was nothing. It was as though the pearls, angered at being ignored, had chosen to disappear.

Anand felt a lump of tears gathering in his throat. Abhaydatta had entrusted him to watch out for him, and what had Anand done? He tried to remember when he'd last examined the pearls. It was at least two days ago, maybe even three. Who knew how long the healer had been in trouble?

At dinner, he whispered what had happened to Nisha.

Her face grew worried. 'Oh no! You must go to Somdatta right away and tell him what you saw!'

Anand knew that she was correct. His mouth grew dry with panic as he thought of what the chief healer would say to him for having failed his trust.

Although the night had turned unexpectedly cold, Anand's palms were sweating as he knocked on the door of Somdatta's hut, which stood apart from the other buildings in a banyan grove. It was a small, thatched affair, far less grand than the Crystal Hall or even the dining hall, and Anand wondered if all the healers lived this simply. He heard the healer's deep voice asking him to come in. Inside, there was a sitting room with little furniture – just a couple of cane chairs and a table – but many books on the shelves that lined the walls. In spite of his nervousness, Anand couldn't help giving the books a curious glance. He remembered hearing that the chief healer's special skill was to interpret ancient books of spells, and he wondered if in one of those books there was a special mantra that would call back the pearls from wherever they'd disappeared to. But Somdatta, who'd been reading by the light of an oil lamp – was already motioning for Anand to sit down.

Anand balanced himself uneasily on the edge of the chair. The healer was asking, in his kind voice, how he was enjoying his first days as an apprentice, but Anand was so nervous he could barely make sense of the words, let alone think of a suitable reply.

'I have to tell you something,' he blurted out.

'I guessed as much,' the healer smiled ruefully. 'New apprentices rarely come to see me unless there's a problem! Tell me what it is, and don't worry so much. Things are often not as bad as they seem.'

But his words didn't comfort Anand. In this case, he knew, they were much worse.

⚜

When Anand had finished telling the healer about the lost pearls and the vision behind the waterfall, Somdatta sat very still, his fingertips pressed together in a steeple. 'Strange,' he finally said. 'Healers have been posted at the Hall of Seeing, morning and night, ever since Abhaydatta left. None of them have sensed anything.'

'I *did* see him, I *did* ...'

'I don't doubt that you saw something. But you are not experienced enough to know what the sending (for that is what it was) means, or who it came from. Perhaps it is meant to misguide us into making a wrong decision. It is a great pity that you cannot find the pearls, for they are objects of power and would have spoken truly. Abhaydatta must think highly of you, to have left them with you.'

Anand hung his head, feeling worse than before.

'You have done right, in any case, to tell me of this. Tomorrow, I will call a council, and together the masters will decide how best to deal with this information. Go now, and sleep. Don't trouble yourself too much about Abhaydatta – he has powers beyond what you might imagine. Look again for the pearls in the morning, and should you find them, bring them to me right away.'

But Anand couldn't forget the look on Abhaydatta's face in the vision as he had glanced up at the darkening sky. If the chief healer had seen that look, he too would have known that Abhaydatta was in a dangerous place, a place where, for some inexplicable reason, his powers didn't work.

By this time it was dark, and most of the apprentices were in their sleeping halls, studying for the next day or preparing for bed. But instead of going to his hall, Anand headed to the hut where

36

Nisha stayed. The hut was dark, and he tried hard to remember which of the windows she had said was hers. Finally, hoping he was right, he tapped on the one facing west. No one answered, so he tapped again, his heart racing at the thought of being caught by Mother Amita. But when the window creaked open, it was Nisha's tousled head that leaned out sleepily.

When she caught sight of Anand, her sleepiness vanished. 'What's wrong?' she whispered apprehensively. 'What did the chief healer say?'

'He's calling a meeting tomorrow, and then they'll decide. But it'll take too long. We've got to help Abhaydatta. He's in deep trouble, I can feel it.'

'But how can *we* help him, Anand? Be practical – the masters are much more skilled than we are. It's best to let them ...'

He shook his head fiercely. 'We helped him before, didn't we, bringing the conch back all the way? And we helped him afterwards, when he wouldn't speak. We're connected to him like no one else is. I'm leaving tonight ...'

'But ...' Nisha's eyes were dark pools of uncertainty. Anand could tell that the idea of leaving the valley, where she had at last found a home, filled her with distress. 'We can't leave just like that, even if we could get past the Gateway. It's against all rules. We'll surely be banished from the Brotherhood – '

'You can stay back if you don't want to come,' Anand said, pretending nonchalance although his heart tensed at the possibility. Nisha's practical, clear-headed approach to problems had saved them many times in the past, and he'd been counting on her more than he'd realized. 'We won't use the Gateway. We'll use a portal.'

'You're crazy! We don't even know where the portals are! And I've heard you need a password ...'

'We'll ask the conch for the password,' Anand stated simply.

࿎

Anand and Nisha stood on the threshold of the Crystal Hall, peering into the dark. The moon had disappeared behind clouds, and the roof of the crystal hall, usually aglow with its light, was a pane of blackness. The conch's shrine was dark, too, but Anand could feel its alert energy focused on them though it said nothing. Holding Nisha by the arm, Anand started making his way toward it, then stopped suddenly. 'There are other people here,' he whispered to Nisha. 'I can sense them.'

Inside his head, he heard the conch chuckle. *There certainly are. A few more steps and you would have tripped right over them. And wouldn't that have landed you in hot water!*

A dim glow appeared around the shrine, enough for Anand to see the shapes of several sleeping healers stretched out on the floor. There were five of them, and they formed a pentagon around the shrine, lying head to toe.

They've been doing that ever since you brought me back to the valley, the conch said. *I guess they don't want someone else making off with me! And what is it that brings you children here, so long after your bedtime?*

We need your help, Anand said inside his head. *But you know that.*

I do indeed, the conch said. *Still, I wouldn't mind being asked politely.*

Anand sighed. *Please, conch, there's no time for jokes. Abhaydatta is in grave danger, but the chief healer won't do anything until the council makes their decision. Nisha and I need to get to him right away. We need to know how to use a portal, and ...* He swallowed nervously. An idea had flashed into his head suddenly, a shocking idea, and also a wonderful one. Or perhaps it had been in his subconscious all along ever since he made up his mind to go?

We need you to come with us. Will you? Please?

I thought you'd never ask! the conch said. Then it began to give him instructions.

✤

Anand focused his mind on doing exactly what the conch had asked him to. If he didn't, he knew he'd be overcome by fear. And then Nisha and he would certainly get caught. He took Nisha by her hand and pulled at her to indicate that they were to step over the pentagon of sleeping healers and go to the shrine. She pulled back, uncertain.

'This is crazy. Are you sure the conch wants you to do this?' she whispered.

He nodded, pointing to the exact place where they were supposed to enter the pentagon. One of the healers had turned sideways and his bent foot had left a small gap in the pentagon. Gingerly, they stepped through this. Anand held his breath, positive the healers would feel their presence and wake up. But nothing happened.

Now they were standing directly in front of the shrine. Once again Anand was struck by its beauty. It was shaped like a lotus, each petal perfect and lifelike in its glimmering detail, the whole enclosed inside an oval. At the heart of the crystal lotus sat the conch. Tonight it looked small and ordinary, a shell someone might pick up at any seashore, but Anand remembered how it could, when needed, shine like a hundred lightning bolts and send forth even greater power.

'How are you going to get it out?' Nisha whispered.

'Shhh,' Anand admonished her. He wasn't quite clear about this part. The last time he'd touched the conch, he'd reached in with his hand. The crystal oval had turned liquid, like water, and allowed him to bring the conch out. But this time the conch's instructions had been different.

Hold on tightly to the girl as you reach in. Whatever happens, don't let go of her … or of me.

When he reached in, the oval wall melted as before, and his hand closed around the conch. He held it tightly, feeling, as always, a deep happiness rise in him, a sense that nothing else mattered as long the two of them were together, the conch and its Keeper. Warmth from the conch was permeating his entire body like a drink of sweet, hot tea on a freezing night. A humming rose around him, and when he looked, he and Nisha were inside the crystal shrine. But how could that be?

Around them, the hall began to swirl. Fast, then faster, until the pentagon of healers was a blur around them. Only, Anand knew that it was he who was being spun around. He could hardly breathe. *Is this the portal that Abhaydatta used?* he gasped.

From far away, he heard the conch say, *No, I have created a new, more powerful one for you. For not only must we travel in space, we must travel backwards in time as well if we are to save Abhaydatta. Remember what I said, and don't let go.*

The spinning speeded up. Shards of light stabbed at Anand's eyes, coming at him from every direction. He shut them tightly and focused on holding on, tightening his right hand around the conch and gripping Nisha's wrist with his left. But the spinning was too intense. He could feel his body coming apart. *Stop!* He cried, but the spinning grew faster. His head snapped back. His hands and feet flailed out, no longer in his control. His fists came undone in spite of his every effort, and he felt both Nisha and the conch slip from his grasp into a whirling, flashing chiaroscuro of light-and-dark.

five

The Village

The first thing Anand noticed when he opened his eyes were the trees that towered above him. From where he lay on his back beside a cracked-earth trail, he could see they had smooth barks that were a very dark brown, and from their branches hung clumps of the large round leaves he'd seen in his vision in the Hall of Seeing.

Shal trees, he thought. It seems the conch brought me to the right place after all.

Remembering the conch sent a shock of misery through him. Slowly, reluctantly, he turned his head to look at his fist, praying that he was mistaken in what he remembered of his dizzying journey through time and space. But his fist lay open and empty.

He'd been unable to do what the conch had asked him to. He'd let go. And now he was alone in a strange village, powerless – and thus useless to Abhaydatta, even if he could find him. *And Nisha, where was she?* He thought of her as he'd last seen her: mouth open in a silent scream, receding into a darkness that flashed like thunderclouds. With a pang he remembered how happy she'd been in the valley, learning to be an apprentice. How reluctant she'd been to leave. But she'd done it for him because he'd been determined to go, and she didn't want him to face the dangers that lurked ahead without a friend to guard his back. Well, he'd lost her, too.

But there was no time to berate himself. Someone was coming. Anand could hear his grunts, and his footsteps. They were loud and heavy and shook the ground, and by the rustle of the bushes as he passed them, Anand guessed he was rather large. Alarmed, he tried to pull himself up to his knees and hide behind a tree, but it was too late.

Around the corner came a boy, dressed only in a pair of ragged half-pants, leading a black buffalo by a rope loosely tied around its neck. The buffalo carried bundles of firewood and grass. The boy was as startled to see Anand as Anand was to see him. He dropped the buffalo's rope with a yelp and retreated behind the animal. The buffalo snorted, advancing on Anand. Its nostrils dilated, foam dripped from its mouth and it shook its great curved horns aggressively. Anand bent over and covered his head with his hands. Any moment now, those sharp horn-tips would be skewering him.

Instead he heard the boy call, 'Kalindi! No, Kalindi, stop.'

Looking up he saw that the boy had grabbed the animal by its neck and was holding it back. Inquisitiveness battled with apprehension on his face – and won. 'Who are you?' he asked, speaking Bengali with a broad village accent Anand had trouble following. 'Where did you come from? Your clothes are funny, though not like the stranger man's.' He grinned. 'You must be hot in them.'

Anand looked down at himself. He was still wearing the thick yellow leggings and tunic he'd put on in the Silver Valley, and indeed, he was sweating. He took off his wool cap and jacket, feeling foolish.

'Who are you?' the boy asked again.

Though the boy looked friendly and safe enough, with a big gap between his front teeth and spiky uncombed hair, Anand was reluctant to tell him anything about himself. 'Where am I?' he asked instead.

'Don't you know? This is the village of Sona Dighi,' the boy regarded Anand with interest. 'Are you like the men who go into the forest and lose their minds? But no, your eyes are different. You must be like the boy in that movie, *Kala Pahar* – Teenu uncle took me to Bardhaman to see it before he became like the others. You know, the boy who gets in a motorcar accident and loses his memory?' He walked around Anand to check for signs of injury, and looked disappointed when he found none.

Anand wasn't sure what to say, but the boy seemed to have reached a conclusion on his own. 'Never mind. You can stay with me until you get your memory back. That's what happens in the movie right at the end. The boy remembers he's a rich businessman's son. And then his father gives lots of money to the people who helped him. That would surely make my grandmother happy! Come along now, and don't mind Kalindi. She won't hurt you. She's very sweet natured. I should know – I've looked after her since she was a baby.'

A bit bemused, Anand followed the boy, keeping a prudent distance from the snorting buffalo, of whose sweetness he was less than convinced. The path wound its way alongside a lake where several women were doing their washing, beating brightly coloured saris against smooth stones. They stopped and stared at Anand as he passed.

'Eh, Ramu,' one of them called. 'Who's that boy with you?'

The boy shrugged. 'Don't know. I found him on the path near the shal forest. He was in an accident. He's lost his memory, and his family.'

Anand felt a little guilty about misleading Ramu, but what could he say? That he'd travelled from the Himalayas through a magic portal to help a master healer and his apprentice? Even if Ramu believed him, word would travel, and the only advantage, frail as it was, that Anand had over the stranger – that of surprise – would be gone. And the part about losing his family wasn't totally wrong. He wondered again where Nisha and the conch were, and if he would ever see them.

'Poor boy!' the woman said. 'He does look addled. Take him to Tara Ma tonight. Maybe she can help him.'

'That's just what I was intending,' Ramu said, drawing himself up to his full, dignified height.

'And what were you doing near the shal forest?' the woman asked. 'Hasn't your grandma told you to stay away from that place?'

Ramu chose to ignore her comments, ducking instead around the corner of a bamboo grove.

Anand, hurrying to catch up, asked, 'Who's Tara Ma? And why shouldn't you go near the shal forest?'

'Tara Ma's the village wise-woman. She knows a lot of things, like how to cure sick people, or help people that someone has put a curse on. But she hasn't been able to help the men who come out of the forest even more addled than you. Once she chanted a petni out of a woman, though. The petni got into the woman and took over her spirit because she walked under the tree where it lived in the evening time. It was a sheora tree, just like the one there, behind that hut ...'

'And the shal forest – ' Anand prompted.

'Oh, that! People think it's bad luck because it's where the stranger takes our men to dig for him. They say that sometimes you can see a strange glow in there, like some kind of fire, only it's blue, not red. Personally, I've never seen anything. Anyway I always stay at the edge. The best grass grows there. It makes Kalindi's milk sweeter, so people pay more for it, and in the marshy parts you can get wild spinach.' He showed Anand a cloth bundle. 'Grandma likes it whenever I bring home some, though of course I don't tell her where I got it. Come on, now. Here's our hut.'

Ramu had stopped by one of the smallest of the village huts, set in a corner of a clearing. It was old and in poor shape, though Anand could see that someone – Ramu, probably – had tried to repair it by daubing patches of mud over the walls and sticking palm leaves into the thinning thatch. Ramu pulled Anand to the back, where an old woman was hunched over a firepit, stirring a pot.

'You took so long!' she said to him.

'Grandma!' Ramu said, 'Look, I've brought home a big bunch of spinach for you.'

The old woman peered shortsightedly at the bundle. 'That's very good, child. Wash it and throw it into the pot. It'll add nicely to the rice and lentils that are cooking in there.'

'I've brought home something else, Grandma – someone, I should say – a boy who's lost. Can he stay with us until he finds his people?'

Ramu's grandmother looked worried. Anand had seen a look like that on his mother's face sometimes, when they'd lived in the slums of Kolkata. It meant there wasn't enough to feed an additional mouth. He was sorry to add to her anxieties, but what choice did he have? If he left now, Ramu would feel shamed. Besides, staying with Ramu would allow him to meet the wise-woman without anyone questioning why.

Ramu's grandmother was a kind woman, for in a moment she said, 'Yes, child. He can stay as long as he needs to.'

When the rice stew was cooked, she divided it into three equal portions. The portions were too small to satisfy anyone's hunger, but the boys took them with good cheer. When the grandmother's back was turned, Ramu scooped a surreptitious handful of food from his plate to hers. Anand did the same, and when the grandmother ate it all and belched with satisfaction, wondering aloud at how full she felt, the boys exchanged conspiratorial grins.

❧

Anand spent the rest of the day accompanying Ramu on his tasks. Ramu lent Anand a pair of half-pants, darned but clean, and a woven cloth to tie around his middle.

'I'm sorry that the pants are so old,' he said apologetically, 'and that the gamcha has holes in it. But you can use it as a turban if it gets too hot, or to dry yourself if we go for a bath in the lake. It also serves as a decent net if we go fishing.'

Anand was thankful to have the clothing. It was cool and comfortable and didn't mark him as a stranger everywhere he went. It was pleasant to follow Ramu around the village. For a few hours, he decided to forget about the responsibilities and worries that weighed upon him and pretended that he was a village boy.

Ramu explained that every morning he took Kalindi around to his customers' homes and sold her milk. 'I always milk her right in front of them, so they can see how fresh and pure her milk is,' he said proudly, 'and I never add in water, like some of the other milkmen do.' Then he went to the village school for a few hours, though judging from his lack of enthusiasm as he described it, Anand guessed that he didn't learn much there.

'The teacher has a long cane and uses it on us whenever we don't do our sums right. But he never really teaches us, and the problems are hard to understand. I think he spends more time thinking up punishments than preparing lessons. He makes us stand out in front of the schoolhouse sometimes, with bricks on our heads, until our necks hurt. And sometimes he makes us stand on one leg until we fall over, and then he canes us some more.'

It sounded horrible to Anand. He remembered the kindness with which the masters in the Silver Valley had treated his mistakes, and a needle of longing pierced his heart. Then he realized that by now they would have found out that the conch was missing, and guessed who had taken it. They wouldn't be feeling kindly towards him any more. Would they send someone after him? And the conch – he could only hope it was safe wherever it was. *Conch!* he called in his mind, as powerfully as he could. But he was answered only by silence.

'Don't the parents protest?' he asked Ramu, to take his mind off his worries.

'Well, he never really hits the children of rich people too hard – it's us that get the worst beatings. And as for my parents, they died during a plague when I was a baby, and I don't want to trouble my grandma by telling her all this. She's so happy that I go to school at all – that's more than she was able to do when she was a child. At least I can read and write a little. She was so proud the day I wrote my name for her.'

Ramu and Anand gave Kalindi a bath in the lake, pouring water over her black hide and scrubbing it till it shone while the buffalo lowed with pleasure. Then they bathed themselves and managed, with a lot of splashing and yelling, to catch a few small fish to take back to Ramu's grandmother who said she'd fry them, crisp and whole, for dinner. In the late afternoon they took Kalindi to the edge of the woods again to graze some more. They gathered more bundles of grass and firewood to sell to the villagers.

'Grandma used to help me do this before,' Ramu said, 'but now she's too old. She gets tired after just a few minutes. So I do it myself.'

He whistled and sang as he went about his task. If he was aware of his hardships, he didn't seem to mind. He knew where to find wild jaam trees, and he taught Anand to climb up their gnarly trunks and pick the ripe purple fruit. He also showed Anand where shalikh birds nested in the bushes, and where the foxholes were. From time to time, Anand peered into the forest, but he never saw anything more unusual than a deer leaping away, or vines swaying silently in the breeze. Once they came across a worn path that led deeper into the woods. Was it the same one that Anand had seen in his vision at the waterfall? He couldn't tell. It was empty, and though he stopped to stare, he could find no trace of the healers anywhere along it.

'That's the path along which the stranger takes the men who work for him. I've heard it goes all the way into the middle of the forest, to the ruins of a very old palace. That's where they've been digging for treasure, though they don't seem to have found any yet.' Ramu shrugged. 'But he pays a good week's wage – that's how long they have to stay in the forest each time – whether they find anything or not. I want to join them the next time he comes for more workers. So far Grandma hasn't let me go, because there's some kind of disease in the forest, and the men come back sick in their minds from it. But this time I'll insist. Maybe the stranger-man will hire me because I can go into small spaces like grown men can't …'

Anand pictured the happy-go-lucky Ramu crawling through a dark passageway somewhere beneath a huge ruined building and shivered involuntarily. He had a bad feeling about the palace already, though he hadn't even gone near it yet. But Ramu's words also gave him an idea.

That night, Ramu took Anand to Tara Ma's hut, which stood at the very edge of the village, near the lake. The night was dark, with no moon, and the wind moaned eerily around the hut. Faraway, the shal trees seemed to beckon menacingly with their branched arms. Standing outside the hut, the boys could hear the wise-woman chanting and moaning.

'She's not been herself either recently,' Ramu whispered. 'She's been telling the men that they must not go into the forest, that they must send the stranger away. But of course they won't listen. Things have been hard in the village. There hasn't been enough rain for two years, and the crops have done poorly. They need the money if they are to feed their families, or buy medicines for those who get sick.' Ramu's face darkened. 'Grandma got sick last winter with a chest cold, and we didn't have the money to get even a bottle of cough mixture. That's why I want to join the digging.'

The door to the hut opened suddenly, and a woman with a shock of white hair haloing her face stood there. 'Foolish boy!' she cried. Her voice was husky, as though she'd been chanting for a long while without rest. 'You want to dig, too? Do you want to lose your soul in the forest and come back a mere shadow, with no light in your eyes? Go home to your grandmother, and speak no more of this nonsense!'

Ramu looked rebellious, but he didn't dare to contradict her. 'I've brought you a lost boy,' he started, but the wise-woman held up her hand to stop him.

'I see everything I need to know,' she said. 'Go home now, and stay away from the dark of the forest that calls to you in its false, enchanting voice. And you,' she caught Anand by the shoulder, 'you come with me.' She dragged him into the dark hut and slammed the door and latched it.

Anand stood blinking nervously in the darkness. Was this the woman he had seen appear before him on the wall of the Seeing Hall? She seemed more unkempt, even a bit crazed. Would she have news of Abhaydatta? Would she know how to help Anand? She was rummaging in a corner of the hut – for a flint-box, he realized, for there was the flash of a flame, and then a small fire leaping in a round stone hearth. Yes, it was the same circle of stones he'd seen. And the woman too, now that she was calmer and had smoothed her hair back and tied it into a bun, he could see in her traces of the beauty and authority he'd noticed earlier.

'I recognize you,' she said now. 'Even though I never saw you before. I felt your aura when I sent my spirit out in search of help. Your spirit calmed my desperate one and gave it hope – I feel that same strong calm in you now. I hadn't realized such a powerful and wise spirit resided in a mere boy's body!'

Anand stared at her. Him, powerful and wise? Why, he had failed in everything he'd been entrusted with. Perhaps she *was* crazy, after all.

'But how did you get here?' she asked. 'Isn't your home far away, in the mighty Himalayas?'

Quickly, Anand told her about the vision behind the waterfall, and how he had felt that Abhaydatta was in great danger and that he had to reach him. He told her about travelling through the portal.

Her eyes widened. 'I have heard of such doorways!' she said, 'and have always wanted to travel along one.' She frowned. 'But how will you return? Do you know how to open another portal from here?'

Anand shook his head. 'I can't return, not unless I find Abhaydatta and help him fulfil the mission for which he came. And Nisha – I have to find her, too.' He described to the wise-woman how his grip had loosened, and how Nisha had gone flying into the unknown, but he didn't say anything about the conch. Some things were better kept to oneself.

'I am sorry about your friend. But it sounds as though you lost her just before the end of the journey,' Tara Ma said. 'If so, she may be somewhere close by. If you want, I will try to locate her.'

Anand nodded. Tara Ma sat silently in front of the fire, eyes closed. But Anand could see her eyes darting this way and that under the lids, as though she were searching. Finally she opened them and gave a sigh. 'She is somewhere close – and yet not so. I sense her presence but cannot reach her. A veil of some kind surrounds her. There is danger around her, but she is not afraid. I cannot tell if this is because she is brave, or because she doesn't recognize the danger. I'm sorry – I wish I could have helped you more.'

Anand lowered his head, dejected. If Tara Ma, using all her powers as a wise-woman, could not find Nisha, what hope did he have?

'But at least I can tell you something about the master healer,' Tara Ma said. 'He and his apprentice arrived here five days ago.'

Anand gave a start. Only five days ago? But Abhaydatta and Raj-bhanu had left the Brotherhood a month earlier. With the help of the portal, they would have arrived in Sona Dighi immediately. Somehow, the conch had managed to send Anand back in time! Perhaps there was still a chance that Anand could reach the healer before it was too late! And if he could help Abhaydatta, then Abhaydatta would have the skills to find Nisha.

'Did he come here?' he asked, looking around at the hut, wondering if Abhaydatta had sat in the very same spot that he sat in now.

Tara Ma shook his head. 'I did not see him, for that would have been too dangerous, but we communicated mentally. He told me that he and his companion were going to enter the forest at dawn, that he would put a spell of dissemblance on them so that their aura could not be felt by the dark magician – for that is what I think the stranger is. But the dissemblance would prevent me, too, from knowing where he went, or whether danger overtook him.'

'Did he say where he would go?' Anand asked.

'To the ruins. That's where the mystery of the forest lies, and the heart of the evil that changes the village men so they come back as though caught in a nightmare. He said he must find what the dark one is looking for before he discovers it, for then the dark one would become too strong even for the Brotherhood to withstand.' She sighed. 'If I had more courage and greater magic, I would go there and look for it, too.'

'I have very little courage,' Anand said, 'and I'm afraid my skills are far less than yours. Still, I'll go into the forest as soon as possible.'

The wise-woman shuddered. 'You mustn't! You have no idea of the force of the evil you are dealing with! The stranger is too powerful, even for me. He almost destroyed me the one time I set my will against his, trying to make him leave the village. See this?' She touched her white hair with a shudder. 'He aged me beyond my years. Next time, he said, he would kill me. Can you imagine what he would do to you?'

Anand's mouth was dry with fear, but he said, 'I can't leave Abhaydatta in there by himself. Even if I can't help him, I have to try. Perhaps, because I'm small and unremarkable, I can escape the stranger's notice. Will you help me?'

Tara Ma gave a small smile. 'You are not so unremarkable! But since you appear to have made up your mind, I will help you, though certainly the stranger will destroy me if he finds out. I know some dissembling, too, though I cannot keep it up for very long. Tomorrow the stranger will come for new men – each Thursday he does so, having sucked all energy from the previous group. I will disguise you as a village boy and hide your aura from him for as long as I can – though it may not be for as long as you need.'

six

Anand Meets the Stranger

Anand stood in the marketplace, glancing around in fascination. A city child, he had never been in a village market before. All around him were stalls – most of them nothing more than a straw mat spread on the ground. Vegetable sellers sat behind piles of purple brinjals and glistening mounds of green chillies, holding up their scales and bargaining vigorously with prospective buyers. Fisherwomen jangled their bracelets, calling out, 'Fresh ilish machh! Caught just an hour ago!' There were buffalo-carts laden with colourful bolts of cloth, and vendors who walked around with trays of hairpins and silk ribbons and glass bangles that glittered in the hot sun. There was a balloon seller who could tie his balloons into intricate animal shapes, and a toy seller who demonstrated wind-up dolls that danced, and puppets that fought with painted wooden swords, and flutes made from palm fronds. In a corner, a juice-maker had set up his equipment and was already passing stalks of sugarcane through a crusher and collecting the foamy liquid in earthen cups. Next to him, a man sold the most delicious smelling fried-onion pakoras, which made Anand's stomach growl, because that morning at Ramu's home he'd had only a handful of puffed rice. Nearby, a sweet-ice man poured coloured syrup on pieces of ice, which he shaved off a huge block of ice that lay sweating under a jute sack, and sold them to children for a few paise. But Anand didn't have any money.

'So many people!' he whispered to Ramu. 'Do they all live here?'

Ramu was not paying much attention to the vendors. He was staring, instead, at the path that ran behind the bamboo grove – the path along which the diggers would return to the village.

'What? Oh, the vendors. No, they come from the neighbouring villages. We didn't use to have much of a market here for the last two years. Everyone was too poor. But now I guess the merchants have heard that on Thursdays the men return from the forest with their pay, and they want to make the most of it.'

Anand glanced around at the crowd. People were examining wares, yes, but it was clear that the buying-and-selling hadn't started in earnest. There was a sense of waiting in the air. Over to one side a group of men sat smoking beedies, flicking the butts impatiently into the gutter. From time to time they gave each other distrustful looks. He guessed that they were hoping to be part of the new digging crew. But there were too many of them, and they knew only a few would get to be the lucky chosen ones.

Would he be one of them? Anand wondered. And if the stranger did not pick him – what would he do then?

He heard a shout, and saw people in the crowd pointing excitedly. The old crew was returning. He pushed to the front to catch a glimpse of them as they rounded the bend of the bamboo grove. But what was this? He saw a straggling line of men, red in colour from head to toe, moving with a strange, shuffling gait that wasn't quite human. From time to time they stumbled as though exhausted. Even when their families ran up to them and embraced them, or led them off, holding a dusty arm – for that's what the red was, Anand realized, dust – their faces remained empty of expression. Each man clutched a bundle of rupees in his fist – but without interest, as though he no longer knew what it was.

Anand felt a chill go through him as he watched them. What had happened to these people? What if the same thing happened to Ramu and him?

Now a hushed ripple went through the crowd and Anand saw that another man had appeared at the edge of the bamboo grove. He looked ordinary enough, though unlike the village men in their knee-length dhotis he was dressed city-style, in pants and a bush shirt and wingtip shoes. In his sunglasses and straw hat, he could have been mistaken for a tourist out for a jaunt in the countryside. But Anand knew right away that he was facing the stranger.

The stranger took off his sunglasses and glanced over the crowd. Anand noticed that there was not a speck of red dust on him. 'So, which of you men wants to put in an honest day's work and make more money in a week than you ever saw in a month?' he said.

All the men who'd been waiting began to shout, calling on him to pick them.

'Take me, I'm stronger,' one called.

'See my arms,' another said, lifting them high, 'they're like tree trunks.'

'I can plough twenty bighas in a day,' a third said.

'Liar!' cried a fourth, and he gave the other man such a hard shove that he fell. A fight broke out. Fists went flying, there were kicks and grunts, and then Anand saw a flash of silver. Someone had pulled out a knife.

'Enough!' the stranger said. Though he didn't raise his voice there was something in it that made the crowd cringe. 'I should just let you kill each other, fools that you are. Quiet now, or I'll go to the next village to get my crew.' He pointed his long index finger at the men he wanted, and each man moved silently to stand in a line. When he had chosen forty men, the stranger turned to go.

'Pick me, please!' It was Ramu. He ran up to the stranger with clasped hands. 'You'll need some boys to dig where men can't go.'

The stranger ignored him.

'Please! I really need the money.'

The stranger had already turned away, but Ramu would not give up. 'I'll work for half of what you pay the others. I'll work harder than them, too! And I have sharp eyes – I may be able to find things that they'll miss.'

The stranger seemed to hesitate.

This, Anand realized, was his chance.

'Me, too,' he cried, mimicking Ramu's village accent the best he could. 'I'll work for half pay, and I have sharp eyes too!' Blood pounded in his head as he stepped forward. Would the dissemblance spell that Tara Ma had used work, or would the man realize that Anand wasn't one of the village boys?

At the sound of Anand's voice, the stranger turned, his brows drawn together. He looked Anand up and down in a measuring way that seemed to the boy very different from the way he had looked at his other workers. His eyes, Anand noticed, were a pale gray, colour of smoke, oddly incongruous on his brown face. Anand tried to lower his head, but there was something in those eyes that prevented him from looking away. The stranger moved closer to Anand and said something that seemed to be in a foreign tongue. The skin on Anand's face began to tingle.

'What is your name, boy?' the man said.

Anand knew he should not tell the man his name. New as he was to magic, he knew that names had power, and that an enemy who learned your true-name gained an immediate advantage over you. So, with Ramu's help, he had already picked a different name for himself. In case anyone asked, he was Bishu. It was a common village name for boys, Ramu had informed him. 'You can keep it until you remember your own,' he had added kindly.

But now Anand found, no matter how he tried, he couldn't say it. Instead, his mouth was opening wide, forming the first syllable of his true name.

The stranger narrowed his eyes, waiting. Anand felt as though a noose were tightening around him. There was no escape.

Just then there was a commotion behind them, and a man seized Anand and Ramu by the arm. It was one of the diggers who'd just come back from the forest. His face was still red with dust, and streaked with runnels of sweat. His eyes were wide and darted here and there, as though the man was terrified.

'No, boys, no!' he cried. 'It's bad enough that he took us men, but don't you young ones go into the forest. It's cold there, cold like death, and the blue fire freezes the heart. Deep underground you can feel the worms crawling over your skin. It's not worth the money, however much he pays you. And never, never, tell him your name. I gave him mine, and now it's ...'

The stranger looked at the man, eyes narrowed, and the man stopped mid-sentence as though a hand had been clapped over his mouth. He gestured wildly for a moment, then fell to the ground, unconscious. The stranger ignored him. The rest of the crowd was too petrified with fear to go to his aid.

'Come!' the stranger commanded his new crew. 'We have wasted too much time here already.' He strode away. The men – and the two boys – followed him apprehensively along the path that would lead them into the dark heart of the forest.

⚜

At first, walking through the forest, Anand was too nervous and excited to do anything but keep up with the crew, but after a while he became aware of his surroundings. To his surprise, he found that the forest was not as gloomy as it had seemed. In places, sunlight dripped down the trunks of trees, turning their brown to gold. Mynahs flew from branch to branch with their shrill calls and iridescent wing-flashes. Striped squirrels – their backs marked, according to the old myth, with the print of Lord Rama's hand – scrabbled for nuts near tree roots. Anand could hear the sound of water. There must be a brook nearby! He wondered if the stranger would let them stop at it and drink, for he was hot and very thirsty. He thought he caught a glint out of the corner of his eye to the left, like light on water, but when he turned to see better, there was nothing there except trees. Disappointed, he resumed trudging. But there was that glint again! Again he turned, only to have it disappear. What was going on?

After he'd gone a bit further, he heard people talking. It sounded as though there was a group of women to his left, a little way off, laughing and out of breath. Again, from an eye-corner, he caught a glimpse of bright garments, aquamarine-blue and sunset-crimson, and heard the tinkle of anklets. This time he was careful not to turn his head fully but glanced sideways, just a little. Now he could see!

What he saw took his breath away. To his left, the shal trees had disappeared. Instead, a group of women were taking a leisurely walk through a rose garden that bloomed profusely around them. Behind them a host of fountains sent up silvery sprays of water that looked so cool that Anand wanted to throw himself headfirst into them. But he knew they would vanish if he tried that.

The women in the garden were dressed in elegant silk garments, loose pants and tunics that were embroidered with gold thread that glittered in the sun. Some of the women wore veils and long skirts, and their glossy black hair swung behind them in braids. One carried a red-crested bulbul on her wrist, stroking its head from time to time. One of them was reciting a poem. Anand couldn't understand the words, though he liked the melodious sound of the language, which sounded not unlike Hindi. It must have been a good poem, because everyone applauded. The woman who had recited the poem laughed and gave a sweeping bow, raising a graceful hand to her forehead.

'Did you see that?' Anand whispered to Ramu.

'See what?' Ramu said, glancing around him. He gave a shiver. 'There's nothing here to see except shal trees and more shal trees. I hate the way they're crowding around us. Makes me feel like I can't breathe.'

Anand looked at the rest of the crew. None of them acted as though they had seen or heard anything out of the ordinary. Even the stranger, who strode on with a look of dark and intent excitement on his face, was oblivious to the beautifully dressed women. Was Anand the only one, then, who saw these people? If so, how was he able to see them? Was he going crazy? And if he was really seeing them, who were they? He turned his head surreptitiously as he walked, wishing to watch them for as long as he could. But soon they had passed beyond his line of vision.

For a few moments, Anand felt strangely bereft. The ladies had been so elegant, their reality so sheltered and beautiful, so different from what awaited him in this hot, airless forest. But then he heard more voices ahead. This time, they were to his right. Slanting his glance carefully, he spotted a boy of about ten years, dressed in a beautiful red silk outfit – a kind of gathered tunic with fitted pants – inside a walled garden. He was playing at sword fighting with his companions. He was obviously someone important – there were gold ornaments around his neck and in his ears, on his head was a jewelled turban, and even his pointed shoes were embroidered with gems. The boys playing with him were richly dressed as well, but they bowed deferentially to him from time to time, and were careful to let him win as they batted at each other with their painted wooden swords. A maidservant kneeled behind them, pouring chilled red juice from a silver pitcher into tiny silver cups.

'Shahzada,' she called to the boy in the red silk, offering him a white silk handkerchief, 'You are hot and tired. Please wipe your face and drink some of this cold pomegranate juice.'

Shahzada! Why, that was the title by which Muslim princes in India had been addressed hundreds of years ago!

'You're always interrupting me when I'm doing important things!' the boy said in annoyance, stamping his foot. He gulped some juice impatiently and dropped the glass and handkerchief on the ground for her to pick up, and ran off to play some more. The red juice spilled onto the green grass. Anand's throat burned with thirst as he thought how wonderful it would have been to drink even one mouthful of it.

'Walk faster!' he heard Ramu hiss. 'The stranger will get angry if he notices you lagging behind.'

Regretfully, Anand quickened his pace, and once again the scene disappeared as he moved ahead. Soon, the path narrowed and was lined by thorny bushes that caught at his clothes and tore his skin as he passed. But he hardly felt the pain. Under his feet, the earth had turned red and dusty, but this too he hardly noticed. His brow was creased in concentration. There was something familiar about all these people, and yet something unusual about them, too.

Their clothes, for one. Even among the rich in Kolkata, Anand had never seen such finery. Yet hadn't he come across clothes like those somewhere?

Then he remembered! One day, when Anand had still been a student in Kolkata, his art teacher had brought a book to class. The book had been titled *Indian Miniatures*. In it were copies of paintings set in the courts of the Muslim nawabs centuries ago. Some of those nawabs, his teacher informed them, had lived near Kolkata about three or four hundred years ago. Anand had been fascinated by the scenes depicted in the paintings: the tiger hunts conducted from the backs of elephants, the musical evenings under golden canopies, the feasts where beautiful women poured ruby wines from long-necked decanters for bejewelled kings.

The people in the paintings had been dressed like the ones he'd glimpsed today!

But why would the people Anand saw want to dress in that old style? What were such elegant people doing in this forest, anyway, outside this poor Bengali village? And most importantly, how was it that they faded in and out of Anand's vision?

Anand was brought back to the present by the stranger's voice. 'Here we are,' he said, gesturing with his hand. Ahead of them, half hidden among the trees, was an enormous ruin – once the residence of someone very important, Anand guessed. It must have been hundreds of years old, for many parts of the structure had crumbled. Broken marble pillars lay on their sides, and walls of stone had been reduced to rubble. Iron grilles that must have protected huge windows stood up here and there like the ribs of a giant skeleton, lending the whole place an eerie air.

Anand shivered involuntarily. There was something both mournful and ominous about the ruin. Something that heavied his heart so that he wanted to drop to the ground and weep, and, at the same time, run from it as fast as possible. But even as he thought this, the scene in front of him wavered and changed. Ahead of him now was a beautiful palace of red stone, its domes shining in the afternoon sun, the proud arch of its main gate guarded by turbaned soldiers who carried spears and burnished shields. He gasped. The scene wavered again, and all that remained was the ruin.

'You will begin digging right away,' the stranger ordered the crew. 'Inside the building, you'll find shovels, pick-axes and other tools. Dig, demolish walls, sift through rock and rubble. Search thoroughly. There may be underground passages, or hidden tunnels. Be on the lookout for those as well. You are to work until I ring the bell for a meal-break. And then you are to dig again until I ring the bell, indicating that it is time for you to rest. Watch out for snakes and scorpions – for each person that gets bitten, that's one less man in my crew!'

The men exchanged looks. Clearly, they didn't like what they were hearing – or the stranger's attitude – but they did not dare protest.

'In the centre of the ruin,' the stranger continued, 'there's a special underground passage I've discovered. You are not to go there on your own. It is too dangerous. Each day, I will take a few men – one at a time, for the passage is narrow – to help me dig there.'

'What are we searching for?' one of the men ventured.

The stranger's eyes glittered. 'Fools such as you don't have the wits to recognize that which I seek. But anything shiny that you find – even if it is only a small piece of metal or glass, bring it to me right away. Don't try to keep even the smallest object for yourself. I have ways of knowing things, and your punishment will be worse than you can imagine. You there,' he pointed to a sturdy young man with a moustache, 'you come with me. The rest of you, get started digging right here. Go on. You've wasted enough time in idle chatter.'

The men did as they were told. Anand and Ramu, too, picked up shovels and headed for a rubble-filled rectangle that must have been at one point a large hall. It was slow work, searching through stone and rock, and hard on their hands. Soon their nails were chipped, and blisters began to form on their fingertips. Every time they moved a shovel-full of debris, red dust rose around them, fine and clingy. Looking at Ramu, Anand saw that his face was already coated with red, giving him a bizarre appearance. He guessed that he must look the same.

In a while the sun had dipped low behind the trees, and the ruin was full of shadows. Anand was very hungry, but worse than that was his thirst. His throat was so dry that he thought he would faint if he didn't get some water soon. But he was afraid to ask the stranger for any. He didn't know if the dissembling spell Tara Ma had placed around him was still effective. In any case, he didn't want to draw any more attention to himself than he had to. Maybe he could find a mouthful of rainwater trapped in a crevice somewhere.

Taking his shovel, he moved away from the rest of the crew into another part of the ruin, behind a wall that had remained standing. On the floor here he could see shallow circular holes, the remnants of huge ovens and firepits. Was he in the palace kitchen, then? From the wall hung hooks that might have at one time held enormous cooking pots, and in a corner – why, in a corner was a large jar made of baked clay, the kind in which, even now, people stored water! Its rim was broken, but its lower half was intact. Anand dropped the shovel and ran to it, but when he looked in, the pot was empty and filled with cobwebs.

This disappointment, on top of his exhaustion and thirst, was too much. He sank to the floor and covered his face with his hands, his eyes stinging. How he wished he'd never come across that cursed vision in the Hall of Seeing! Then all of them would be safe now, Abhaydatta, Nisha, Raj-bhanu, the conch and himself. They would all be in the Silver Valley, probably enjoying a wonderful meal in the dining hall. The memory of the valley, with its beautiful parijat trees and clear rivers – and its tables that were always laden with food – filled him with sorrow. Would he ever see it, or his friends again?

'I hate this godforsaken place!' he cried into his grimy palms. 'I wish I could get away from it!'

He felt a hand cuffing his ears. 'And what place is it that you are calling godforsaken, you young rascal?' bellowed a voice. 'I hope it is not my kitchen!'

Startled, Anand opened his eyes to find himself in a room bright with many oil lamps and filled with the bustle of meal preparation. Servants dressed in white kurtas and pyjamas were busy chopping onions and garlic or cleaning goat meat in a corner, while assistant cooks were stirring large bubbling pots or rolling out parathas and frying them on sizzling iron tawas. Oh, all the different fragrances in that kitchen! Had he ever smelled anything as good? But he didn't have a chance to notice anything else, because a huge man with a bristling moustache was leaning over him, a scowl on his face.

But as Anand shrank back in fear, the scowl changed to a warm smile, and the man guffawed and clapped him on the shoulder. 'I don't think it is, for it is to my kitchen you run whenever you have a moment off from your duties, young Abbas, is it not? And sometimes you are here even when it is your duties you should be attending to!'

Anand gaped at the man in astonishment. He acted as though he knew Anand, though he called him by a strange name. He looked down at himself and saw that he was dressed in the same kind of kurta-pajama that the other servants wore. He guessed that it must be the uniform of those who worked in the palace, for the chef, too wore a similar outfit, though on his head was a silk fez cap, possibly to signify his superior standing.

'Hungry again, I suppose? And thirsty too, no doubt. You're lucky that I have a soft corner in my heart for boys who have come from my home village, you ragamuffin!' The chef turned from him to yell to a servant. 'Bring our Abbas a bowl of the leftover chicken qurma!'

'At once, Zafar Miah!' the servant replied.

'I must go and attend to dinner,' Zafar told Anand. 'The Begum has invited a number of important guests tonight, including the chief minister. He's hard to please, that Haider Ali, so Her Majesty has specifically asked that I make the mutton biriyani myself. The rice has been soaking in saffron water all afternoon. It should be ready now. Be off as soon as you eat the curry, for certainly all the punkah-pullers – even an inexperienced one such as you – will be needed on such a warm night!'

Someone brought Anand a steaming bowl of chicken curry and a thick piece of naan. Thankfully, he dipped the bread in the delicious gravy and ate it, and then scooped out pieces of spicy chicken with his fingers, thinking all the time of what the chef had said. In this world, into which he had sipped by some miracle, he had a name, and a job – that of a fan-puller – and, most important, a friend. He drank a cup of cool water from the water-jar that stood next to him, and closed his eyes with a satisfied sigh. He hadn't had a meal like this since he'd left the Brotherhood. He wasn't quite sure what this place was, or how he managed to enter it, but he was certain of one thing: he wasn't going to leave it again, to return to the stranger in that dangerous, desolate ruin! The last thought that came to his mind before he fell asleep was that of the conch.

Conch! He called, not really hoping for a response. But through the drowsiness that wrapped his mind in a sheet of lead he felt its presence. Though it did not speak, he smiled in his sleep, knowing it was very close. If he just extended his hand in the right direction, he could reach it.

⚈⚈⚈

A hand was shaking his shoulder, a voice calling him urgently. 'Bishu! Bishu! Wake up! Thank God I found you before the stranger did! He would have given you a good whipping if he'd caught you resting. Don't do this again! You'll get us all in trouble. Come, it's time for dinner.'

It was Ramu, his red-streaked face filled with concern. Behind him, light flickered from a fire the crew had built on the floor of the ruin to keep snakes, and worse creatures, away at night. They were cooking rice and lentils over it – and not very expertly either, if the charred smell were any indication.

With a sinking heart, Anand realized that he was back in the present, dressed in his ragged digging clothes, his hands swollen with blisters. He wanted to weep for that cheer-filled palace kitchen he'd been in a few minutes ago. Had he merely conjured it up out of his longing? But surely not – for his raging thirst had left him, and he wasn't hungry either. At dinner, he gave his bowl of khichuri to Ramu when no one was looking. He barely heard Ramu's whispered thanks.

If I could go there once, he was thinking, *I can do it again. I just have to figure out how.*

seven

The Pit of Blue Fire

Their days took on a sameness. In the morning they dug, then ate a brief lunch made up of something from the store of dry foods that the stranger had shown them – mostly it was lentil stew – and dug again until dark. For dinner, they had potatoes and rice. If they were lucky enough to come across wild squash growing along the edges of the ruins, they celebrated with a vegetable curry. After dinner, no matter how tired they were, they had to dig some more. The stranger, complaining that they were not progressing fast enough, had provided them with helmets fitted with lights. They brought him what they found – shards of window glass, pieces of beaten metal that might have been parts of shields or serving trays, even a silver jewellery box from a corner of the ruin where once the ladies of the palace must have lived. He looked at the objects, his mouth twisting, then flung them from him, yelling at them to search more carefully. In between digging, the crew watched for snakes – several dangerous varieties had been spied already, including a cobra or two. There were scorpions, also, and fire-caterpillars, their fine red hair bristling with poison, and spiders in various sizes. In spite of the heat, to keep themselves safe at night, the crew was forced to cocoon themselves tightly inside bed-sheets – the same sheets the previous crews had used and left behind. Anand's blisters burst, then dried into calluses. Sometimes, looking at them, he couldn't believe he'd been here for just a few days.

Each day, the stranger took several men, one at a time, to dig in the underground tunnel he'd spoken of. He must have worked them really hard, for when they returned to the group, they were too exhausted to eat, or even talk. The rest of the crew would barrage them with questions, for everyone was curious about the pit – that's what they called it – because the stranger had forbidden them from going near it on their own. But the men who'd been there wrapped themselves in their sheets and turned their faces away from the fire. They ate without seeming to taste their meal, and in the following days, though they continued to dig mechanically, they seemed to have gone away to some far space inside their heads. They would not respond when called, and sometimes one had to shake them by the arm in order to get their attention.

※◎�※

The very next morning after he had experienced the magical world of the palace kitchen, Anand tried to go there again. He slipped away when no one was looking and went back to the ruined room with the broken water-jar. He sat down next to it, squeezed his eyes shut, and wished with all his might to be pulled into Zafar Miah's time. He kept his eyes closed, listening for the chef's booming voice, hoping to smell lamb roasting on a spit, but all he heard was a nearby rustle. He opened his eyes to see a cobra slithering over dead leaves to disappear into a crack between two broken walls.

He tried again the next day, and the next, but the kitchen did not appear again. Whatever cruel magic had allowed him in that one time had shut itself off from him. Even the scenes he'd glimpsed out of the corner of his eye the first day were gone. He was trapped in the ruins with only their memory to taunt him. *Maybe you did dream it all*, he tried to console himself. But a part of him knew it was not so. That other world existed! He just didn't know how to get back into it. What made the torture worse was his growing conviction that the conch was there. He played over and over in his mind what he'd sensed that day in Zafar's kitchen: the conch's faint, cool presence. Had it been trying to communicate something to him? Oh, if only he had not fallen asleep so stupidly!

'What's wrong with you, Bishu?' Ramu asked irritably, after he'd called him several times without receiving a reply. 'You're acting like you're touched in the head, like the men who've been to the pit.'

Anand mumbled an apology, but his mind raced on. Where was Abhaydatta? Anand had hoped to find him by now. He'd been convinced that the healer was hiding somewhere in the ruins – or in the surrounding forest – but if so, why hadn't he shown himself to Anand? And if he wasn't here, then where could he be? Anand tried to use the few divining skills he'd learned in the valley to sense Abhaydatta's presence, but he was unsuccessful. With each day that passed, he felt more desperate. *Nisha was right*, he thought. *This problem is too big for me. I should have left it to the Brotherhood.*

Perhaps it was because he was distracted by his thoughts that he found himself in a different part of the ruin this afternoon. It was darker here. Trees had grown out of cracks in the marble floors that showed traces of a mosaic pattern. Many of the walls here still stood, though some of them leaned crazily, as though waiting to topple onto the heads of unwary passers-by. Anand shivered. It was chilly here, and damp, which was surprising because it was so hot and dusty everywhere else. Around his feet, the floor was slippery with moss or fungus – he couldn't tell what it was in the gloom, only that it squelched unpleasantly between his toes and stank of rot. The passageway sloped sharply, walls crowding in around it. Why, it was the beginning of a tunnel!

His heart speeded up. Was this the tunnel the stranger had warned them to stay away from?

Anand knew he should turn back and run as fast, and as silently, as he could to the central hall where the crew was digging before he got into trouble. A power throbbed here in the heavy, clinging air, physical, electric. He knew it to be evil, though he could not have explained why. The back of his neck prickled with premonition. But a strange fascination had come over him. He had to know what was at the end of the tunnel! He had to! He moved forward, feeling his way like a blind man through the dark, his fingertips scraping the rough walls.

Then, suddenly, he could see. There was an underground chamber ahead of him, lit by a flickering glow like a fire – only this fire was an unnatural blue. He remembered the man in the forest warning him of it. But why did it seem so familiar, as though he'd seen it somewhere? Ahead, he glimpsed silhouettes outlined in blue. One was the stranger's; the other, with a shovel, was one of the men from the crew. They were standing at the edge of a large hole from which the cold glow emanated. As Anand watched, huddled against the wall, the stranger patted the man on the back. 'You've done well,' he said. 'We've advanced much today. Here's a bonus for you.' He flipped something shining into the air and the man dropped his shovel to catch it in both his hands. He stared at it incredulously, then bit it.

Anand, too, stared. From where he stood, it looked like the stranger had given the man a gold coin. But where, in this day and age, would the stranger get a gold coin?

'And what is your name, my good man?' the stranger asked. His tone was casual, but Anand felt the air in the room grow still, as before a storm. The throbbing increased in intensity. The blue glow was suddenly brighter, more alert. No. Surely he was being fanciful! How could a light be alert?

The man had not noticed any of this. Still staring at the coin, he said, 'It's Abdul.'

The stranger cupped a hand behind his ear. 'I'm sorry, I don't hear very well nowadays.'

'Abdul,' repeated the man.

'Ah, Amal!' the stranger said, nodding. 'A good Hindu name, that!'

'No, no, sir, I am not a Hindu! I am Muslim. My name is Abdul!'

No sooner had the man said his name for the third time than a finger of blue light leapt from the pit. It seemed to fasten itself onto his mouth. The man fell to the ground and heaved as though he was having difficulty breathing. The coin spilled from his hand and rolled along the floor. The light grew brighter. A terrible coldness radiated from it, making Anand's teeth chatter. The man pulled at his mouth, trying to dislodge the light. Finally, he stopped struggling and lay still. Soon after that the light snaked back to the pit like a fat, satisfied tentacle.

The stranger chanted a few words over the man before pulling him roughly to his feet. 'Go! Rejoin the crew,' he ordered, and the man stumbled blindly toward the tunnel.

Anand shrank back into the shadows, but there was no place to hide. The man was bound to spot him and cry out, and then the stranger would know that Anand had seen everything! Anand dreaded to think of what would happen to him then. But the man lurched past Anand without seeming to notice him.

The stranger picked up the gold coin and slipped it into the pocket of his shirt. He continued to stand at the edge of the pit, looking down into its depths as though waiting for something to happen. What was he staring at? Anand wondered with a shudder.

'O great jinn! O Ifrit!' the stranger called. 'I have given you one more spirit today, bringing the tally to one hundred. Why do you not help me avenge myself, as you had promised?'

A harsh, hissing sound came from the pit. It was a voice, but not a human one. It made Anand's insides turn to ice. 'O fool of a Kasim, with less brains inside your head than would fit inside a chickpea, you bring me only weak and untrained minds. They can add but little to my strength. To gain my full powers I must feast upon the spirits of powerful beings. Where is the magician whose presence I sensed, and his apprentice?'

Anand listened intently, his whole body held stiff. The being in the pit was referring to Abhaydatta and Raj-bhanu. He was sure of it!

The stranger paced angrily around the pit. 'Why do you taunt me? You know they escaped my net, despite my greatest efforts. I injured the younger one, but the old man was stronger than he appeared. I had almost caught them when he threw a cloak of protection around himself and his apprentice and disappeared. I do not know where they went. Perhaps they have gone into the forbidden world.'

Anand let out a grateful sigh. Abhaydatta and Raj-bhanu were safe – at least for the moment!

A sound, like metal grinding into metal, came from the pit, setting Anand's teeth on edge. The jinn, he realized, was laughing. 'Then they succeeded at what you have failed to accomplish for all these years, fool! Even now, with an entire village digging for you, you have not discovered the gateway. But no matter – bring me more men so I may suck out their spirits, and when I am strong enough, I will break the chains that Nawab Alibardi's magician Bismillah – curse his soul! – forged with his spells. The spells that threw you forward in time when you conspired against Alibardi, the spells that bound me to this infernal pit of torture because I aided you! Then will I blast you a new gateway, and together we will travel back four hundred years to the time of Alibardi and rule that world with our combined power.'

Kasim shook his head. 'Much as I would love to avenge myself on him, we cannot return to Alibardi's time. Bismillah is too powerful for us – we both know this, to our sorrow – so powerful that even after his death, the spell he set in motion will continue to guard Alibardi's realm for one hundred years. But when a hundred years have passed and Alibardi's grandson Nazib becomes nawab, the spell will diminish and fade. The new nawab will grow weak with an illness none can cure, and the court will be full of dissension. That is the world we must enter. In that world there exist no magicians with enough skill to counter our combined force – the Kabala has revealed this to me. Now tell me for certain, how many more men will you need?'

'Perhaps many, perhaps a few, perhaps only one,' the jinn replied. 'I sense among those you have brought this time a being of power, raw and unschooled, yet filled with the potential for great doings. Bring him to me. He may be enough.'

Anand didn't wait to hear any more. He ran back through the tunnel as fast as he could, no longer concerned about being quiet. He had very little time left. Now that Kasim had been instructed to search, as soon as he saw Anand he would know that Anand wasn't a mere village boy. And if he got Anand to the pit, Anand knew he would not be able to withstand the hypnotic pressure of that evil blue light. He would give it his name, and his spirit as well.

Emerging from the tunnel, he looked around him wildly. He had to find a place to hide until he decided what to do next. He didn't have much time. Behind him he could hear the echo of footsteps. Kasim was coming.

Desperately, he called to the conch. *Help me! Now more than ever I need your magical powers!*

He didn't hear it reply, but suddenly in his mind, clear as though it was outlined in fire, a sentence arose. *I am close, but to use me you must step into yourself.*

His heart leaped in excitement, then fell. What on earth did the words mean? Did the conch say them? It must be the conch, but why, oh why did it have to resort to riddles when what Anand needed were simple directions?

The footsteps were very close now, ringing on stone. To elude Kasim, he ducked into a crumbling doorway and found himself inside a room with large windows decorated with marble friezes. The roof here had once been supported by carved pillars. Most of them had fallen, but one still remained. He hid behind it, trying to control his panting. The footsteps paused outside the door. Had Kasim heard something? Could he sense Anand's presence? Anand pressed himself against the pillar. *No one is here,* he thought. *Only stone.* He closed his eyes and imagined himself to be part of the pillar, cool and solid and strong, enduring even when an entire civilization had passed away. After a while he heard the footsteps move off.

Anand let out the breath he'd been holding. Impulsively, he threw his arms around the pillar. *Thank you!* he whispered. *Now if only you could show me how to step into myself.*

It was a beautiful pillar, though he'd been too preoccupied to appreciate its elegance until now. It was carved from bands of black and white marble and inlaid in places with precious stones. As he looked at it, a pair of rubies detached themselves from the bottom of the pillar and rose up.

Anand jumped backwards, and only the fear of Kasim kept him

from crying out. What he'd been looking at were not rubies but the eyes of a snake. A cobra, to be exact. He stared, too petrified to run, as the snake unwound its long body from around the pillar. Had it been there all this while? Why hadn't it bitten Anand, then? However, it seemed ready to make up for that oversight right now as it glided towards him with lightning rapidity. Anand tensed his body. To have escaped the stranger only to be poisoned to death by a cobra! That would be a cruel joke, indeed, on the part of the universe.

The snake stopped in front of him and raised itself up. Anand flinched, waiting for the sharp fangs to strike, but the snake did not bite. It looked at him with its unblinking ruby gaze – in a reassuring kind of way. *A reassuring gaze from a cobra! Now I know I've gone crazy!* Anand thought. Still, he felt his body relax a little. The snake dropped to the floor and crossed the room with a sinuous grace, its scales glinting. It paused by a pile of rubble, then disappeared into it.

Anand knew he shouldn't go near the rubble. The snake probably had its nest inside the pile. *And just because it didn't bite me last time doesn't mean it's going to put up with me poking in there*, he told himself. But already he'd started removing the stones. Though he worked cautiously, gingerly, ready to pull back and run at any moment, he did not see the snake. It was as though it had vanished. He saw, instead, in the failing light of evening, a glint. Was it a piece of metal?

His heart beat unevenly. Kasim had insisted that they bring him anything metallic that they find. Could this be what he'd been looking for? He cleared the rubble feverishly, uncaring of his broken nails or his scratched fingers, and finally lifted out a square of metal about two handspans in length and width. When he turned it over, he realized that it was a mirror. He dusted it off carefully with his gamcha, amazed that it hadn't cracked under the weight of all those stones. When he held it up to look into it, he gave a start. Because it wasn't his own face he saw. Instead, it was as though he were looking through a small window. And on the other side of this window was a narrow, cobbled alley. Along it, men in turbans and long robes were leading mules loaded with sacks. At their head their leader, a bearded man in a flowing white robe and a headdress, rode on a black horse. When he stopped before a doorway, one of his men ran forward and knocked on it. A man opened the door, and a delicious aroma wafted forth.

'Tell Zafar Miah that Sheikh Asaf Ali has arrived from Peshawar with the juiciest dates, the whitest cashews, the sweetest dried apricots and the crispest pistachios in all of Allah's good world,' the man said.

'Zafar Miah will be glad to hear it!' the man cried. 'The nawab has taken ill and will eat nothing our cooks prepare for him. But perhaps with such delicacies, Zafar Miah will be able to tempt him.'

It was the world that Anand had been longing for and dreaming about, the world of Zafar's wonderful warm kitchen, the world of the rose gardens and veiled court ladies and the shahzada with his bejewelled shoes! The world from which Kasim had been banished, and which he was determined to re-enter and control. The world, Anand suspected, that Abhaydatta had escaped into, the world where the conch was hidden. Could Nisha be there, too? he wondered, his heart giving a leap.

Holding the mirror, Anand turned around. Immediately, the scene outside the window changed. Now he was looking into an enclosed courtyard shaded by many palm trees. There was a large pool in its centre, and women in fitted blouses and long colourful ghaghras that floated up around them in the water were bathing, splashing each other playfully. This must be the zenana, where the ladies of the court lived, safe from the gaze of men. Anand turned some more until he was looking into a large hall. A man was sitting on a huge, jewelled throne. He was dressed in a long coat embroidered with gold, but he leaned listlessly on the red velvet pillows that surrounded him and paid little attention to the supplicants that kneeled in front of him with their requests.

Was that Nawab Nazib, the one who was too ill to eat any of Zafar Miah's delicious creations? And had Anand found the gateway into his world?

eight

The Gateway

Anand turned the mirror this way and that for a while, marvelling at the different scenes that appeared in front of him. The mirror was a window through which he could see into the world of the past, he understood that much. But so far he was unable to understand how he should use it to enter that world. When he tried to reach through the mirror to what was on the other side, his fingers came up against solid glass, cold and quicksilver. He remembered the words he'd heard: *To use me you must step into yourself.* Could they have referred to this mirror? But how was he to step into himself when he couldn't even see his reflection in it?

Perhaps he was on the wrong track altogether. Perhaps the words had meant something subtler, as magical instructions often did. Perhaps he was supposed to use the mirror as an aid to meditation, to going deep inside oneself. He did not know much about meditation – he had just practised it a few times before he left the Brotherhood, and not very successfully. He would have to find a quiet place, away from the crew, and try it again tomorrow. Right now, though, darkness was falling fast around him, and shadows shivered behind broken doorways and pillars as though they were alive. Instinctively he knew that it wasn't safe to be alone in the ruins after dark. It was also dinnertime, and he didn't want the crew to notice his absence.

Anand wrapped the mirror carefully in his gamcha and made

his way to the centre of the ruin, where the crew huddled near the fire. He planned to slip the mirror into his bedroll before anyone questioned him about what he was carrying, and for this reason he ducked down the pillared outer passage, circling the hall area until he was close to the corner where the men stowed their bedding. He need not have worried. Most of the men, gathered around the fire, were too involved in a heated argument to notice him. The others – the unfortunate ones who had been to the pit in the past few days – sat leaning against their bedrolls, some only an arm's length from where Anand was crouching. But Anand knew that they, with their apathetic stares, were no threat to him.

Having hidden the mirror, he was about to make his way to the large pot where dinner – khichuri once again – was bubbling. By now he was so hungry that even the thought of overcooked lentils was a welcome one. He was curious, too, as to what the men were arguing about with such intensity. Usually they were too tired by the end of the day to do much except talk about how they would spend the money the stranger would be giving them. But just as he stood up, he felt a sharp tug on his elbow. It was Ramu. He held a finger to his lips and motioned for Anand to follow him out into the passageway.

'What's the matter?' Anand asked.

'Where were you all this time?' Ramu whispered. 'The stranger came to the digging area a while back. He was behaving very oddly. First he came close to each one of us and stared into our eyes. It gave me a dizzy feeling, as if he was reaching all the way inside my head. Then he walked around us, his nose wrinkled up, almost as though he was smelling us. Then he asked if anyone was missing from the group. Well, someone told him that the Mondol brothers were digging down on the eastern side where they'd found a big heap of stones, and that you'd gone off on your own, like you usually do, they weren't sure where. His eyes went all glittery when he heard that. He asked the men to tell him all about the three of you. Well, the Mondols have lived in the village for three generations, so the men had a lot to say about them. But halfway through he said he wasn't interested in them. He asked who you were, and where you'd come from. I kept quiet, but some of the others said you weren't from the village. The stranger said that we were to call him as soon as you came in. See that gong in the corner, we're supposed to ring it. And if you tried to run off, we were to tie you up. He said he'd give every one of us a reward if we did this.' Ramu stared at Anand curiously. 'What does he want with you? Did you do something you shouldn't have? Did you find something he wants and keep it for yourself?'

Anand couldn't help giving his bedroll a quick, guilty glance. 'I saw the pit,' he whispered. 'I think the stranger – his name is Kasim – guesses that I was there.'

'What's in the pit?'

'A demon – Kasim called it Ifrit. He's feeding the men's spirits to it.'

Ramu's mouth fell open for a moment. Then he laughed. 'You're making that up to scare me, aren't you?'

Anand's spirits sank. If Ramu, who was his friend, didn't believe him, what chance did he have of convincing the others of the danger they were in?

'I wish I was making it up!' he said. 'Come with me! I must tell the men about it right away. All of us need to get away from here as soon as possible.'

'Don't go there ...' Ramu started. But already Anand had walked into the circle of firelight.

'Here you are finally, boy!' said one of the men. 'What took you so long?'

'Where is it that you skulk off to each day while the rest of us are breaking our backs digging?' another asked with an unfriendly glare. 'And now you've done something to make the master angry with all of us!'

'Trouble,' said a third man, spitting into the fire. 'That's what he is, coming to our village from God-knows-where. Let's tie him up right now, like the master said.' Anand saw a thick coil of rope lying by the fire, waiting.

'Please!' he said urgently. 'I'll answer all your questions. But first I must tell you something that's far more important.' Quickly, he described the scene at the pit, speaking as clearly and logically as possible through the dread that arose in him at the memory of that cold, blue light. 'That's why your friends who go to dig at the pit have been silent and strange ever since they returned,' he ended. 'Their spirits are lost, and so will yours be if you don't escape right now.'

A heavy silence hung around him when he stopped speaking. The men looked at each other, and Anand could see some of them stealing glances at the men who'd been to the pit, who now sat in a corner, picking at their nails or staring into the darkness. Then, just as he'd begun to hope that he'd persuaded the crew, a voice shouted, 'The boy's lying!'

'Yes!' said another. 'He wants us to go back to the village without getting our money! What'll we tell our families?'

'He's planning something. Maybe when we're gone, he'll go to the master and ask for double pay.'

'He looks like a tricky one! I always told you these outlanders couldn't be trusted. Well, men, what do you say that we earn ourselves that reward the master promised?'

There were cheers.

'You don't understand,' Anand started, but his voice was lost in the commotion.

'Get the rope,' someone shouted. 'Grab his arms!'

A man caught Anand's arms roughly and held them down at his side. Someone else was throwing a black rope over his shoulders. It slithered unpleasantly across his back as though it were alive. Anand struggled, but there were too many of them for him to fight.

Then a figure rushed toward Anand, throwing himself headfirst onto one of his captors. It was Ramu.

'Run, Bishu, run!' he yelled as he sank his teeth into the arm of the man who was tying Anand up. The man swore and the rope slipped from his hand. Anand didn't wait to see any more. He shrugged out of the rope and ran as fast as he could, stopping only to grab the mirror. The gamcha had fallen off, and the mirror shone with sudden brilliance in the firelight.

'Look!' one of the crew shouted. 'He's got something in his hands!'

'Maybe it's the treasure! That's why the master was so upset! After him! And you, Hassan, strike the gong!'

A deep, melancholy ringing pursued Anand as he ran from the hall. It reverberated in his ears as he ducked into one ruined room after another. But nowhere could he find a satisfactory hiding place. Behind him, he could hear the men shouting and running, looking for him. He heard Kasim's voice, chill and efficient, directing them. 'Idiots! Grab a lighted helmet, each one of you! You two go to the right. And you, go down that passageway under the peacock arch. I'll take the left corridor.'

The left! That was the way Anand had taken. What ill luck led Kasim to choose the same direction? Anand tried to move through the dark as quickly as he could, and as silently, though it was hard to be silent when he couldn't see where he was going. On several occasions he stubbed his toes or banged into piles of stone, toppling them. From time to time he darted a glance over his shoulder to see if Kasim was catching up. Yes, he could see a light bobbing not too far behind him. Desperately, he sprinted through a doorway, caught his foot on something that felt like a tree root, and fell. He tried to save the mirror, which was still in his hands, but it hit the floor with a crash. Despair filled his heart. Surely the mirror could not have survived such a fall! The room he was in was roofless, and a little moonlight pushed past the towering shal trees to lend a glimmer to the scene. In that faint light, Anand saw – miracle of miracles – the mirror was unharmed! Not even a crack marred Anand's face as he peered into it.

It took him a moment to realize that he was seeing his reflection.

He held up the mirror to look closer. Immediately, his face was replaced by a busy market-scene, men selling live chickens and goats, yelling out prices. But when he put the mirror back on the floor, he could see himself in it again.

The mirror had to be laid on the floor for it to become a gateway!

Elated, Anand put out his hand, expecting it to go through the mirror this time. But once again his fingertips touched solid glass.

Passing through the gateway was not going to be as simple as he'd thought it would be.

Behind him, he could hear Kasim grunting and cursing as he searched the ruins for him. The bobbing light was getting closer. Anand closed his eyes, trying desperately to concentrate. What had the words said? *You must step into yourself.*

The light was very near the room now. He could hear Kasim breathing hard. There was only one thing Anand could think of doing. If it didn't work, he was doomed. He stood up.

'Boy!' Kasim called. 'I can feel you – you're somewhere very close! Come out from your hiding place now, and I'll make sure you don't get hurt. But if you don't, then when I find you – and I *will* find you, have no doubt of that, because there's no place for you to escape to – you'll be truly sorry. By the time I'm finished with you, you'll be begging for death.'

A numbness spread through Anand's entire being when he heard these words, and he faltered. Images of the pit rose up in his mind. Would Kasim throw him in there as punishment? He heard the jinn's grating laughter again, and for a moment all he could see was that chill blue light. Perhaps he *should* give himself up, he thought. Kasim was right – there *was* no way out of here – at least not one that Anand knew how to use. Fear cramped his stomach, and he clutched at it, remembering how once he had carried the conch in a pouch tied around his middle. How he wished that it were with him right now!

With that thought he gained a moment's strength. *If I give up,* he thought, *then who will find the conch?* Holding his breath, he raised his right foot above the mirror. He could see the reflection of his sole – filthy, callused, red with dust from the ruins. He stepped down onto it.

Two things happened then: the mirror began to glow, and Kasim came into the room. When he saw what Anand was doing, his body stiffened and his eyes went wide with anger and incredulity. The mirror was flashing intermittently; bright strobes of light blinded Anand, disorienting him. He felt a moment of terror, recalling the portal the conch had opened for him, that crazy spinning into nowhere. And this time he'd be alone on this journey, without the conch to protect him. What if he was trapped in-between two worlds?

Kasim had recovered from his shock. He ran towards Anand, arms outstretched to seize him. There was no more time. Anand put his left foot down on the mirror. He felt Kasim clutch at his shirt and heard the old fabric tear. Then somehow Kasim's hand was gone, and blackness was all around him.

This time the sensation was that of falling down a bottomless tunnel. His stomach flipped over, and bile rose in his throat. He tried to hold on to something, but the walls around him were like black glass and his fingers slid off. But it wasn't completely dark in here, as he had thought at first. There was a little square of light above his head. Looking up, he realized he was looking through the mirror in reverse. Though he knew he was travelling with great velocity, the mirror seemed only an arm's length away. Was it moving with him? But no, he could see Kasim, his face contorted with rage, bent low over it, trying to see in. He was chanting something – a spell, possibly. Then he stood up and brought his foot down on the mirror, just as Anand had done. Anand could see the underside of his boot pressed onto the glass. Once more, the mirror began to glow.

He was going to follow Anand through the gateway! Anand's palms grew damp at the realization. With his superior magical skills, Kasim would probably catch up with Anand in the time-tunnel. Maybe he would kill him right here, before Anand could reach the other world and warn anyone of what was happening. And then Kasim would be free to go to the court of Nazib and wreak vengeance and chaos.

And Anand had enabled it to happen! If it weren't for him, Kasim would still be searching for the gateway.

Kasim raised his other foot.

'No!' cried Anand. He raised his hands and, trying to remember what he'd learned of telekinesis, pushed upward with his whole mind, trying to keep the gateway closed. But he wasn't strong enough. He could feel an opposing pressure bearing down on him

– the will of the sorcerer, he guessed. It was too strong for him. It forced him to his knees. *Conch!* He called in anguish, and then, *Mirror!* But his voice reverberated in the glass tunnel, going nowhere. Horrified, he watched as Kasim brought his other foot down.

He had expected to see Kasim's feet come through the square into the tunnel, but instead the mirror exploded into a thousand pieces. The blast lifted Kasim like a rag doll and threw him somewhere beyond Anand's sight. The square of light was disintegrating. Shards from the mirror fell everywhere. Anand caught at one and gasped as the sharp edge cut his finger.

The tunnel was completely dark now. Anand felt a rushing around him like a strong wind. It threw him to the ground. In it he heard faint, faraway sounds like the clash of swords, and the blowing of war-trumpets. Finally – who knows after how long – the wind died down. Slowly, shakily, Anand rose to his feet, blinking in the sudden light. He found himself in a narrow alleyway, clutching a piece of mirror about the size of his thumb in his bleeding fingers. Over the tops of the cramped buildings that looked like shops, he saw a looming red palace, its sandstone walls glittering in the late-morning sun. He had crossed over the barrier of time into Nawab Nazib's world! He looked around cautiously, but there was no sign of Kasim anywhere.

For some reason he couldn't fathom, the gateway had repelled the sorcerer, even though that action had caused its own destruction. For the moment, Anand was safe. But now that there was no gateway anymore, how would he ever get back to his own world?

nine

In the Palace of Nawab Nazib

Anand looked around the alleyway, his entire being charged with
excitement. He couldn't believe that he was actually here, in a world
hundreds of years before his time! He would worry about the
shattered gateway later. Right now, the scene in front of him was too
fascinating for him to think of anything else. The narrow lane, with
its floor of packed dirt, was crowded with tiny shops, each crammed
against the other. He couldn't tell what kind of items they sold, for
their doors were shut, and he was unable to decipher the letters of
the painted wooden signs that hung above them. It seemed that
families lived upstairs from the shops, for he could see washing
hung out to dry, and parrots calling from cages set on balconies. For
a moment he was worried that someone might have seen him
appear from nowhere. But for some reason, though it was the
middle of the day, the alley was empty. He could hear a large group
of people, however, somewhere close by. They were yelling good-
naturedly, their voices happy with anticipation. Anand decided to
go and explore. Fortunately, he found that he was dressed once
again in the white clothes that all the palace servants wore. It would
allow him to blend in easily with the crowd.

He looked down at the shard of mirror in his hand. His finger had stopped bleeding, but there was dried blood along one edge of the glass. He started to toss it into a pile of rubbish on the roadside, then hesitated. Even if it could be of no further use to him, it had once been an object of power. It seemed disrespectful to throw it on a heap of household sweepings, to end its days among dust balls and vegetable peels. Moreover, it had saved his life. If it hadn't been for the mirror, he would have been in Kasim's grasp by now. Perhaps even at this moment the jinn would have been sucking his spirit away. He glanced around and noticed a small store at the edge of the alley. Its walls were cheaply built, with gaps already appearing between the bricks and mud. Anand chose a large gap into which he could fit the fragment, which was about four inches long. *Strange!* He thought as he slipped it in. *Hadn't it seemed smaller just a few moments back?* But he was impatient to join the crowd, so, with a whispered word of thanks, he ran towards the commotion.

He found himself on a wide and stately avenue paved with stone blocks. It was lined with gulmohur trees in full bloom. The red flowers filled the sky with their cheerful, fiery colour. The street was equally colourful, lined with people dressed in their holiday best – men in long jubbas and bright turbans, women in gathered ghaghras that swirled around their ankles, their thin veils sparkling with sequins. Vendors had already set up their stalls under the trees, and Anand could see lamb roasting on spits. He could also smell the delicious odours of wheat parathas and potato tikkas browning on flat tawas. His stomach gave a small, protesting growl. Giddy with excitement, children ran along the edges of the street, begging for treats, while their mothers shouted at them to get back before they were trampled to death by the elephants, who would be here any instant. By standing on tiptoe and craning his neck, Anand saw that the crowd was being held back by sentries carrying ceremonial spears, resplendent in red turbans bordered with gold, staring straight ahead with their impassive, moustachioed faces.

'What is going on, uncle?' he asked one of the men in the crowd.

'Why, don't you know? It is the young shahzada's birthday, Allah grant him a long and healthy life! A procession will be coming down this road soon with the prince at its head. I've heard he will distribute coins to all who have gathered to honour him. Have you never seen a royal procession before? Oh, it is a splendid thing, indeed! Come, I'll make a bit of space for you next to me.'

Gratefully, Anand squeezed to the front of the crowd – and just in time. Down the avenue he could see the musicians with their drums and shehnais, dancing as they advanced. A group of horsemen followed them. The riders had on the same red and gold turbans as the sentries. Anand guessed this to be the uniform of the nawab's men-at-arms. The horses wore plumes and bridles decorated with shiny brass bells and stepped proudly in time to the music. Behind them – Anand's eyes widened as they fell on them – came the elephants.

Anand had only seen an elephant once, a long time ago in the Alipore chiria-khana, when he lived in Kolkata. That had been a sad-eyed, dusty beast that wandered listlessly around its cage, and he had felt sorry for it. These elephants were quite different! They were massive animals that swayed majestically as they carried silken howdahs on their backs. The lead elephant was an elegant beast with gleaming tusks that looked like they had been polished. Her forehead was decorated with an elaborate, painted design, and around her neck she wore a silver collar. On her back sat a mahout who directed her from time to time by tapping her with a trident. Behind the mahout, on a silken howdah covered with a canopy to keep out the sun, sat a boy – the same boy Anand had seen drinking pomegranate juice earlier, when he'd first glimpsed Nazib's world. Today, he was dressed in a sherwani coat so thickly embroidered with gold thread that Anand couldn't even see the cloth beneath. He wore a matching turban on his head. In its centre was a jewel the size of a pigeon's egg. But in spite of all his finery, in spite of the people cheering and bowing to him, he looked bored and restless.

Behind the shahzada sat a lady. A jewel-studded veil covered her entire upper body, but her hands, their slim fingers sparkling with many rings, were beautiful. She leaned forward and whispered something into the shahzada's ear while smoothing back a lock of hair that had escaped from his turban. Anand guessed that she was the begum, the prince's mother. Her small, affectionate gesture brought his own mother – whom he would probably never see again – to Anand's mind, and a lump of sorrow rose in his throat.

The begum must have been reminding the prince of his duties, for now he opened a large box that sat in front of him and lifted out a fistful of silver coins. He threw them out over the crowd. The people applauded louder, crying out to Allah to bless their handsome, gracious shahzada, as they scurried for the coins. The boy smiled, pleased with the praise, and threw out more money. It amused him to see people grovelling on the road to pick them up, and sometimes, though his mother shook her head, he threw the coins straight ahead of him, in the path of the elephant, and laughed as people darted in dangerously close to the beast's giant legs to get them. But in a few minutes he grew tired of this game, too. He pulled at the mahout's shirt, gesturing for him to make the elephant go faster. The mahout reluctantly prodded the beast, and the elephant raised her trunk and trumpeted her displeasure. The begum was displeased, too. But when she pointed to the box of coins – probably telling the shahzada his task wasn't done yet – he sulkily up-ended the box, letting all the coins fall in a heap close to where Anand was standing.

When the crowd realized what had happened, there was a stampede, everyone rushing for this last chance to fill their pockets. Someone shoved Anand roughly onto the road so that he stumbled right onto the elephant's path. Looking up, he saw that the beast's raised leg was inches from his head. Any moment, it would come down, smashing his skull like an egg. Frozen with fear, he closed his eyes.

But instead of a crushing weight on his head, he felt something soft and rubbery touching his cheek lightly. It was the elephant's trunk! She wrapped it around Anand's arm and pulled him up gently until Anand was standing beside her. Anand held onto the trunk for balance and looked for a moment into the elephant's eyes, black and kind and infinitely wise. *Thank you*, he whispered in the beast-language that he had learned in the valley, though he wasn't sure that would work in this world. He couldn't tell if the elephant understood him, for right then the mahout yelled a command and she moved on.

Anand stood staring after the elephant, still dazed by his near-accident and unexpected rescue. He was brought back to the present by more cheers. Another elephant, larger and darker than the first, was approaching, carrying a howdah that looked just as sumptuous as the prince's. On it sat a tall man with a stern face and dark, intense eyes that darted over the crowd. His outfit was as elaborate as the prince's, and on his turban he wore a diamond that sparkled blindingly when it caught the sun. He, too, was throwing coins to the crowd – Anand moved back quickly from the edge of the road when he saw this – but even their cheers did not bring a smile to his lips.

'Uncle,' he asked one of the men near him. 'Is that the nawab?'

'Where did you come from, you dim-witted lout!' the man exclaimed. 'Even children who have barely learned to talk know that this is Haider Ali, the nawab's chief minister.' He lowered his voice. 'Some say he is the most powerful man in the kingdom, more so than even the nawab.'

Behind the chief minister's elephant came others, carrying the rest of the courtiers. The last few elephants, he was surprised to see, carried children. They, too, were lavishly dressed, a stark contrast to the street urchins who ran about in their ragged garments and bare feet.

'Who are these?' he ventured to ask.

'The children of the courtiers, of course,' his informant snapped. 'Who did you think they were?' Then, taking pity on Anand's ignorance, he pointed out the more important ones – the sons of the army commandant and the treasurer, and the daughter of one of the nawab's other wives.

'And this is Paribanou, niece of the chief minister,' he said, pointing to a girl who was sitting on the last elephant.

The girl looked as though she was Anand's age. Dressed in a sky-blue salwar kameez shot through with gold threads, and covered with a gauzy blue veil, she sat between two other girls, who were whispering into her ear. Behind them sat a woman attendant, keeping a watchful eye on them. The girls must have said something funny, for Paribanou threw her head back to laugh. Her veil slipped. The scandalized attendant quickly pulled it over her head again, scolding her all the while. But Anand had already seen her face. In spite of the elaborate braids and jewellery, the kohl that lined her eyes and the betel leaf juice that reddened her lips, he recognized her.

The girl was Nisha!

'Nisha! Nisha!' he cried, running alongside the elephant, pushing past the people who lined the street, uncaring of danger, of what people might think. One of the girl's companions noticed him and pulled at her sleeve. She turned and looked at him through the veil, then turned away without interest.

She didn't know who Anand was!

Anand's head swam. Had he made a mistake? Had his longing to find his friend clouded his vision and made Paribanou look like Nisha? No! He was sure it wasn't so. Somehow Nisha had taken on an alternate identity in this older world, just as he had, and in doing so had forgotten who she really was. If only he could speak with her!

Paribanou's elephant had moved on ahead by now. One of her companions looked back at Anand and made a comment, and all the girls laughed. Anand's face was hot with embarrassment, but he was determined not to give up. Maybe when the procession ended and the girls dismounted from the elephant, he'd have a chance to speak to Paribanou. He began to run once again, but a rough hand grasped his shoulder and spun him around. The sharp, shiny tip of a sentry's spear was inches from his face.

'How dare you run behind the chief minister's niece and call out to her, you insolent servant boy!' the sentry cried. 'Have you no fear, or has the sun's heat addled your brain? It is Allah's great mercy that Haider Ali did not see you, or he would have had you beheaded before nightfall. Now run back to your duties, before I give you the beating you deserve.'

Anand made his way through the dispersing crowd, not sure what to do next. Paribanou was an important personage in this world, cherished and guarded by her powerful uncle, and Anand was only a servant boy. How would he ever get near her? His growling stomach made him realize that he hadn't eaten in a long while. He cast a longing look at the street vendors' wares and searched the pockets of his tunic with hopeful fingers, but he did not find even a single coin. Apparently his alter-identity was no good at saving money! Then he remembered Zafar Miah in his bustling kitchen with its mouth-watering smells. That's what he would do – he'd go to the gruff, kind chef, and ask for something to eat. Perhaps a meal would give him the energy to come up with a plan. He asked a boy who was sprinkling water in front of a cloth-merchant's shop in order to keep down the dust if he could show him the way to the nawab's kitchens.

The boy looked at Anand curiously, wondering, no doubt, why a palace servant didn't know this basic information, but finally he pointed to an alleyway. 'It leads to the back gate of the palace. That's the closest to the rasoi-khana,' he said. Following it, Anand found himself in front of a set of huge metal-studded doors. He walked up to them fearfully, afraid that the gatekeeper posted there might ask him questions to which he had no answers. But the man was busy picking his teeth and barely spared Anand a glance as he slipped through. Servant boys must use this entrance all the time, Anand thought. No one even notices them. For the first time, he realized that the ordinariness of his identity gave him an advantage. It was almost as good as a spell of invisibility!

※◎※

It wasn't difficult for Anand to find his way to the kitchens; he had only to follow his nose. In a few minutes, he stood at the threshold, observing the scene in front of him with pleasure, breathing in the delicious fragrances of basmati rice and curries simmering in large pots. But Zafar was nowhere to be seen.

One of the cooks looked up from grinding meat, gram flour and chillies into a paste for kebabs. 'What do you want, boy?' he said, his voice annoyed. Then, as Anand hesitated, he added, 'Off with you, unless you have a good reason to be here!' He took a step towards Anand, ready to speed him on his way with a cuff to his head. 'No-good rascals, coming to the kitchen all the time, expecting free food, taking advantage of Zafar Miah's soft heart …'

Anand tensed, ready to flee, but just then he heard the booming voice of Zafar coming down the corridor. In a moment the big man could be seen, walking along with a companion. The new man must have been a palace employee, too, and an important one, for his white jubba was tied at the waist with a wide silk cummerbund, crimson as a sunset and embroidered with gold.

Zafar was shaking his head dejectedly. 'Something is wrong with the nawab, mark my words, Latif Miah. Today I prepared a pista-pulao specially for him, using fresh pistachios from Kabul and aged basmati rice so that it would be easy to digest. But he sent it back untouched! This has never happened before. I must make him some lassi tonight, with fresh yogurt and roasted cumin powder. Hopefully, it will settle the ill humours in his body. It is too bad we no longer have a great magician at court like the fabled Bismillah. He would have chanted a spell and cured our nawab in no time!'

'You are not the only one with problems, Zafar Miah,' the other man said in a dejected voice. 'Look at me – six punkah-pullers fallen sick on the same day – no doubt from too much drink at the moon-watching festival last night. And the afternoon session of the court will start in an hour! I have somehow managed to find three men to work the fans there, but I desperately need more. And where am I to find them? It is enough to make a man's beard turn gray. How I wish I had listened to my bibi and retired to my home village last monsoon season!'

'Don't worry so much, my friend,' Zafar said soothingly. 'Let me make you a glass of my cardamom tea. It will calm you, and then you will know what to do.' He caught sight of Anand and clapped his hands. 'Look! Here is one solution to your problem – our young Abbas!' He beckoned Anand over. 'You may not have noticed this fine young man before – he's been here only for a month now – but he's a diligent worker. And no wonder – he comes from the same village as I do! I know he has never been in the courtroom before, but he is smart and will learn what to do quickly.'

Latif gave Anand a dubious look. Then, shoulders slumping, he sighed.

'What choice do I have?' he said in melancholy tones. To Anand he said, sternly, 'Boy, can you follow orders and, more important, can you remain quiet and not draw attention to yourself?'

'Yes, sir,' Anand replied, giving an awkward bow. Here was an unexpected development! He wasn't sure what it would lead to, but at least it would allow him to observe the nawab and his courtiers closely. Might Abhaydatta be among them? His heart speeded up at the possibility. He longed to see the old healer again, to tell him about Nisha and her strange amnesia. Surely Abhaydatta, master of forgetting and remembrance, would know what to do with her.

'Don't let me down, or else I'll give you a whipping you'll remember for a long time!' Latif warned. 'Be ready in half an hour. Ask the other punkah boys to get you the appropriate clothes for court – and you'd better not dirty them, like you've done with these. Ask Rahman to guide you to the court hall. Now, brother Zafar, how about some of that cardamom tea you promised?'

ten

The Durbar

Half an hour later, Anand, fortified by a delicious meal of fried fish,
vegetables and pulao (the same pulao that the nawab had – foolishly,
in Anand's opinion – rejected), was on his way to the hall where the
afternoon session of the court was to be held. He was dressed in a
kurta made of stiff white silk – the expected attire, he guessed, for
servants who had to be in attendance at the durbar. His guide,
Rahman, a boy slightly older than him, had been a punkah-puller
at the nawab's court for several seasons now. Anand confessed to
him that he didn't know his way around the palace at all.

'Don't worry,' Rahman said. 'All of us felt overwhelmed at first
when we started working here. This is the summer palace of Nawab
Nazib, so it is only half the size of the main fort in Murshidabad.
But it's still large enough that it's easy to get lost in, so be sure to
take note of the turns we are taking.'

Anand stared in awe at the maze of corridors and courtyards
that led off in different directions. The palace wasn't just one
building, as the ruins had led him to believe, but a huge compound
of many structures joined by walkways or separated by gardens, all
of it surrounded by high walls of stone. It had obviously been

carefully designed. Leafy tamarind trees and jacarandas heavy with blue flowers were planted along the avenues to provide shade. The main roads were paved with stone or brick, often laid out in intricate designs, and bordered by man-made canals that kept the city cool. The residential quarters of the rich were particularly resplendent, with arched marble gateways and fountains, though the common people, as Anand had already seen in the alleyway, lived quite differently.

'It's like a city in here! Do people live in all these different buildings?' he asked.

'Oh yes,' Rahman said. 'It's quite crowded in the palace. Because the nawab stays here for several months each year, his ministers come with him, so the work of the court can continue. Though recently the nawab seems tired all the time, and pays little attention to the business of ruling. The nobles bring their families, their favourite animals – mostly horses and elephants, though some of the court ladies keep pet deer, and birds are always popular – and, of course, their servants. Each of the nobles has quarters in the palace assigned to him, the biggest and best ones being for the nawab's favourites. This building,' here he pointed to high walls topped with spearheads beyond which Anand couldn't see, 'is where the nawab's queens and their maidservants live. He has more than fifty wives ...'

'Fifty wives!' Anand interjected, amazed. Although he had read a little about the lives of nawabs and kings in history class, the reality of their lives had never struck him with such force before.

'Yes. That's nothing! His father had almost a hundred! But only a few accompany the nawab in the summer. I've heard it's really beautiful in there, with a marble pool to swim in, peacocks roaming everywhere, and the whole place smelling of jasmine and roses. But don't even think of going in – not that you'd get past the guards – because the punishment for any man or boy who enters the zenana is immediate death!'

This was truly a different world he found himself in, Anand thought as they hurried along, a world with different rules – rules he had better learn fast if he wanted to survive.

They were passing another imposing, enclosed building. This time there were sentries at the massive gates, which were reinforced with silver and steel. The upstairs windows were covered by a filigree of marble, so that no one could see in. The sentries carried sinister-looking muskets and, unlike the more relaxed palace guards Anand had seen earlier, seemed to mean business.

'Who lives here?' Anand asked.

'The chief minister, Haider Ali. You had better not stray in here, either, if you value your life! The chief minister has the reputation of being ruthless with trespassers.'

'Does he have many wives, too?' Anand asked.

'Not he! His only family is his niece, the beautiful Paribanou. I've heard he dotes on her – though it's hard to imagine the iron-fisted Haider Ali showing affection to anyone!' Rahman said.

Anand stared at the windows with new interest. Perhaps Nisha – he couldn't reconcile himself to thinking of her as Paribanou – was up there right now, looking at him. He thought he saw a shadow darkening one of the squares, but the filigree made it hard to be certain. His heart fell as he eyed the sentries at the gate. More than ever, it seemed impossible that he would get close enough to Nisha to speak to her.

'See, back there are the servants quarters,' Rahman said, 'and over in the corner are the stables for the nawab's horses. He uses them when he hunts roebuck and wild boar, though of course when he goes after tigers, he always rides one of his elephants. He is a fine rider and hunter, the best in the land, but this summer he hasn't ventured out even once.'

'Where are the elephants kept?' Anand asked, thinking of the shahzada's elephant, which had saved him from being so grievously injured. It would be good to see her again.

'The hathi-khana is near the gate which opens onto the lake, because the elephants love to take baths early each morning,' Rahman said, pointing to fenced-off area in the distance that bordered the palace wall. 'And now, here we are at the durbar.'

The durbar was a great hall with high ceilings, polished marble and granite walls, and pillars inlaid with coloured stones that glittered expensively. At one end of the room was a raised dais with a massive gold and silver throne on it. The seat was covered with thick silk quilts; silken bolsters served as armrests. A rich Persian carpet in jewel colours covered the dais. Behind the dais, the entire wall was covered with the most exquisite filigree work that Anand had ever seen. Two beautiful silver doors were placed in the centre of the wall, a little behind the throne. A silver railing ran around the dais, fencing off the throne area from the rest of the court. The room was further divided into sections by a bronze railing and an iron railing – probably to separate the less important nobility from the more important ones. All through the hall, large leaf-shaped fans made of embroidered cloth hung from the ceiling, attached to ropes. Punkah-pullers were at many of the fans already. The punkahs near the throne were especially sumptuous, made of silk with iridescent peacock feathers stitched into them.

Anand had expected to be sent to the back of the hall, but as they entered, one of the court officials called out, 'You, boys! Take the two punkahs on either side of the throne. Move fast! It's almost time for the courtiers to come in!'

'The punkah-pullers don't like to be close to the nawab,' Rahman whispered as they made their way toward the dais. 'More chances of things going wrong – of a whipping, or maybe even being thrown into jail! There are stories about punkah-pullers who had their arms chopped off because they didn't pull the punkahs fast enough, causing the nawab to sweat. But don't worry – that was only during the time of our nawab's grandfather, who was known for his fiery temper. Just follow me and do exactly what I do. Remember to keep your eyes lowered, and move as little as possible. As long as no one notices you, you'll be fine.'

Filled with misgiving, Anand went to his station, picked up the thick cord attached to the end of his punkah, and gave it a tentative tug. It was heavier than he had expected. The punkah swung jerkily. He darted a glance at Rahman and tried to copy his hand movements and the way he swayed his body back and forth. This time the punkah moved smoothly, releasing the fragrance of roses. Someone must have sprayed the fans with rose attar! But the work was hard – in a minute, Anand could feel his arm muscles beginning to burn with the unaccustomed strain. He grit his teeth and tried to fall into a rhythm, as Rahman had.

A great gong sounded, and a line of men dressed in form-fitting pants and glittering tunics that fell in folds of swishing silk past their knees entered and took their places. They wore turbans of many colours, some set with stones, but all went barefoot as a mark of respect to the nawab. The ones wearing the finest attire stood closest to the silver railing. Anand guessed that these were the most favoured nobles. He had expected Haider Ali to be at their head, but, surprisingly, the chief minister wasn't there.

The space behind the bronze and iron railings was filling up with other courtiers – Anand darted a quick look at them, hoping to see Abhaydatta. But there was no sign of him either. Beyond the courtiers, milling around in the open compound outside the hall and kept in check by sentries with spears, were the many commoners who hoped to beg the nawab for a favour or even to just see him for – as Rahman had explained earlier to Anand – a single glimpse of the nawab, chosen by Allah to rule his people, was considered to bring good luck.

Now a second gong rang, and at the sound a hush descended on the hall. The nawab was coming! The carved silver doors Anand had noticed earlier swung open behind the dais, and musicians playing on shehnais and drums ushered in a standard bearer who carried a tall flag, a silver crescent moon on a field of green velvet. Behind him came the nawab's personal guard, a line of armoured men holding up shining, unsheathed swords. They positioned themselves strategically around the dais. Two boys followed, strewing the ground with colourful petals, and upon this walked the nawab. He was a short, slight man with a kind mouth but a weak chin. He was dressed in a cream silk kurta embroidered with beautiful gold lotus flowers and wore gold shoes that curled up at the end. A turban with a large diamond at its centre sat on his head. The assembly cheered as he entered. The nawab raised his hand and smiled, but Anand could see that he walked slowly and falteringly, and the smile took some effort.

At his elbow strode Haider Ali, his clothing almost as resplendent as the nawab's. As the nawab climbed onto the dais, he stumbled. He would have fallen if the chief minister's arm had not shot out to catch him. A look of concern passed over Haider Ali's face, softening his otherwise proud, impassive expression.

When the nawab had settled himself on the throne, leaning against a bolster, Haider Ali, who stood at the foot of the dais, made a sign. At once the court announcer stepped forward with a parchment from which he read the first set of petitions for the day. Rich and poor, Hindu and Muslim, subjects of all kinds came to the nawab with requests. A nobleman had died childless, leaving a rich jagir behind, and a neighbouring nobleman wanted the nawab's permission to take over the estate. In return, he offered to pay a hefty tax to the state treasury each year. A merchant's caravans had been captured by a band of Borgee mercenaries, and all his goods seized. He prostrated himself in front of the nawab and wept and tore his hair, crying out for justice. A poor widow, veiled in a burkha, begged him for enough money to enable her to send her eldest son to a famous madrasah where he could study to become a clergyman. A shopkeeper brought a complaint against a trader of silks who had taken his money but not delivered the goods he had promised. A dacoit caught while robbing a zamindar's mansion was dragged before the throne, his face still darkened with the lampblack he had rubbed on it to keep people from recognizing him. The zamindar, a fat, oily man, demanded that he be sentenced to a long and painful death. An emissary from the East India Company requested the extension of a trading treaty.

Each time a case was announced, the nawab would lean toward Haider Ali and consult with him. They would discuss the matter for a moment, then the nawab would nod, and Haider Ali would call out the decision reached in his sonorous, confident voice. Though his bearing was one of complete respect to his monarch, it was clear to all that the chief minister was really the one in charge. Listening in fascination to the judgements, Anand had to admit they were just ones. Haider Ali had the instincts of a good leader; he knew when to be merciful and when to be severe.

The nobleman was given the jagir, but in exchange for a higher tax than what he had offered. The commander-in-chief of the nawab's army was ordered to launch an offensive against the Borgees, for they were becoming a serious threat to law-abiding citizens. He was not to stop until he captured the Borgee captain – or killed him. A full payment of fees was to be made to the madrasah for the widow's son. The trader of silks was to be arrested, and forced to refund all the money he had taken from the shopkeeper. In addition, the trader would pay a large fine to the treasury for his unlawful acts. The dacoit, whose band had killed several of the zamindar's guards, was sentenced to death – but swiftly, by hanging, though his body was to be left on the gallows for a night and a day, to instil fear into the hearts of other lawbreakers. The zamindar was sternly admonished to take better care of his villagers so that hunger and need did not drive them to break the law. The East India Company was granted an extension, but warned that there had been complaints against their agents for being too harsh with the farmers from whom they bought spices, dyes and tobacco, and paying them too little. If this continued, the nawab would revoke their permit and ask them to leave the state.

The plaintiffs – even those who were not pleased with the decisions – accepted the judgements without protest. They bowed thrice to the nawab, and once to Haider Ali, but as though in recognition of his power, their kornish to him was even more deferential. Then they backed out of the nawab's presence, being careful not to turn their backs, which would be a grave show of disrespect, on him.

As the durbar progressed, Anand grew aware of small sounds from behind the wall with the filigree. He could hear whispers, the tinkle of bangles, once even a smothered laugh. The women of the zenana were back there, observing what went on in court! He imagined them commenting on events, or gossiping about the various people who appeared in front of the nawab, their clothes and jewellery, their mannerisms, their business. Was this the highlight of their day, the one chance in their sheltered women's existence to see how the outside world functioned, to watch the play of power? But perhaps he was wrong in thinking this. It could well be that the world of the zenana was exciting in its own right. Anand remembered reading in his history book about the political intrigues that went on in there, about wives or concubines who were so influential that they were known as kingmakers by later generations. Was the begum such a woman, in spite of her delicate appearance, her slender jewelled fingers? Was she, even at this moment, watching the proceedings carefully, observing the interaction between her husband and his chief minister, troubled by the nawab's dwindling health and the growing power wielded by Haider Ali? Perhaps her son was sitting by her – for the prince was still too young to attend the durbar. But she would want him to begin learning about how to govern a kingdom while he was young. Anand imagined the shahzada to be sulking with boredom, looking for a chance to play pranks on the other children there.

Then a thought struck him. Was Nisha there, too? It was very possible. Unless being in a different world had changed her personality totally, she would insist on being in the centre of the action. And as Haider Ali's niece, she was sure to command a seat in the front row, directly behind the filigree, to allow her a clear view of the durbar. That meant she would be able to see Anand clearly, too! The last time she hadn't recognized him – but that was understandable because it had happened so quickly, in the midst of a crowd that pushed and shoved around him. Surely this time if she saw Anand's face, she would know who he was!

Cautiously, he tried to angle his body so that it was sideways to the zenana wall. Though he had been warned against it, he raised his face a little so Nisha would be able to see his profile. In attempting all this, he almost lost the heavy rope that he'd been pulling, and had to lunge for it with his aching fingers. Luckily, he caught it before the weight of the punkah whisked it too far from him. Heart pounding, he could only hope no one – no one except Nisha, that is – had noticed him.

In the middle of the reading of a petition, the nawab leaned toward Haider Ali. Anand heard him say that he was too tired to continue. He had to lie down for a while.

'Send me a new hakim, Haider,' he added. 'The last doctor was of no use in curing this pain that chews on my insides. Each day it gains in intensity, so that I can fall asleep only with the help of opium, a larger dose each time.'

Haider Ali looked concerned. 'Indeed I will, your majesty,' he said. 'I will search for the best hakim in all the land and send him to you as soon as I can. Meanwhile, I shall ask the announcer to end the durbar session, and have your palanquin brought here, and personally accompany you to your resting quarters.'

The nawab gazed at all the people still waiting to have their petitions presented to him. 'No, don't ask for the palanquin to be brought into the durbar, Haider,' he said. 'It is not good for the people to see how unwell I am. And don't cancel the durbar. Many of these poor souls have travelled for days to get here. I am aware – though I do not like it – that many have paid a large bribe even to be allowed into the durbar. Too often lately they have been turned back because of my ill health. My bodyguards will accompany me back, and the begum will take care of my comfort. I would like you to remain here – for I trust you as I trust myself – and respond to the petitions.'

Haider Ali bowed low and said, 'As you wish, Your Majesty.' If he was pleased by the nawab's words, his face did not betray it.

The nawab added, 'Perhaps I will call the shahzada from the zenana to sit on the throne in my place, so that he may observe you and assist you in making decisions. It may help him when I am gone and the burden of governing falls on him.'

Haider Ali bowed again, more stiffly this time. From where he sat, Anand could see that there was a frown on his face. The nawab noticed the frown, too, for he said, quickly, 'But perhaps the shahzada is still too young and headstrong. I will have him learn the craft of statesmanship another time.' He beckoned to the court announcer and spoke softly to him.

'By order of His Majesty the illustrious Shah-en-shah of Bengal, Nawab Nazib, his vizier Haider Ali al dauleh, Pillar of the State, will preside over the rest of the durbar today, so that the business of the state might continue and the nawab's loyal subjects receive timely justice.'

A ripple of whispers went through the crowd, and people glanced in surprise at each other. Such a thing had obviously not happened before. But most of them did not seem unhappy. Some of the ministers may have been concerned at this development, for it established Haider Ali's power over the court even more firmly, but they were careful to hide their dissatisfaction. All bowed in the kornish, to show that they accepted the nawab's decision.

When the nawab rose to leave, Haider Ali helped him down from the dais. The nawab put a hand on the chief minister's shoulder to support himself, and pulled a silk scarf from his pocket to wipe his face. As he did so, a small, jewelled snuffbox dropped from his pocket to the floor. The box came to a rest near Anand, who gazed at it in confusion, not sure what he should do. Should he ignore it and wait for one of the nawab's guards to pick it up? Should he pick it up himself and return it to the nawab? But that would mean he would have to let go of the punkah's rope. As a punkah-puller, perhaps he wasn't supposed to do that. He glanced toward Rahman, hoping for a hint, but the guards, standing at attention with their eyes fixed straight ahead, blocked the older boy from his view. The nawab had almost passed him now, and no one else seemed to have noticed the snuffbox.

Anand gathered up his courage and picked up the snuffbox. He stood and bowed as deeply as he could – though his bow was still awkward – and offered the box to the nawab. The nawab looked startled, as though he hadn't been aware of Anand's presence until this moment.

Then a furious hand snatched the box from Anand, and a voice cried, 'How dare you approach the nawab, you insolent cur? How dare you touch one of His Majesty's possessions with your filthy hands? A hundred lashes of the whip would not be sufficient punishment for such disrespect!' It was Haider Ali, his eyes blazing.

Trembling and unnerved, Anand didn't know what to do. He felt every eye in the durbar fixed on him. He had obviously violated an important rule of this society! Oh, why hadn't he just left that unlucky snuffbox alone! What would happen to him now? He wanted to explain to the chief minister that he had meant no harm, but even if he could have managed to get the words out, he was afraid they would only anger Haider Ali even more.

Then he heard the nawab's soft voice say, 'Don't be so hard on the boy, Haider. He is probably a new servant, and does not know our court's etiquette. At least he is honest. Many would have kept the box for themselves. Make sure he is rewarded for his honesty. Asaf, help me to my palanquin.'

The captain of the bodyguards rushed to help the nawab. The silver doors opened, and the nawab disappeared behind them. Haider Ali glared at Anand, obviously still angry with him. But he could not go against the nawab's command. He threw a coin at Anand and returned to the dais. His knees wobbly with relief, Anand sat down and resumed pulling the punkah. The crisis seemed to be over, at least for the moment. With any luck, the chief minister would forget him soon, for surely a mere punkah-puller was not worth such an important man's attention.

Haider Ali nodded to the court announcer to read the next petition, but before the man could start, a blinding bolt of lightning flashed across the sky. A huge thunderclap followed, so close that it shook the foundation of the durbar hall, and glass from one of the large windows shattered, showering sharp shards over the crowd. People shrank back and cried out in alarm and wonder, for the sky was a bright blue, without a single rain-cloud in it. 'Bad luck,' someone whispered, and others took up the words, glancing sideways at the chief minister who stood on the dais. He, too, looked startled – and displeased. But in a moment he pulled himself together and told the announcer to resume reading.

The business of the court continued, but Anand, sitting at the punkah-station, found it hard to pay attention. A new thickness was in the air, a smell like gunpowder, making it hard for him to breathe. Did no one else sense it? Dread prickled the back of his neck. The lightning was no freak accident of nature, he was sure of that. Could it be that Kasim's jinn had grown strong enough to break through the barrier? Was it possible that the sorcerer was now in Nawab Najib's world?

eleven

A Visit to the Lake

The feeling of uneasiness grew on Anand over the next few days. From time to time, he felt that same strange prickling at the back of his neck. He couldn't shake off the belief that he was in grave danger that someone was searching for him. An ominous heaviness weighed upon his heart, and he went about his daily tasks with an increasing sense that time was running out. It slowed his limbs and took away his appetite so that a concerned Rahman asked him if he was falling ill. 'Perhaps you've caught the same heat-sickness that is going around,' he said. 'Do you want to go to the hakim who looks after the palace servants? He can give you some of his neem-juice potion. It's bitter and foul-smelling, but I've heard it removes impurities from the blood.'

Anand shook his head. The hakim couldn't help him, he knew that. What he needed was the conch. If he could hold its cool white beauty in his hands just once and listen to its soothing voice, surely it would cure whatever was ailing him. He tried to remember the sound of that voice, the many wise things it had said to him in the past. But all that remained in his mind was the last instruction the conch had given him: *hold on and don't let go*. But he *had* let go – and that had been the start of all his troubles.

What tantalized him further was the sense that the conch was not far from him. He couldn't have explained how he knew this, for he hadn't seen the smallest proof of its presence anywhere in this world. Nor had it appeared in his dreams, although every night when he lay down on his straw pallet in the crowded room where the punkah boys slept, he sent out a wish for this to happen. Neither had he found Abhaydatta anywhere, though he searched diligently for him wherever his duties took him in the palace. And Nisha – well, he knew exactly where she was, but he hadn't yet come up with a plan that would take him there.

His days had been exceptionally busy, for the heat-sickness had struck many of the palace servants, including the punkah-pullers. They vomited and grew delirious with fever, and had to be quarantined in a different part of the palace. The rest of the punkah-pullers had to work double shifts, for the weather was so oppressive, even in this garden-city, that the noblemen and their families demanded fans at all times. Latif, their overseer, grew haggard with stress.

'Can you imagine!' Anand heard him exclaim angrily to Zafar. 'I received a message from the vakil's residence, asking for some pullers to work through the night! Apparently His Eminence was unable to sleep all last night because of the heat. Where do they think I'll get more workers? Do they think I am another Pir Bismillah, to manufacture men out of thin air?'

Zafar clicked his tongue soothingly. 'These noblemen, they never think, that's the problem. They just order, and expect us to come up with a solution! Yesterday afternoon the shahzada suddenly demanded kulfi for all his friends. Did he even consider for a moment that to make so much kulfi I would need a cartload of ice-blocks, not to mention half a day to boil, cool, sweeten and freeze the milk?'

'What did you do?' Latif asked, his own worries forgotten for the moment.

'I went to the nawab's residence to explain this to the shahzada. Of course he wouldn't listen. He stomped his feet and screamed and threw a hookah at me. Fortunately, his aim is so poor that I was in no danger. Fortunately also, the chief minister, who had come to see the nawab on some business, heard him ranting and gave him a severe scolding, saying that this was no way for a future monarch to behave. And right he was! If only his own parents disciplined the shahzada more often, it would be good for him. But being their only child and future heir, he has been indulged since his birth, and we servants have to suffer the results! Anyway, Haider Ali asked me to send the shahzada some chilled watermelon juice instead, to cool his system. And so I did! I have some left over, if you would like to try a glassful.'

'Indeed I will, Allah bless you, Zafar Miah. This oppressive heat is unlike anything I remember. This beautiful garden-city has always been known for its mild climate, but ever since that strange lightning flash during the afternoon durbar, something seems to have gone wrong with the weather – and with the people also, for they are more short-tempered than usual.'

Anand agreed with the last statement. The heat had made everyone irritable, and several squabbles broke out among the punkah boys each day. Being the new boy, and one of the younger ones, Anand was often the target of their temper, and as a result he had acquired several bruises on his arms and legs. It would have been worse if Rahman had not taken his side and made it clear that anyone who fought Anand would have to fight him, too. Anand appreciated this, but it did not lessen his longing for the Silver Valley and his courteous fellow apprentices. He smiled bitterly to himself when he remembered how dissatisfied he'd been during his early days there. *When I get back to the Brotherhood,* he promised himself, *I'll never ever complain about anything again*! But deep inside him lurked a doubt he dare not give voice to: would he ever get back?

This morning Anand awoke tired and miserable, for the low-ceilinged room in which the punkah-pullers slept was crowded and smelly, with only a few small windows. The sun had barely risen, but already the room was hot. His duties would not begin for another two hours, but he couldn't bear the thought of lying for another minute on his tangled, sweaty bedclothes. He craved a cool drink, a long, soapy bath, a strong wind to drive the stink from the room. But since none of these were available, he decided to go and see the elephants instead.

It took Anand a little while to find the hathi-khana, for he was still learning his way around the labyrinth of the palace. When he finally got there, he was disappointed to see that the barn-like structure that held the elephants was empty. A surly-looking sweeper was cleaning out the stalls and putting in fresh dried grass. Anand had to ask him twice where the elephants had gone before he pointed his shovel irritably at one of the tall arched gateways that controlled entry into the fort.

Anand ran to the gate, which was fortunately still open. The guards standing around chatting glanced at him but didn't ask any questions. Anand's eyes widened at the scene beyond the gate. A large lake stretched all the way to the edge of a forest of towering trees – the same forest, he guessed, that would grow to cover the ruined palace in future centuries. Was this the lake he'd glimpsed in the other world, as he followed the digging crew into the forest? In its silvery water, a herd of elephants were bathing. He couldn't help smiling – his first smile in days – as he watched them.

Clearly, the elephants loved the water. Even the enormous war-elephants playfully squirted water over each other and romped around, stirring up huge billows of mud. They pulled out bunches of grass that lined the lake's edge, knocked them clean against their legs, and ate them with gusto. Elephant calves held onto their mothers' tails with their trunks as they ventured deeper into the water. The older calves chased each other in the shallows.

Anand could see that the animals were very fond of their keepers. They trumpeted in pleasure when the mahouts massaged their skin with oil or scrubbed their heads. They let them climb onto their backs, and did not mind it if they pulled on their fan-like ears for leverage. Sometimes they circled them with their trunks, as though embracing them, or blew gently on their faces, as though talking to them. Some of the younger mahouts used their elephant's trunks as slides, yelling in laughter as they careened down them into the lake-water, their brown, glistening skin matching the water-darkened skin of the elephants. Watching them, Anand felt a pang of envy. Why couldn't fate have made him a mahout in this world, instead of a punkah-puller? He tried to locate the shahzada's elephant among the herd, but all the elephants looked the same to him.

Just then there was a commotion at the gateway, and a covered palanquin, carried by four bearers, appeared. Some nobleman or other must have come to watch his favourite elephant being bathed. This surprised Anand. In these few evenings of working the fans at the homes of various courtiers, he'd already noted that the nobles lived an indolent life. They liked to dine and drink until late at night, conversing with friends, plotting for power, listening to poets and singers present their latest compositions, or watching the dancing girls. They rarely woke up early.

As soon as the palanquin was lowered, an impatient hand pushed open the curtain and a veiled figure, a girl, jumped out. Why, it was Nisha! And for once guards didn't surround her. Anand's heart began to beat fast as he wondered if this was the chance he'd been looking for. But now someone else was climbing out of the palanquin, an older woman who stepped down gingerly, trying to avoid getting mud on her fine clothes. She was probably Nisha's chaperone, for she wrung her hands and entreated the girl to return to her quarters. Nisha paid her no attention. She raised her long skirt and rushed to the edge of the lake and clapped imperiously, calling out a name Anand couldn't hear in the melee of elephants and mahouts. But he had no trouble recognizing the man who appeared in response to the summons, though he was clad in the mahout's knee-length dhoti and wore a close-cropped beard, as was the fashion in this world. It was Abhaydatta!

Delighted, Anand was about to rush forward and throw his arms around the healer. How wonderful that both his friends were in the same place at the same time! But what he saw next made him pause.

Abhaydatta gave Nisha a long, low kornish, the way a servant would, and she acknowledged it with a curt, superior nod. Then she pointed to one of the elephants – hers, Anand guessed – and began to give him orders. Abhaydatta listened respectfully, nodding from time to time. He motioned to a younger mahout to bring the elephant out of the water so that Nisha could pat its trunk. She took out a banana from the folds of her clothing and held it out to the elephant, who picked it up daintily and tossed it into its mouth, then trumpeted and raised his trunk in a salute that made her laugh.

'Make him pick me up, old man!' she ordered Abhaydatta. The healer clicked his tongue in a particular rhythm, and the elephant curled its trunk around Nisha's waist and lifted her off the ground. She clapped, shouting in glee, and when the elephant put her down, she threw Abhaydatta a coin. He caught it deftly and bowed to her again.

Why were Abhaydatta and Nisha behaving as though they didn't know each other's real identity? Was it a strategy they'd devised so that onlookers wouldn't grow suspicious? Were they communicating in code all the time, a code Anand didn't know how to decipher? Or was it – his mouth grew dry at the thought – that they'd both forgotten their true selves?

He waited behind a bush, unsure of what to do. Nisha's attendant wrung her hands again, pointing to the sun, then back towards the city. Anand guessed she was telling Nisha how late it was, and how they'd better get home. Finally Nisha fed her elephant another banana, gave Abhaydatta a final set of instructions, and climbed reluctantly into the palanquin. Once her palanquin had passed through the gates into the palace compound, Anand made his way to Abhaydatta, torn between excitement and anxiety. What would he do if the old man, too, didn't recognize him?

But Abhaydatta's eyes crinkled in a smile as soon as he caught sight of Anand. He put both his hands on Anand's shoulders and gave them a squeeze, and Anand knew if there hadn't been so many people watching, the old man would have given him a hug as well.

'I can't talk much now, there're too many people around,' the healer whispered. 'But I am indeed glad that you were able to find your way into this world! Some other time, you must tell me how you did it – and without losing your memory, too! As you can see, in this world, I am an elephant trainer. What are you?'

Quickly Anand told him about his alternate identity in Nazib's world. 'I'm so glad you know who I am!' he added. 'Nisha doesn't seem to recognize me.'

'She doesn't know who I am either, but she's drawn to me, though she doesn't understand why. So she comes to see me often.'

'But why haven't you reminded her? After all, you *are* a master of remembrance and forgetting ...'

Abhaydatta shook his head sadly. 'There is a protective shield around Nazib's world. I think the master magician Bismillah activated it after he banished the sorcerer – the same man who attacked me in the forest, I suspect – so that he wouldn't be able to return. It was very hard to pierce, and when I passed through it, I lost my powers. Fortunately, I didn't lose my memory, not like Nisha or Raj-bhanu – yes, he's in the hathi-khana, too, as one of the assistant mahouts. I've told everyone he's my nephew. In this world, my name is Saleem and his is Hosain.'

The elephants were done with their baths and were lumbering out of the water one by one. Anand knew he had only a few more moments to speak to Abhaydatta.

'Kasim – the sorcerer who attacked you – has broken into this world now. I'm sure of it!' he said.

'I felt the disturbance in the atmosphere,' Abhaydatta said, his face grim. 'But how could he have penetrated Bismillah's shield?'

'The shield was supposed to disintegrate after a hundred years – Kasim knew that and timed his entry accordingly. Also, his jinn must have helped him.'

'A jinn!' Abhaydatta's face darkened. 'No wonder Raj-bhanu and I failed to defeat Kasim in the forest! Raj-bhanu was badly injured in the process – I'll have to tell you about that later.' The last of the elephants was lumbering out of the lake. Looking at it, the healer said, 'I must go, or ...'

'Wait!' Anand interrupted anxiously. 'You've got to do something to stop Kasim! I heard him tell the jinn that he's determined to take control of the nawab's court.'

Abhaydatta shook his head sadly. 'I don't have any powers here. And even under normal circumstances, I would not be able to stop a jinn on my own. But you might – '

'Me!' Anand cried in disbelief. 'That's impossible! How can I possibly do what you, a master healer, cannot?'

'Ah, Anand, you have strengths you aren't aware of. They aren't fully developed yet, but they're there. I felt them the very first time, when I met you in the slums of Kolkata. Besides, you have the conch, do you not? Isn't that how you found your way to this world, and to me?'

Anand hung his head guiltily. 'Not quite.' As quickly as he could, he told Abhaydatta about losing the conch as he travelled through the portal, and about finding the mirror that brought him to Nazib's world.

Abhaydatta looked disturbed. 'I'm sorry to hear that. It will make things much more difficult for us.'

'I know the conch is somewhere close,' Anand said. 'But I don't know where to look for it!'

He was interrupted by a gray trunk that bumped gently against his cheek. Looking up, startled, he saw that the last elephant had stopped and was regarding him with its shiny black eyes.

Abhaydatta raised an eyebrow. 'That's Matangi, the shahzada's elephant! She seems to have taken to you. Strange! She's not usually friendly towards strangers.'

'She saved my life on the day of the procession,' Anand said. Then he gave a gasp as he felt Matangi's trunk circling his waist tightly. The next moment, she had lifted him off the ground! His heart skipped a beat as he swayed wildly in the air. But then she placed him securely on her back. He clung to her great ears and grinned with delight. Most of the mahouts had gone through the gate by then, but the few who saw him gestured and spoke excitedly among themselves.

'Amazing!' Abhaydatta said, shaking his head in disbelief. 'That's the first time I've seen her do that! Usually I have to bribe her with sugarcane before she'll allow even the shahzada to climb on her back.'

A current of warmth spread through Anand's body. How beautiful the elephant was! There was a mark on her forehead like a white star. He stroked it and whispered, 'I don't know why you like me, Matangi, but I'm certainly glad you do!'

A shout from one of the guards interrupted them. 'You, old man!' he called rudely. 'Enough of your chatter! It's time for us to close the gates. Get inside! And you'd better get that boy off the elephant's back right away. If our shahzada finds out that you let a servant climb onto his elephant, you'd be out of the job, or worse!'

It upset Anand to see the guard speaking so roughly to the master healer, a man who was universally respected in his own world. But Abhaydatta only winked at Anand, as though it didn't matter. He made a clicking sound with his tongue, and Matangi lowered Anand to the ground. The heavy wooden gates, reinforced with iron bands, were already being pulled together.

'Put all your energies into finding the conch,' the healer whispered urgently to Anand as they hurried through the gateway behind Matangi. 'Without it, we're helpless against Kasim.'

'But how shall I find it?' Anand asked. 'I don't even know where to look.'

'Trust in yourself! You are the conch bearer – you have a connection to the conch that no one else has. Try to make your mind receptive to its energy. And remember, often something may be hidden in the most obvious of places.'

'Wait – ' Anand cried. There was so much more he needed to ask.

But Abhaydatta shook his head. 'I'm late and must catch up with the other mahouts. Already I saw them giving us curious glances. Matangi's behaviour has made them all wonder who you are. If we talk together any longer, it will make them even more suspicious – and gossip travels faster through the palace than a wildfire. That is why you must not come to see me again until you find the conch.' He clasped Anand's arm briefly. 'Be careful! Kasim saw you go through the mirror into Nazib's world. He'll be searching for you.'

Anand watched forlornly as Abhaydatta strode toward the hathi-khana without a backward glance. The healer was right. In the future, it would be too dangerous for them to meet. He felt as though he was losing his companion all over again. All this time he'd been thinking that if only he could find the healer, all his worries would be over. But now that Abhaydatta had lost his powers, there was no one that Anand could depend on except himself.

twelve

An Unexpected Dinner Party

As the sun rose higher, the day grew hotter, and the punkah-pullers were kept busier than ever. Anand spent all morning working in the treasury, which was located in an old part of the palace, with aged, creaking punkahs that were hard to pull. His muscles burned with fatigue, and even the sight of the tahsildars counting out stacks of gold and silver coins to pay the salaries of various palace retainers failed to hold his interest. His mind wrestled vainly with the problem of finding the conch. Abhaydatta had said, *Often something may be hidden in the most obvious of places.* But what would be an obvious place for a conch shell with magic powers?

The punkah boy who was to relieve him took his time in arriving, and by the time Anand got to the dining hall where the servants took their meals, most of the food was gone. He dipped a hardened roti in some lukewarm dal and chewed it dispiritedly. The vegetable curry was too salty, and the buttermilk too watery. He wondered if he might be able to slip away to Zafar's kitchen later for a snack. But when he reported back to Latif, he was sent straightaway to work at one of the minor courtrooms in the palace, where a long, complicated and boring case about a border dispute between two noblemen was going on. By the time he returned to the punkah-pullers-quarters, it was evening and he was bone tired. He drank thirstily from a water pitcher and leaned against the wall, hoping Latif would dismiss them soon so that he could crawl into bed.

He was half asleep by the time Latif entered the hall, looking more harried than usual. 'I need more pullers for tonight!' he cried. 'I know all of you have worked two shifts already, but something crucial has come up – and unfortunately, the rest of my workers have already been commissioned for other tasks. Who would like to volunteer?'

No one answered. Anand guessed that all the pullers were as exhausted as he was.

'Come, my boys,' Latif said, 'don't let me down! There's a very important dinner party tonight, and the host wants every punkah in his dining hall manned, to keep his guests comfortable.'

Still, no one answered.

'It's Haider Ali!' Latif cried in desperation. 'You know he won't take no for an answer! He'll pay you handsomely – he always does. And I'm willing to throw in a bonus, too.'

Anand forced open his eyes and struggled to stand up. A dinner at the chief minister's? It was an opportunity that he couldn't afford to pass up, tired though he was. He guessed that the dinner would be for men only, as was the custom, and Nisha would not be present at it. But he had to try to see her once again. He raised his hand.

'Thank you, Abbas!' Latif said in a relieved voice. 'And here's Rahman, and Yusuf, and Hamid. Boys, you won't be sorry!' He tossed them each a silver coin, gave them instructions, and hurried off to handle other emergencies.

❦

As he followed Rahman into the building, Anand thought that Haider Ali's house was even more impressive inside than it was on the outside. The servant's entrance was large and imposing, with an arched gateway where the sentries searched them thoroughly before letting them in. ('Powerful men like the chief minister have powerful enemies!' Rahman whispered to Anand as a sentry made them remove their turbans and waistbands.) The kitchen, through which they had to pass to get to the dining hall, was not as large as Zafar's, but it bustled with just as much activity and smelled just as delicious. Anand's stomach gave a protesting rumble – they'd only had time to grab a bowl of rice-and-dal before leaving for this assignment.

'Will they give us something to eat?' he whispered to Rahman.

The other boy nodded. 'The chief minister's cook is a good-natured man. He usually allows us to take leftovers from the party.'

The dining room was oval shaped, and its marble floor glittered with a mosaic of colours. In the centre was a beautiful carpet decorated with fantastic beasts. On it, twelve low, carved wooden tables, each set with a gold plate and gold goblets studded with jewels, were arranged in an oval. In a corner, musicians were already tuning their sitars. A servant ran through the room, spraying it with sweet smelling perfume from a pichkari. Hardly had Anand seated himself at one of the punkah stations when he heard the guests coming in. They were greeted at the door by attendants and led to their seats. Cool water with rose petals floating in it was brought in silver bowls for them to wash their hands. When all were seated, Haider Ali entered, dressed resplendently in a tunic encrusted with gold and jewels, a magnificent turban with a diamond on his forehead. Rings glittered on his fingers, and ropes of pearls hung from his neck.

He bowed courteously to his guests, who had risen to their feet to show him respect. 'Salam alekum! Welcome to my humble home, noble friends. I am most appreciative that you have chosen to join me for this simple meal.'

He clapped his hands, and servants appeared bearing dish after covered dish. Each servant brought his dish to Haider Ali and knelt in front of him, uncovering it for his inspection. After he examined the dish and nodded his approval, it was served to an official taster who checked it for poison, then to the guests, and finally, to him. Anand's mouth watered as he watched the gold plates being piled with fragrant rice pulao, savoury fried chicken, goat and lamb curries, and vegetable kurmas of several kinds. A simple meal, indeed! He wondered if Nisha – who must be eating in the zenana quarters – was being served all these dishes, too. Between courses, clean plates were brought for the guests and warm lemon-water for them to wash their hands. At the end, after many kinds of sweets, fruits and nuts had been served, each guest was given a hookah. They settled back onto their pillows, smoking contentedly, praising the chief minister's chefs, and gossiping about the latest goings-on in court.

Anand noticed that Haider Ali did not eat much. Nor did he drink the wine that was lavishly poured into his guests' goblets. His hawk-like eyes watched the courtiers as they laughed and talked, their tongues loosened by drink. Anand felt that he was assessing each man carefully for his own future purposes. But none of them realized this, for he was a gracious and solicitous host, laughing at their jokes and making sure they had everything they wished for.

It was after midnight when the party broke up, the guests taking a reluctant leave because there was a durbar session for them to attend the next day. Haider Ali was the last to exit, and before leaving he whispered something to one of the attendants. Watching him disappear down a corridor, Anand let go of the fan's rope and flexed his tired fingers. Now for those leftovers from the kitchen! And after that, might there be a chance for him to slip away from the others and look for Nisha's room? Deep in thought, he didn't notice that the attendant had walked over to him.

'You, boy!' the man cried, making Anand jump guiltily. 'Are you asleep, or are you slow in the head? Didn't you hear me calling you? Come with me!' When Anand stood up, he slipped a silver coin into his hand and whispered, 'His Eminence needs a puller to attend to the fan in the emerald meeting room, and he asked specifically for you.'

'For me?' Anand whispered back, puzzled. 'But he didn't even look at me.'

'Little escapes the attention of our master,' the attendant said. 'Come! He will be angry if you are late.'

Anand hurried behind the attendant, wondering what kind of meeting would be taking place so late at night. He was led into a small, narrow room no wider than a passage, its stone walls and floor bare of any decoration. Fear struck his heart. Was this a prison cell? Had Haider Ali somehow guessed Anand's plans to meet his niece and decided to imprison him here? He looked around wildly for escape, but there was only the door he had entered through, which was blocked by the attendant. Then he saw the thick rope of a punkah. It disappeared into a hole cut into the top of one of the walls. The hole was just large enough for the rope to go through. He began to understand. He was in an annex next to the emerald room, built so that a punkah-puller could do his job without seeing or hearing what was going on in there. But what could Haider Ali be discussing that was so secret?

'Listen carefully, boy!' the attendant said. 'You are not to mention to anyone that there was a meeting tonight. If anyone asks why you were late returning to the punkah-pullers' quarters, tell them that you were working the fan in the chief minister's bedchambers. If a single soul comes to know of this, you will be sorry you were born. Our master never forgets a face – and he never forgets a betrayal!'

He shut the door behind him, leaving Anand to his task.

Anand worked the fan-rope, wondering at the unexpected turn in events that had landed him in this strange situation. Surely it wasn't coincidence! This meeting – whoever it was with – was important. He could sense that. He had a nagging feeling that he needed to know what was going on in the emerald room. He stood on tiptoe, trying to get as close to the hole as he could, but he couldn't hear even a whisper. The walls of the emerald room had been built extra thick to protect against eavesdroppers. He had to find another way.

Abhaydatta's words came back to him. *Trust in yourself,* the healer had said. He'd said that Anand had inside him powers greater than he knew. But then, he hadn't seen Anand fumbling during his lessons in the Silver Valley. Why, he'd been the most inept of apprentices! And whatever little power he had was probably lost when he entered this world. Still, since there seemed to be nothing else to do, he creased his brows, thinking back on what the healers

had taught him. The lessons seemed so far away. He was afraid he'd
forgotten crucial parts of the few spells he knew. In any case, none
of them were appropriate for seeing and hearing through a stone
wall. But finally, he pressed his left palm to the wall in front of him,
awkwardly working the fan with his right hand, and concentrated
as he'd been taught in the Hall of Seeing. He was sure it wouldn't
work, but to his surprise the wall seemed to waver, as though seen
through ripples of heat. In a few moments he could see what was on
the other side, though very dimly, as if he was peering through
smoke. He could even hear the faint drone of a conversation.

The emerald room, in contradiction to its opulent name, was
severe in its plainness. Its walls were bare and its furnishings
consisted only of a few cushions set out on a carpet and a small table
that held a jug of water and some glasses. Looking into the room,
Anand thought, was like seeing into a hidden part of Haider Ali's
being, but as yet he was unable to decipher what it revealed.

There were three men seated in the room – Haider Ali and two
of the noblemen who had come to dinner.

'Haider, you must listen to us,' one of them said, leaning
forward passionately. 'The nawab was a good ruler in the past, but
of late he has grown ill and weak. The neighbouring kings know
this. You yourself have heard about the skirmishes on the border. It
is only a matter of time before one of them invades us. You must
take over the kingdom and make sure our army is strengthened.
Qutb and I will pledge you our full support. I know that most of
the other nobles will accept you as the new nawab – '

The muscles of Anand's right arm burned from pulling the
heavy fan. He didn't know how long he could keep up what he was
doing. But he had to hear the minister's response to this
proposition! He gritted his teeth and pressed his left palm hard
against the wall.

'So, Hamid, you want me to rebel against my king?' Haider Ali
asked, a forbidding look on his proud face.

'Don't think of it as rebellion,' the other nobleman said
placatingly. 'You are the only one among us who can unite Bengal
and make it a powerful kingdom once again. We need a strong

leader, Haider! People are suffering in the provinces – law and order are falling apart – '

'And what would you have me do with the royal family, once I take over?' Haider Ali asked. 'Imprison them? Kill them? No, Qutb, I pledged my allegiance to Nazib when we were both young men. What honour would I be left with if I betrayed him now?'

Hamid waved his hand impatiently. 'But his fortunes are failing – and ours – and our kingdom's – will fail with him! A war with one of our neighbours – a war for which we are ill prepared – will cause more suffering to all. Is that what you want, Haider?'

Haider Ali shook his head.

'Then you must see why our plan is best,' Hamid said. 'Nazib doesn't have to be killed – you can exile him, along with his family – and make sure his last days are comfortable – '

'Let me think further, Hamid,' the chief minister said. 'There may be a more honourable way out of this dilemma. Meanwhile, I appreciate the trust you have placed in me. Go now, and rest assured that I will hold all you have said in the strictest confidence. Once I come to a decision, you two will be the first to know.'

He struck a gong that sat close to his hand, and an attendant appeared. Hamid and Qutb bowed and left with him. Haider Ali remained sitting, a deep crease between his brows. Then slowly, his face cleared, as though he had thought of something. He reached for the gong, but before he could strike it, there was a knock on the door. He looked up, surprised, and one of his hands went to the dagger he wore at his waist.

The door opened. Anand couldn't see the face of the man who entered, for his back was to him. He was dressed like a nobleman, except that over his tunic and pants he wore a long, wine-red cloak. It seemed to Anand that he glided rather than walked across the floor.

'Who are you?' Haider Ali asked angrily, rising to his feet, holding his dagger ready. 'And how did you get past my guards?'

'Call me a well-wisher, O noble chief minister,' the man said with an ironic bow. As he rose, he turned slightly, with a smile that stopped Anand's breath. It was Kasim, but a Kasim that had grown many times more powerful. Even through the wall, Anand could feel the malevolence that radiated from him. 'Getting past your guards was child's play! I can do much more than that.' He moved his hand and the dagger, jerked from Haider Ali's hand by some invisible force, skittered across the floor. 'Fortunately for you, I am willing to use my powers for your benefit. But do let us sit down first. It is so uncivilized to converse while standing.' He gestured again and Haider sat down abruptly on the carpet.

Kasim settled himself comfortably, leaning against a cushion and taking his time to arrange the folds of his cloak. Anand could see that he was taking pleasure in making the chief minister wait. 'It has come to my knowledge,' he said finally, 'that certain noblemen whose names shall remain unspoken have made you an offer. The offer tempts you. You would like to be king, except for the small matter of your reputation. You do not want people to think that the great and honourable Haider Ali stooped to betray his friend and liege lord. I have a solution to that.'

'I don't want to hear your solution,' Haider Ali said. His words came out stiff and slow, as though he had to force them through a barrier.

'You should listen to my offer before you reject it, should you not, o great one?' Kasim said mockingly. 'It is an important lesson in statesmanship, and those who do not learn it cannot survive for long.' The veiled threat in his words was clear. 'What if I dealt with the nawab for you? As I said, I have certain powers. All I need is to be in his presence. I can plant the seed of a spell in him, and within twenty-four hours he will be dead. Don't worry – it will look perfectly natural. A stoppage of the heart, perhaps, in front of the court, or maybe dizziness that causes a fall down a staircase, leading to a broken neck. There will be no whisper of suspicion, and as you are the most powerful of the nobles, all will naturally turn to you to lead the kingdom out of this tragedy.'

'And what do you want in return?' Haider Ali's careful voice did not betray any emotion.

Kasim gave a triumphant laugh. 'Ah! I thought you would be interested in my little plan! All I ask in return is that you retain me as your court magician – and secret advisor – when you become nawab.'

'If you are so strong,' Haider Ali asked suspiciously, 'why do you need my help at all? You could go to the durbar tomorrow on your own and do what you say – '

Anger darkened Kasim's face. 'It is the cursed charm of Bismillah. Its remnants endure even now. It creates a barrier around the nawab, so that I cannot approach him unless I am invited by someone whom he trusts implicitly. This invitation – that is all I need from you! Think how much you have to gain in exchange for this little act – '

Kasim must have relaxed his control on Haider Ali, for now he stood up and extended a hand. He was going to accept the sorcerer's offer!

No! Anand cried inside his heart. *Don't give up on your honour! And don't trust Kasim!*

The chief minister didn't react, but Kasim looked around suspiciously, as though he sensed something amiss. Anand knew he must remain very still and keep his mind blank if he wanted to remain undetected. He shrank back so that only his fingertips touched the wall. The scene wavered and darkened, but he could still see what was going on.

Kasim reached for Haider Ali's hand with a triumphant smile, but the chief minister shoved him away and pointed at the door. 'Get out!' he shouted. 'By Allah, how dare you think that Haider Ali would stoop to using your paltry conjurings to gain a throne! Besides, I see very well what your real plan is – to control the kingdom, using me as a pawn. Leave now, or I'll summon my guards.'

Anand stiffened, expecting a terrible outburst from Kasim, but he only smiled. Somehow that cold smile was more frightening than any amount of ranting and raving would have been. 'I will leave now, O magnificent Haider! Not because I am afraid of your guards, but to give you a chance to try out the plan you have hidden in the secret recesses of your mind. The plan that you think is better than mine. I will be back in three days. I have a feeling that you might

| 119 |

be singing a different song by then. I know you are too intelligent to discuss our visit with anyone, but just in case – ' he drew a finger across his lips – 'I'll take some precautions.'

He opened the door and vanished into the corridor before Haider Ali could respond.

Haider stood stone-still for a long moment, staring at the open door. Then, just as Anand was beginning to wonder if Kasim had placed a freezing spell on him, he rubbed at his eyes as though waking from a trance and rang the gong. To the servant who appeared, he said, 'Ask the Lady Paribanou to come to me at once.'

Anand sat up straight. Had he heard right? The chief minister wanted to see Nisha?

'But sire,' the servant ventured, 'what if she is asleep? As you know the Lady Paribanou has – uh – a rather fiery temper – '

'Tell her attendant that it is the most urgent matter,' Haider Ali said brusquely. 'As for her temper, I will deal with it.' When the servant left, he paced up and down the room. On the other side of the wall, Anand waited with equal impatience for Nisha to arrive. What urgent matter could her uncle want to discuss with her at this late hour?

thirteen

Haider Ali's Plan

Even before he saw her, Anand could hear Nisha's footsteps along the corridor as she hurried toward the emerald room. He wondered a little at this, for Haider Ali, who was still pacing, had obviously not detected any sounds. Was the seeing-spell making Anand's hearing grow keener, or was it because the two of them were connected by the joys and sorrows they had shared in another world? He smiled a little as he listened to her quick, impetuous footsteps. They seemed to say, *my uncle had better have a good reason for dragging me out of bed at this hour.* Even in this incarnation as the niece of a chief minister, his Nisha was still the same!

Now she burst into the room, the loose white kurta that she must have worn to bed partly covered by a long shawl. 'Wait outside, Layla Bibi,' she commanded her attendant, 'and be sure to shut the door behind you.' Once she was alone in the room with her uncle, she threw off the shawl and ran to him. 'Is something wrong, Uncle?' she asked, putting out her hands to clasp his. 'Are you not well? Shall I pour you a glass of water?'

A rare smile lighted up Haider Ali's face as he looked at her. 'No, beti,' he said, stroking her head. 'Nothing's wrong. But something important has occurred that I must tell you about right away, for you need to prepare yourself. Paribanou, I need your help.'

'What is it, Uncle? You know I'll do anything I can for you.'

'I did not intend for this to happen so soon – but someone – ' Haider Ali broke off and looked confused. Anand could see the spell Kasim had cast was working, preventing the chief minister from mentioning his name. After a moment, he shook his head, as though to clear it. 'As I was saying,' he continued, 'the nawab's ill health has pushed matters to the cliff's edge. I must take precautions to ensure that the kingdom will be safe in case he should die suddenly. I will go to him therefore and ask his permission to betroth you to the shahzada.'

'What?' Incredulity and distaste battled each other on Nisha's face. 'You want me to get married? To that spoilt brat? Why, he's ...'

Haider Ali held up his hand. 'He can be difficult at times, I realize that. But the betrothal will stabilize the kingdom by allying our families. Should the nawab suddenly die, the shahzada would be able to ascend the throne peacefully. The other nobles would not dare to rebel against him when they see that he has my support.'

'But Uncle, that Mahabet, he's a pest! He's always bullying the other boys, and he throws a tantrum whenever he doesn't get his way. The last time we met, he told me that girls had no intelligence. It was only by practising the greatest restraint that I stopped myself from boxing his ears.'

A smile flitted over the chief minister's thin lips. 'I commend you for that, niece!'

'Besides, I don't want to get married, not for a long time. I don't want to leave you – '

'The marriage itself will not take place for a few years – you're both too young for that – so nothing will really change for you. You'll still live here with me. And hopefully the shahzada will mature as he grows older. You can help him with that!'

'Uncle,' Nisha pleaded, almost in tears, 'please don't force me to – '

'No more arguments!' Haider Ali declared. 'I have made my decision. In my day, the young listened silently while their elders spoke. In my love I have been too lenient with you until now! The sons and daughters of courtiers must marry when and where it is necessary for the good of their families and the good of the country. You have always known that. Besides, did you not say, a moment back, that you would do whatever I wanted?'

When she hung her head wordlessly, he touched her shoulder with a gentle hand. 'Do not be so distressed. One day you will see that what I do is for your good. You will be a great begum and rule over a great kingdom, I know it. But it is late now – I must go to bed, and so should you. Compose yourself before you leave this room. I will tell Layla Bibi to wait outside. It will not do to let her see how upset you are. No one must gossip about our late night meeting until I have had a chance to speak to the nawab.'

He opened the door and strode out. Nisha sank to the carpet and put her hands over her face, her shoulders slumping dejectedly. Anand watched her with sympathy. He guessed that she'd been used to getting her own way around Haider Ali's house, but this time her ambitious and powerful uncle wouldn't allow her to go against his will.

Then he realized that this was probably the closest he'd get to being alone with her.

'Nisha! Nisha!' he called as loudly as he dared, letting go of the fan and placing both his hands on the wall. He didn't think she would hear him, but to his surprise she raised her head and looked toward the wall. It was clear, though, that she couldn't see him, for she frowned. 'I thought I heard something,' she muttered to herself. 'It sounded like someone was calling a name. I must be really tired. I'd better get to bed, as Uncle advised.' She wiped her eyes and rose tiredly to her feet. In another moment, she would be gone.

'Nisha!' Anand called desperately. 'It's me, Anand! I'm here in the punkah-puller's annex, behind the wall.'

Nisha looked around suspiciously. 'Who are you?' she asked. 'And how is it that I can hear you through this thick stone wall? And who's Nisha?'

Anand sighed. This wasn't going to be easy. 'You're Nisha,' he said. 'But you've forgotten.'

'What nonsense!' Nisha said. 'My name is Paribanou. Whoever you are, you are obviously crazed. Perhaps I should call a guard to take you away. Who knows, you might be dangerous!'

Anand stiffened, but Nisha didn't move to the door as he had expected. Instead, she said, her eyes sparkling with curiosity. 'But maybe first you should tell me your story – about how you can speak through walls, and how I've forgotten myself. Crazy people sometimes make up the best stories. But be careful! If I don't like your story, I'm going to shout for the guard.'

'Maybe first you should tell your attendant outside to go away –'

'Why? So that you can rush in and attack me?' Nisha asked.

'No! So that we can talk without her coming in and finding you conversing with a wall!' An idea struck Anand. 'Come close to the wall, put your palms on it, and concentrate all your attention on the stones in front of you. I don't know if this will work, but if it does, maybe it'll make you trust me a bit more.'

Looking suspicious but intrigued, she did as she had asked. For a moment nothing happened. Then suddenly her face cleared and she gave a delighted laugh. 'Why, I can see you!' she said. 'What a fine trick! Are you a magician? My uncle was telling me that we used to have a great magician at this court once, long ago – '

'It's no trick, Nisha,' Anand said urgently. 'And I'm not the one who's working the spell. You are! You're from another world, from the Silver Valley, where you were being taught to develop special powers by the Brotherhood. Surely you remember the valley, how beautiful it was, with the golden parijat trees?'

A thoughtful look came over Nisha's face, and for a moment hope leaped in Anand's heart. Then she shook her head. 'I don't know anything about a Silver Valley,' she said. 'But it certainly sounds interesting. Let me get rid of Layla Bibi. Then we can talk some more.'

She went to the door and said something in her imperious voice. Anand could hear the attendant protesting, but after a few minutes Nisha returned by herself. 'She's gone for now,' she grinned. 'But I had to promise her that I'd be in my bedchambers in a few moments. She's going to check, so you'd better come along with me. I'll hide you in my room. That way, after she goes to bed, you can tell me the story.'

She hurried into the corridor. In a moment she had pulled open the door to the annex. She stared at his face for a long moment. Anand hoped that up close like this his old friend would recognize him, but she merely said, 'Aren't you the boy that picked up the nawab's snuffbox in the durbar? Well, you certainly seem to have a talent for getting into trouble!' She threw him her shawl. 'Put it over your head,' she ordered. 'It's long enough to cover you almost to your feet. Luckily, the corridors are lit only by a few sconces this late at night. If a guard sees you, let's hope he'll mistake you for Layla Bibi!'

Anand draped the soft silken shawl over himself. It caressed his cheek, smelling of rose and musk. As he followed her down several corridors, he mused on the life Nisha was living in this world. What a privileged and luxurious existence she had! How would he make her believe that she used to be a sweeper girl who lived on the streets of Kolkata until destiny brought her to the Silver Valley to become a healer? And even if by some miracle she believed him, would she want to go back to that Spartan existence?

'Here we are,' Nisha said finally, opening a door. Anand peered into the room, which was lit by hanging oil lamps. There were thick, soft carpets on the floor and a canopied divan in one corner. Beside it was a mahogany table with a matching chair. On the table were several books and pieces of parchment, as well as an inkwell and a quill made from an eagle feather. Curiously, he opened one of the books. The curvy writing was in that same unfamiliar language he had seen on the storefronts. He couldn't read it; he guessed that his alter-identity Abbas must not have had a formal education.

'These are my textbooks,' Nisha said. 'My uncle is not like the other nobles, who don't want the women of their family to be educated. In fact, he is always making sure that I work hard at my studies. Right now my tutor has me studying *The Shahnama* – you know the story, right, of the hero Rustam who kills his son Sohrab by mistake – and of course, here is the Koran.' She looked at Anand's blank face. 'Oh, I'm sorry,' she said pityingly. 'Of course you wouldn't know how to read.'

Anand bristled. 'I do know how to read – just not in this language! Back in the Silver Valley, our books were all written in – '

'No, no,' Nisha said, settling herself on the divan and pointing Anand toward the chair. 'Start from the beginning. How did you get to the Silver Valley? Or were you born there?'

Anand had to laugh. 'No one's born in the Silver Valley! We all come there to learn how to use magical skills to help people in the world.'

'Magical skills!' Nisha's eyes sparkled. 'In your story, do I have magical skills?'

'Well, you were just beginning to learn them. You were particularly good with the use of spices and herbs – '

Just then there was a knock on the door.

'Quick!' Nisha said, pulling the covers up to her chest. 'Hide under the divan!'

Anand had barely managed to crawl under it when the door opened. He heard Layla say, 'I'm glad to see you in bed, young lady, though I'd be happier if you were asleep. You're going to be sick tomorrow, mark my words, with all this traipsing around after midnight. And why, may I ask, was it so important for you to walk back alone from the emerald room?'

'Layla Bibi,' Nisha said, making her voice small and pitiful, 'I'm trying to sleep, but I'm so hungry – '

The trick worked. Layla Bibi forgot what she was saying and clicked her tongue in motherly concern. 'You poor child! No wonder you're hungry! Your body's rhythms have been agitated by being up so late. I'll get one of the maids to bring you something to eat right away.'

She bustled down the corridor, complaining. 'I don't know what your uncle was thinking of!' Anand heard her say. 'Whatever it was, it surely could have waited until morning. Men! They have no commonsense!'

Nisha grinned. 'She's actually a dear, kind person. She fusses a bit sometimes, but she does take good care of me. She's looked after me ever since I came to Uncle's house as a baby when my parents died, and so she has a soft spot for me. I'm afraid I take shameful advantage of it!'

Anand stared at her. How could Nisha have had such a long past here? He himself knew almost nothing about the background of Abbas. For a moment, his confidence faltered. Maybe the girl in front of him really was Paribanou and only looked like Nisha due to some cruel coincidence. 'Do you actually remember that time?' he ventured.

'Not really! I can barely remember what happened last year! Layla says I have such a bad memory because I had brain fever as a child. She's told me everything, though – '

There was another knock on the door, and Anand had to hide again. This time when he came out from under the bed, he saw that a large silver platter filled with mangoes, lychees and several kinds of sweets and savouries had been set on the table, along with a goblet of sweet buttermilk.

'Eat!' Nisha said. 'It's for you – I thought you looked hungry. I'm sorry there are only snacks here. The kitchen must be closed –'

Anand laughed as he bit into a sweet. 'Believe me, it's a lot better than what punkah boys usually get! Maybe that's why they gave us such bad food from time to time at the Silver Valley, to get us used to any kind of situation we might find ourselves in later.'

'There you go again, jumping into the middle of the story!'

So Anand started at the beginning – though it was hard to do that. Stories went on and on, each hooking on to the one before it, and to the one after. It was hard to separate them. This story in which he found himself, where was its true beginning? With his entry into Najib's world? With the call of help from the wise-woman Tara? With Bismillah's banishment of Kasim centuries before Anand was born? But there was no time now to puzzle all this out, so he told Nisha how he had first met her when she was a street sweeper in Kolkata, and how they had helped Abhaydatta in his quest to return the conch to its rightful home in the Silver Valley. A shiver went through Nisha as he described the sorcerer Surabhanu, who pursued them with black fury in his heart. But was that because a part of her mind recalled how he'd hypnotized her to use her for his purposes, or was it merely that she was drawn into the story? Anand described the evil talking apes that captured them, and the mysterious red-gold mongoose that helped to free them. He described the guardian in the river, and the pass in the mountains that could only be opened by placing one's palm on a particular rock-face, and the final, most difficult test that faced him when she was unconscious.

Nisha listened fervently, her shining eyes fastened on him without blinking, as he went on to describe their current adventure. He explained how he'd received a message of danger in the Seeing Hall, how Abhaydatta had left the Silver Valley to investigate it and fallen into trouble, and how he, Anand, had lost both Nisha and the conch in the process of travelling through the portal to help Abhaydatta. He told her about Kasim in the ruins, and how he had almost caught Anand and fed his spirit to the jinn. 'They're in this world now, and Kasim is planning to hurt the nawab,' he ended. 'He came to see your uncle tonight, to enlist his help. Your uncle didn't agree, but Kasim is sure to come up with another plan. I've got to find the conch before that happens!'

Nisha let out the breath she'd been holding. 'Quick! Take a piece of parchment and the quill and draw me a picture of the conch.'

A puzzled Anand tried to do as she asked. He wasn't a very good artist, and the result, he thought, was pitiful. The shell on the parchment looked small and lonely and had none of the conch's beauty or magnetism. But Nisha clasped her hands together tightly. 'I've seen it!' she breathed.

Anand jumped to his feet. 'Where is it?' he said. His heart hammered with excitement as he looked around, wondering if perhaps it was hidden in this very room. He'd lost them both at the same time. It would make sense if they ended up together. Why hadn't he thought of that before!

But Nisha shook her head regretfully. 'I'm sorry! What I meant to say is that I saw it in a dream – '

Anand was sorely disappointed, but he still held on to a glimmer of hope. Perhaps the dream would give him a hint of where to look. 'Tell me what you saw in the dream,' he said.

'I was digging through a jewellry chest of some sort, and it lay at the bottom, among gold chains and pearls – and a diamond studded turban, I think. I couldn't see the chest, or the room it was in. What a strange coincidence this is – '

'It's no coincidence!' Anand cried. 'The conch is trying to send a message. I'm not sure why the message came to you instead of me – maybe because on my own, I could never find it. You've got to help me! You have access to places where I can't go. Maybe that chest belongs to Haider Ali. In that case, Nisha, you could easily – '

'I'm not Nisha. I'm Paribanou!' Nisha interrupted, her mouth set in an obstinate line. 'And I'm not sure I believe your story.'

Anand looked at her anxiously, not sure if she was about to call in a guard, as she'd threatened earlier.

'But it's a good story, and I like you – though I don't know why I should like a common punkah boy!' she said after a moment. 'And I did have that dream, so I'll try to help you. It'll be fun – like a treasure-hunting game! Let's sleep now. Tomorrow I'll think up an excuse to look among my uncle's jewels.'

Anand made himself comfortable on the carpet with the extra pillow and quilt that Nisha gave him. Exhausted, he fell into a dreamless sleep at once. It seemed that he had only slept for a few minutes before he felt a hand shaking his shoulder.

'You must get up and go now,' Nisha said. 'It's morning. This is the time when the night servants leave and the day servants come into the house. You'll be able to mingle with them and get away. In case you're questioned, say that you were pulling a punkah in one of the bedchambers.'

Anand rubbed his eyes, trying to get his brain to function. 'Wait! When will we meet again? How will I know if you found the conch?'

'I'll come to see my elephant tomorrow morning at the lake – and if I find the conch, I'll bring it with me.'

Before he could thank her, she opened the door, checked both ways, and pushed him quickly into the corridor. 'Go that way,' she pointed. Anand hurried along the corridor, not daring to look back. What if someone caught him and asked what he was doing here, outside the Lady Paribanou's room? What if he couldn't find the way out? But as the corridor joined a larger one, he saw several tired-looking servants walking in a particular direction. He followed them, apprehensive that they might be suspicious of him. But they were interested only in getting to their beds. Hidden among them, he passed safely through the gateway of Haider Ali's mansion and found his way to the punkah boys' quarters, where he slipped in through an open window, his mind still reeling with all that had happened since last night.

fourteen

In the Hathi-khana

For Anand the day passed with desperate slowness. Not only was he weary from lack of sleep, he was also afire with impatience as he imagined Nisha searching her uncle's coffers for the conch. Every hour he thought to himself, *maybe she's found it by now!* But there was no way for him to know.

It didn't help that for the entire day he was assigned to the guest quarters, where a group of singers who had been invited to perform at the upcoming full moon festival were staying. The festival was only a day away, so they were all practising feverishly under the eagle eye of the old maestro, who made them stop and repeat their lines each time he felt they were not up to par. He shook his walking stick at them and shouted the most terrible threats about how he would beat them and turn them out on the streets without a paisa. Anand suspected that he didn't mean it; he could see that the old man loved his students like his own children. Still, it made the singers jumpy and irritable.

They complained that the tea Zafar sent them from the kitchen was not sweet enough; the betel leaf rolls had been stuffed with too many spices; the day was so humid, it was dampening their voices;

the punkah boys were not doing a good job – see how their kurtas were soaked with sweat! Anand could tell they were very skilled, and he liked their songs, especially one about how the moon, seeing all the people of earth gazing at her beauty, grows shy and pulls a shimmery veil of clouds across her face. But after they had repeated it for the twenty-third time, he felt he couldn't stand to hear it ever again.

It was dark before he had a moment to himself. He should have followed the other punkah boys to dinner, but a great yearning came over him to see Abhaydatta. Perhaps he could share a meal with the old healer – like old times – and describe his encounter with Nisha. Abhaydatta would be delighted to hear of her dream of the conch! But most of all he wanted to tell Abhaydatta about Kasim and his plot to kill the nawab. The healer would know what they could do to forestall him.

Anand wanted to see Raj-bhanu, too. He remembered the dynamic young man from his morning in the wind-tower. He had known so much and been so confident and kind. How Anand had envied him, and wished he could do half the things that Raj-bhanu could! But now Raj-bhanu didn't remember anything about that life. Anand shuddered. *It must feel like being at the bottom of a well with darkness all around, not understanding how you got there. Thank heavens that that didn't happen to me!*

He hastened in the direction of the hathi-khana, wondering at the undeserved luck that let him slip through Bismillah's barrier without harm. Had the mirror protected him somehow? He remembered with regret how it had shattered while repelling Kasim, and in his heart he thanked it once more for saving him from the sorcerer.

In the approaching dusk the slender minarets rose into a magenta sky like pointing fingers, and the last of a muezzin's prayer call drifted in the air. Torches lined the more important streets, the ones with the looming sandstone or marble mansions, throwing flickering shadows onto the flagstones. The courtyard gardens had been watered, and the scent of jasmine and rose and wet earth rose up around him, bringing relief after the long, hot day. Anand felt a moment of well being, and he took the turns with confidence, proud of the fact that already he was learning his way around the palace grounds.

As he approached the area where the animals were housed, he was surprised to note that a large crowd had gathered outside the stalls. People were pointing at the stables and speaking to each other in uneasy whispers. Anand wanted to find out what had occurred, but he knew it wouldn't be wise to draw attention to himself by asking questions. He hurried to the elephant compound. Abhaydatta, he was sure, would be able to tell him what he wanted to know.

The compound was made up of a barn where the elephants were kept chained, a large field walled in by thick wooden stakes where the mahouts took the elephants for exercise and training, and a line of small buildings on the other side of the field, where the mahouts lived. Through gaps in the stakes, Anand could see several of them cooking meals over open fires outside their rooms. Even from across the field, he could smell roasting meats and simmering curries. They made his mouth water, reminding him that he hadn't eaten since midday. The elephants had all been chained up in their stalls by now – he could hear them shuffling and trumpeting – so he quickly slipped through a gap between two stakes and ran across the field.

'Can you tell me where Saleem lives?' He asked one of the men who was cooking. The man jutted his chin at the building at the very end of the row. Then he narrowed his eyes and stared at Anand.

'Aren't you the boy who was at the lake yesterday?' he asked. 'The one Matangi picked up and placed on her back? How'd you get her to do that? She's been mean-tempered, that animal, ever since one of her calves died! What's your name, and where are you from? And why do you want to see Saleem, anyway?'

Anand was taken aback by the volley of questions. He mumbled something about being Saleem's grandson.

'Grandson, eh?' the man gave him a suspicious glance. 'Then how is it that I've never seen you visit your grandfather before?'

'Uh-I just got here from-uh-our village,' Anand stammered, wondering what he should say if the man asked him what the name of their village was. But fortunately at that moment the piece of meat the man was roasting fell off the spit, and while he was rescuing it from the flames, Anand made his escape. He felt the man's gaze on his back, though, as he walked. And when, having reached the last building, he glanced quickly over his shoulder, he thought he saw the man hurrying off toward the compound gate.

Anand meant to tell Abhaydatta about the interrogation. But when he saw the old man squatting on his verandah, roasting the chapatis that a young man – Raj-bhanu, Anand guessed, though the man's back was to him – rolled out, he was so delighted that he forgot. He ran toward him, about to throw his arms around him, but Abhaydatta stopped him with a frown.

'What brings you here?' he whispered in a displeased tone. 'Didn't I warn you not to come and see me again?'

'But so much has happened!' Anand said, his face falling. 'I just had to tell you!' He glanced at Raj-bhanu, wondering if he was angry with him, too. But Raj-bhanu did not turn around.

Abhaydatta sighed and took the pan off the fire. He put out his hand and drew Anand close in a hug. 'It isn't that I'm not happy to see you. But I'm worried for your safety. Something strange occurred here this evening – '

'Was it at the stables? I saw a crowd gathered there.'

'Yes. A few hours earlier, all the animals – including the elephants – started acting strange. They whinnied and trumpeted, and tried to break out of their stalls. It's as though they could sense something dangerous and wanted to get away. I could feel it too. It was like a cloud of cold, black hunger, an emptiness seeking to pull you into it.'

'What was it?' Anand asked. 'Could you see it?'

'No, without my powers I could see nothing.'

'Do you think it was the jinn?' Anand whispered.

The healer shook his head. 'No. This power brought a numb fear into my heart, but a jinn's presence would have overwhelmed me. I suspected that Kasim had created a Searcher and sent him to find me.'

The word sent an icy shiver down Anand's spine. 'What's a Searcher?' he asked.

'It is a shadow-being with no soul, only a space cut out in its centre in the shape of the person it is searching for. When it finds him, it sucks him into the hole inside of it, and carries him to the sorcerer who sent it out.'

'What did you do, then?'

'I started by chanting the protective sutras. They are ancient, and powerful enough to work even if the one who chants them has no magical abilities. Then I ran into the elephants' stalls and concealed myself. As you might guess, elephants are sacred beings. It is not by chance that Lord Ganesha, the remover of obstacles, is portrayed with an elephant head! Our scriptures say they were created out of the earth's energy; thus, some of its insulating power remains in them. If you stay close to them, you can be hidden from evil. After a while, the cloudy feeling passed. But by then one of the Arabians had managed to break out of his stall. Horses were created from fire energy, and therefore they are particularly nervous animals. He was berserk with fear, crashing into walls, striking out at everything near him with his hoofs. When his groom tried to catch him, to stop him from injuring himself, he trampled him to near-death.

'The incident made me realize that we must be far more careful than before. Kasim is close by, and he is stronger than I assumed. He will not forgive us for escaping from him, and thus preventing his jinn from eating our spirits. He would like to crush us like bugs – that is the kind of thing that gives pleasure to a man like Kasim. Our only advantage is that he does not consider us dangerous. He knows about the shield, and so he guesses that we are powerless. And he is right. Without the conch we're no match for him.'

'That's what I came to tell you about!' Anand said excitedly. Then he broke off and peered at Raj-bhanu, trying to gauge if it was all right to speak in front of him. Abhaydatta had said he no longer knew who he was. Might he accidentally give away what Anand told the old healer?

'Hosein,' called Abhaydatta. 'We have a guest.'

Slowly, awkwardly, Raj-bhanu turned toward Anand. His face was the same familiar one Anand knew, but the expression on it was totally different. This Raj-bhanu gave Anand a sweet but vacant smile, drooling a little through loose lips, then looked away and began to rock.

Anand was horrified. This was worse than anything he had imagined. In entering the nawab's world, Raj-bhanu had lost not only his memory but his mind as well.

'You can safely say whatever you want to in front of him,' Abhaydatta said sadly.

'What happened?'

'He was already injured when I pulled him through the shield. The shock must have been too much for his brain. I've tried everything I can think of – herbs, chants, even a visit to the local holy man – but nothing works. Our only chance is the conch. If we can find it – '

'We just might!' Anand said. Quickly, he described Kasim's visit to the chief minister, and then his own meeting with Nisha and the dream she'd told him about. 'She's agreed to help me, even though she doesn't remember me,' he ended. 'She's searching for the conch right now in her uncle's treasury. That must be where it is! Why else would the dream come to her?'

Abhaydatta looked uncertain. 'The ways of the conch are mysterious, and dreams are slippery messengers unless you've been trained as an interpreter. I would like to believe as you do, but I have a feeling that finding the conch will not be as easy as that. Certainly I believe Nisha has to play a part in this. But so do you, because you are the Keeper of the conch. Perhaps the dream came to Nisha so that she would be drawn to help you. Let us keep an open mind and see what happens.'

'Well, she'll be at the lake to see her elephant tomorrow morning. Then we'll know if she succeeded or not. But at least we have three days before Kasim returns to Haider Ali. That gives us a little time.'

'A little, yes,' Abhaydatta said. 'Though not as much as I would like. I will hope that Haider Ali remains strong-willed. But it would be hard for any man to withstand Kasim if he really wanted to bend him to his will. But enough of doom-saying.' He gave an exaggerated bow. 'Young sir, I hereby invite you to partake of this banquet of chapatis and cabbage that I have prepared!'

The three of them ate in a companionable silence. To Anand, in spite of Abhaydatta's joking, the simple meal did taste like a banquet. He would have liked to curl up next to the old man on his blanket and spend the night in more talk, but Abhaydatta would not have it.

'We've tempted fate enough already,' he said. 'If Kasim or his jinn are indeed searching for me, you need to be as far from me as possible. Besides, your absence from your quarters for two nights in a row will raise many questions. You must go now. Walk as fast as you can without attracting attention. I will chant a sutra for you. No matter what you hear, don't look back, and don't stop.'

Reluctantly, Anand started off into the night. To take a short cut, he slipped through a gap in the stakes into the training field. It was eerily quiet in there. Not a single sound came from the elephants. They must all be asleep, Anand thought, with a great yawn. The day's tiredness hit him suddenly, and he quickened his pace, wanting to get to bed as fast as possible. Dark clouds had covered the moon, filling the area with shadows. Maybe it'll rain, Anand thought, and provide some relief from this heat.

He was almost halfway across the field when he thought he saw a movement out of the corner of his eye. He turned, but there was only the bare field, streaked with shadows. But when he continued, he sensed the movement again. He whirled around. Nothing. But had one of the shadows moved a little?

The clouds must have shifted in the sky, he thought. Still, a feeling of disquiet came over him and he began to run. Out of the corner of his eye, he felt the shadow moving faster. This time, when he turned to look, it did not stop but kept coming toward him, an opaque, amoebic blackness. But in its centre was a hole – Anand could see the lights of the mahouts' quarters glinting faintly through it.

The Searcher! It was looking not for Abhaydatta but for him!

A paralysing fear struck Anand's heart, and it became harder to move his legs. He felt himself slowing down. The shadow had grown larger, as though it fed on his fear, and had taken on a vaguely human shape. He could see two small pinpricks of red where its eyes might be. They seemed to have a strange magnetic power – it was hard to move his eyes away from them. He shuddered, remembering too late that Abhaydatta had told him not to look back. He closed his eyes and called up a picture of the old healer. He saw Abhaydatta kneeling on his verandah, arms raised high, chanting. Anand could almost hear the words, though he did not know their meaning. Soothing yet energizing, they calmed his mind and gave him strength to keep going.

But the Searcher was too close. He could feel its dark presence in the tightness of his back muscles. He'd never make it to the other end of the compound in time. And even if he did, it could easily catch him in one of the alleyways leading to the palace and paralyse him. Then nothing could save him from Kasim.

What should he do? He looked around wildly as he pushed forward. It was hard to move. His back felt as though it was made of iron, and there was an enormous magnet behind him, pulling. Then a wave of angry roars broke through the dark. No, not roars. Trumpeting. The elephants had sensed the Searcher's presence!

In his head he could hear Abhaydatta saying that the elephants possessed the sacred energy of the earth.

Anand ran into the barn where the elephants were kept. The cavernous building was dimly lit with a few smoking torches. In their light he could see the elephants chained in rows, each with its own hay and basin of water. The whole place smelled at once musty and wild, and Anand wrinkled up his nose as he went in further, stepping gingerly over piles of dung. One of the elephants trumpeted angrily and swiped at him with its trunk – almost as though he knew that Anand was the reason the Searcher was there. As though in response, several other elephants trumpeted, raising their trunks and rattling their chains as though to break them. One huge tusker stomped a leg thick as a tree trunk, making Anand flinch. He backed away, eyeing their massive, curved tusks. To protect himself from the Searcher, to throw it off-track, he had to get closer to the elephants. But he wasn't sure they would allow it.

Then he heard a soft snuffling sound from the other end of the stalls. An elephant was waving its trunk at him, almost as though inviting him to come nearer. Anand narrowed his eyes, trying to see more clearly. There was a white star on the elephant's forehead.

'Matangi!' he cried and ran toward her. She trumpeted imperiously, as though asking the others to let him through, and when he got close, she gently tousled his hair with her trunk. He put his arms around one of her legs and held it tightly. It felt as solid as a pillar, and as safe. He closed his eyes and leaned against the elephant's side, his tensed muscles relaxing as he felt the rhythmic beat of her heart.

He awoke with a start and found himself half-lying on the ground, his head resting against one of Matangi's legs. He must have dozed off from exhaustion! He had the vaguest memory of a disquieting dream, something about the nawab and his begum arguing bitterly, but he couldn't remember any more than that. He stretched and stood up, peering into the dark compound outside. He must have slept for only a little while, though he felt rested. But the Searcher was gone. Somehow he was sure of that.

Matangi regarded him with her shiny black eyes and offered him a trunkful of hay, making him smile. He stood on tiptoe and stroked her ears and neck. 'Thank you for saving me once again,' he whispered. 'I'd better get back to my quarters before anything else happens.'

This time Anand ran all the way back, making sure not to stop or to look behind him. Every sound or shadow made his nerves jangle with fright, but fortunately he encountered nothing more dangerous than a couple of stray dogs. The lamps in his sleeping hall had been extinguished and most of the punkah boys were asleep already, but as he crept in and lay down on his pallet, Anand could hear whispers. Rahman, whose pallet was next to his, was speaking with one of the other punkah boys.

'No, I have no idea what the nawab and chief minister were talking about,' the boy said. 'They met in one of those sealed chambers where you can't hear anything from outside. But I did catch a glimpse of the chief minister when he was leaving. His face was white with anger and his hands were shaking. His groom took a few minutes to bring his horse to the front entrance from the stables, and for that he cuffed him so hard that the poor boy fell to the ground!'

'I've never heard of Haider Ali losing his temper like that!' Rahman said. 'He's always so controlled. And the nawab and him have been close friends ever since they were boys. What could Najib have said, I wonder, to make him so furious? Oh well, if it's important enough, we'll know soon enough. Nothing remains a secret for long from the punkah boys!'

The two of them drifted off to sleep, but Anand lay awake for a long time, his stomach clenched with worry. The nawab must have refused Haider Ali's proposal of betrothing Nisha to the shahzada. Strange! Why would he reject his friend's offer? Even Anand, knowing as little as he did of court matters, could see that the match would have strengthened the nawab's position and gained his son an important ally. But what worried Anand more was the thought of what the enraged chief minister might do, now that he had been turned down.

fifteen

In Search of the Treasure Chest

Anand stood hidden inside a grove of banana trees near the lake, watching the elephants play in the water. No one appeared to have noticed him. The mahouts were busy cleaning up the elephants, for they were to lead the procession tomorrow night at the full moon festival. The elephants were busy spraying each other and their mahouts, churning up mud and trumpeting their delight as the cool water ran over their bodies. Only Matangi turned her face to the banana trees once, snuffling enquiringly, but when Anand sent her a thought to look away, she joined the elephants next to her in a chase-and-spray game.

Anand searched for Abhaydatta. There he was, right in the centre of the melee, sitting atop an elephant – Anand thought it was Nisha's – whose back he was scrubbing. He longed to tell the old man about the incident with the Searcher last night, but it was impossible to get close to Abhaydatta. He watched for Nisha's palanquin, wondering why she was taking so long, worrying about how he was going to speak to her in the midst of so many people.

The elephants had finished bathing by now. They emerged from the lake in a single file, their mahouts on their backs. In a few minutes they would disappear through the gates. Anand scanned the gateway again, but there was no sign of the palanquin. Where was Nisha?

Then he saw a horseman – a boy, really – coming through the gates, riding so fast that dust rose from the horse's hooves. When he looked closer at the slight figure on the horse, he realized it was Nisha! She was dressed in a long tunic and pants, and wore a turban with a veil hanging from it. He watched in amazement as she rode her horse right to the river's edge, then reined him in sharply. How did she learn to ride so marvellously? Or was it a skill she put on, along with her new identity, when she entered this world? If so, had Anand, too, inherited skills he did not know about yet?

Nisha was shouting commands at Abhaydatta, who had just led her elephant out of the lake. She pointed to the elephant's side and shook her head angrily. Apparently she was telling him that the elephant wasn't clean enough, for Abhaydatta took him back into the lake and began to wash him again. Nisha rode her horse into the water, too, and pointing with her riding crop, gave him loud instructions. Anand edged out from the cover of the banana trees so that she'd be able to see him.

Nisha did not pay him any attention, though. 'What's wrong with your eyes, old man?' she yelled angrily. 'There's a streak of mud on his ear – didn't you see it?' She leaned forward to point to the elephant's ear. At the same time, she gave her turban a furtive tug, so that it slipped from her head.

'My turban!' she cried. 'Pick it up quickly, before the muddy water ruins it!' When Abhaydatta retrieved the turban and handed it back to her, she gave a shout of dismay. 'Oh no! The jewel in the centre of the turban is gone! It must have fallen into the lake! Find it for me!'

Abhaydatta knelt and searched in the water, but didn't find anything. 'I'm sorry, My Lady Paribanou,' he began apologetically, but she cut him off.

'Oh, you'll never find it,' she said in an impatient voice. 'Your eyes are too weak.' She looked around and clapped her hands. 'There's a boy by the banana trees – maybe he can help you. Boy! Come here right now!'

Anand suppressed a smile as he salaamed and ran over to the lake. Nisha was a good actress – and a fast thinker. Now they'd get a few minutes to talk.

'Don't worry about the jewel,' she whispered as soon as he reached them. 'I have it here in my hand. I wish I could say the same about the conch! It's nowhere in my uncle's house. I went through his treasure chests item by item.'

'What'll we do now?' Anand asked, his heart sinking.

'Look more carefully, you idiot!' Nisha shouted suddenly, making him jump. 'Sorry!' she added softly. 'I'll have to do that from time to time, so that people don't get suspicious. As it is, I'll be in a heap of trouble for riding out here alone. Uncle is in a really foul mood, and he has ordered me to stay in my room until he gives further instructions. I'm sure the gossip has reached you – '

'I did hear that the nawab turned him down – ' Anand started hesitantly. He wondered if Nisha was upset at the developments, but she only made a face.

'Apparently the begum has set her heart on the shahzada marrying her cousin's daughter. Her cousin is the begum of one of the neighbouring territories, so I guess she thinks it's a good alliance. I'm perfectly happy about it – I never liked that spoiled brat anyway! I was going to grit my teeth and go through it just for my uncle's sake. But my uncle – ' her face grew concerned – 'he's taken the rejection really hard! I've never seen him so angry! And then something else happened.'

Abhaydatta, who had been silent all this time, spoke flatly. 'He met with Kasim.'

A cold hand squeezed Anand's heart. But Kasim was only supposed to come back to Haider Ali after three days! That's what they'd all been counting on.

Nisha stared at Abhaydatta. 'How did you know? Anand said you're a very powerful healer in the world you come from. Is that true?'

Abhaydatta nodded. 'Yes. It is your world, too, child – but we'll talk of that later. Tell us what happened.'

'My uncle and I were at dinner – not that either of us felt like eating! My uncle had asked the steward to bring him wine, which surprised me, for he's a devout Muslim and never drinks, unlike the other noblemen. He kept saying that he would be avenged for this insult to him and his family. He said he'd been a fool to think of honour and friendship all this while, for it was clear such things were not important to anyone else at court, especially not to the nawab. Then the door opened and a man I'd never seen before walked in. I guessed he was Kasim. He wore a red and black cloak that shimmered around him, but his eyes, when I looked into them, were like chiselled holes.' She gave a shudder, remembering.

'A red and black cloak!' Abhaydatta exclaimed. 'The last time it had been only red! It is a sign that he is gathering more evil energies to him.'

'I don't know how he got in,' Nisha continued, 'because there are always guards outside every door wherever my uncle is, and no one is supposed to come in without being announced – '

'He probably wove a dissembling spell around him,' Abhaydatta said. 'It would make him look like someone the guards knew – maybe a servant or a cup-bearer.'

'My uncle was surprised, though not displeased the way I would have expected him to be. But they didn't talk about anything important – only a few minutes of polite chit-chat about court events – '

'I doubt that!' Abhaydatta said dryly. 'Try to remember the exact words they used, child. It might help me understand what Kasim is planning.'

Nisha creased her brows, trying to recall the scene. 'Kasim asked my uncle who I was, and he told him. Then Kasim said, *Only a fool would reject such a beautiful pearl necklace.* My uncle's face went white when he heard that. He said to Kasim, *I, too, have been a fool to turn you down so churlishly. Permit me to take you as my guest to the full moon festival tomorrow night. There you may see the royal family as closely as you wish.* Kasim smiled and said, *The entire royal family? This is beyond what I had hoped for!* Then he bowed and left, and my uncle put his head down on the table, clutching it as though he had a blinding headache. It was probably the wine. When I asked him if he was all right, he snapped at me to go to my room and stay there.'

Anand and Abhaydatta exchanged glances. 'Kasim's planning to do something at the full moon festival, isn't he?' Anand whispered.

'Yes, I'm afraid so,' the healer said. 'He's probably going to try to kill the royal family, or put them under some harmful spell. Haider Ali's invitation to Kasim has nullified Bismillah's protective spell. Now, with the jinn to aid him, there'll be no stopping Kasim. It is quite possible that he will kill Haider Ali as well, now that the chief minister has given him what he needed. Or he might control his will and force him to do whatever he wants. In either case, before we know it, Kasim will become the real ruler of Bengal.'

'Kill my uncle? Control his will?' Nisha cried. 'We can't just stand by and let Kasim do that!'

'Our only hope is to find the conch,' Abhaydatta said. 'Think carefully, child. What did the room in which the treasure chest was kept look like? Perhaps that will give us a clue.'

Nisha shook her head. 'I don't know. I saw nothing but the chest in my dream.'

'If only the mirror that brought Anand to this world was not lost to us!' Abhaydatta said. 'We might have been able to look into it and find where the treasure chest was located, for such mirrors have many different powers.' His shoulders sagged. 'But without it, there is no way for us to search through every nobleman's treasury by tomorrow night – even if we could work a spell of dissembling twice as strong as Kasim's.'

'Wait!' Anand said, suddenly remembering. 'The mirror shattered, but there was a shard left. I hid it in a crack in a brick wall. Could that work, if I found it?'

'I don't know,' the healer said. 'In this world, all the magical rules I learned are inverted. But we'll have to try – we have no other option.'

There was a shout in the distance. A group of horsemen, accompanied by a palanquin, were riding toward the lake. One of them pointed at Nisha and shouted again. The riders were slowed down by the palanquin, but they would still arrive at the lake in a few minutes. Nisha grimaced. 'Layla Bibi must have discovered that

I was gone. She's going to be furious! She's probably not going to let me out of the mansion for the rest of my life!'

'How will we meet again, then?' Anand asked. 'If I do find the mirror, you're the one who will have to look into it. Even if Abhaydatta and I see something, we won't know which part of the palace we're looking at. We'll need you for that.'

Before Nisha could reply, the palanquin had arrived. Layla Bibi shot out of it like a plump, quivering lightning bolt. 'How could you do this to me, Paribanou!' she cried indignantly. 'Going off riding on your own, without even a chaperone! Thank the Prophet that your groom noted the direction you'd taken, or else it would have taken me hours to find you. You're too old for such adventures, now that you're of marriageable age. Your uncle will be absolutely livid – with you, and with me, I'm sure. He'll probably tell me to leave his service, saying that I have failed in my duty. And I have! Allah! What if something had happened to you? What if some ruffian'– here she shot a dagger glance at Abhaydatta – 'had kidnapped you?'

'But Layla Bibi, as you see, I'm quite safe and – '

Layla Bibi ignored Nisha and turned on the other two. 'You! Old man! What are you grinning at? And you, servant boy! You shouldn't even be standing this close to a noble-born lady. Off with you both! Right now!'

'They were only helping me to find the diamond brooch that had fallen off my turban,' Nisha said.

'Hai Rabba! Not the diamond your uncle gave you for your last birthday? Now I shall lose my position for sure!'

'Calm down, Bibi! We found it.' Nisha opened her hand. 'See, here it is!'

Layla Bibi snatched the jewel out of her palm. 'I'll keep that until we get back home, young lady. And now, off the horse and into the palanquin with you! No, I don't want to hear another word. Let's hope we can return home before your uncle sends for you to join him for breakfast. From now on, I'm going to make sure there's a servant-maid with you at all times, so you don't run off like this again.' She pushed Nisha into the palanquin, climbed in herself, and pulled the curtains shut with a decisive snap. Anand and Abhaydatta could hear her scolding Nisha all the way to the gate.

Anand grimaced in sympathy. 'Well, she's not going to be able to come to the lake again,' he said.

'That's right,' Abhaydatta answered as he guided the elephant out of the water. 'You're going to have to find the mirror shard and take it to her. Then the two of you can put your heads together and try to make it work.'

'Wait!' Anand cried. 'I can't do it without you! I don't know enough magic. And how on earth am I to get to Nisha? You know how closely Haider Ali's mansion is guarded! And now she's going to have a maid-servant watching her all the time – '

'Hurry up over there, you two!' came the gruff voice of one of the gatekeepers. Now that Nisha had gone, they weren't inclined to keep the gate open for mere servants.

'I won't have a chance to see you again,' Abhaydatta said as he swung on to the elephant's back and clicked his tongue to make it go faster. 'We'll be busy getting the elephants ready for the parade. But I'm sure you'll find a way to do what needs to be done. Believe in yourself, Anand! After all, you are the conch bearer!'

≈≈⊚≈≈

Anand mopped at his sweaty forehead as he glanced around the alley. Could this be the one where he had hidden the mirror? It was in the right area, behind the avenue where he had watched the procession and almost been trampled by Matangi on the very first day he had entered the nawab's world. But, as he had discovered in the last couple of hours, several alleys ran alongside each other behind the avenues, and they all looked alike with their cramped storefronts, dillapidated homes, winding dirt roads and worn brick walls that appeared as though they might tumble down at the slightest push. He remembered hastily slipping the shard into one of the gaps in one of the walls. But where? He'd searched the walls in each alley, feeling between the bricks until his fingertips were raw and aching, and had found nothing. It was an impossible task!

He lowered himself wearily onto the steps of a closed-down tavern. It was almost midday. He was hungry and thirsty, and in a lot of trouble besides. After talking to Abhaydatta, he hadn't gone back to the punkah boys' quarters to get his daily assignment. *Latif must be furious with me for not showing up!* He thought ruefully. *I've probably added a new swatch of gray to his head.* Latif was sure to have reported his truancy to Zafar by now, so Anand couldn't run to the kitchen for a bite to eat, either. Not that he felt like eating, famished though he was. Hunger was the least of his problems right now. Unless he found the mirror, Nisha and he had no chance of getting to the conch. And without the conch to help them, they would have to stand by and helplessly watch while Kasim did whatever he wanted to the nawab and his family.

Anand felt like slapping himself. *If only I hadn't been so hasty and shoved the piece of mirror somewhere, without taking care to mark the spot!* He thought angrily. *Why hadn't I been more careful? I knew the mirror was an object of power. I should have guessed I might need it again.* Abhaydatta had told him to believe in himself, to remember he was the conch bearer. But what good was that when he didn't know how to get in touch with the conch any more?

Conch, conch, he cried inwardly, trying one more time. *Where are you? I really need you to help me find the mirror.*

The silence inside his head was deafening. Dejected – though he hadn't really expected anything else – he sat on the steps, not knowing what to do next. He should search the walls in this alley, he supposed, but it would take hours before he would be done with all of them. By then, it would be too late. Hopelessly, he put his face in his hands.

Anand wasn't sure how long he'd been sitting there, lost in his thoughts – but no, *thoughts* was not the right word. His mind had been strangely blank. *Like swimming in an underground lake*, he thought. But now, emerging from it, he realized that there was a light flickering against his closed eyelids. What could it be, and how long had it been there? Was it just his tired eyes playing tricks on him? But no, there was definitely a light. He observed it intently, afraid it would disappear if he shifted his attention from it. It moved a little to the right and flickered again, the way sunlight might, if reflected in water – or a mirror!

His heart beating rapidly, Anand opened his eyes just a little. Immediately, the flicker vanished. He clamped his eyes shut, cursing himself for being so stupid. Fortunately, after a moment, he could see the flicker again. It moved a little to the right and stopped – almost as though it wanted Anand to follow. Gingerly, with his eyes closed, Anand took a few steps in the direction of the flicker. That seemed to be the correct thing to do, for the flicker grew brighter and danced ahead. Holding his hands out in front of him like a blind person, Anand followed. He wasn't going to risk losing the light by opening his eyes again. He hoped he wouldn't step onto a pile of cow-dung or get run over by a donkey-cart, or be stopped by some passer-by and asked if he had gone daft. He seemed to be crossing the alley and turning into another, and then another one. The paved stones under his feet gave way to gravel and dirt. Then suddenly, the flicker stopped. It was very bright now. He stretched his hand out further – and touched a wall.

Anand opened his eyes and found himself in front of yet another alley wall. Though this wall seemed no different from the others he'd searched all morning, he began peering into the gaps between the bricks with new excitement. What was that glimmer in there? Scarcely daring to hope, he reached in and felt a welcome sharpness against his fingertips. Manoeuvering carefully, he pulled something thin and shiny out of the gap. A broken piece of mirror the size of his palm lay in his trembling hand. It was larger than he recalled it being, but he knew at once that it was the same fragment that he had picked up and saved! He could feel a slight warmth emanating from it, an energy that throbbed as though the mirror had a heart that was beating.

Anand didn't understand why the power had led him to the mirror, or why that power hadn't led him directly to the conch. He was just thankful, because on his own he wouldn't even have got this far. He took off his turban and wrapped it around the shard with care; he still remembered how its edge had cut his finger before. Was it really larger now? But everything that had happened on that day was a blur. He could easily have been mistaken about the fragment's size. And even now it was tiny. How would he or Nisha locate *anything* through it?

But he would have to worry about that later. Right now, he had to get the mirror to Nisha. He wiped more sweat away. Now that the turban was gone, the sun's rays beat mercilessly upon his head, even though by its position he could see it was late afternoon. Late afternoon already? How long had he sat in a trance on the steps? He trudged as fast as he could through the heat to the back gate of Haider Ali's mansion, with a strong premonition that time was running out.

The guards at the gate, two large, burly men, looked at him with disgust when Anand said that Latif Miah had sent him to replace one of the punkah boys on the afternoon shift who had been sick last night.

'What is Latif thinking of,' the older of them exclaimed, 'sending us bareheaded boys who look like they've been playing danda-goli in the dust all day! You had better go to the servants' quarters right away and change your clothes and wash up.'

'It wouldn't do to have you filthy and rumpled in front of the chief minister's special guests,' said the other one. 'They've been meeting all morning, and they will be thirsty and short-tempered by now. If Haider Ali sees you looking like this, old Latif would lose his job for certain.'

'I will do as you say, sirs!' Anand said, salaaming deeply to both of them. As soon as he was out of the guards' line of vision, he planned to sprint up the staircase that led to Nisha's corridor. With luck on his side, he should be able to get to her room without running into any of the servants, who must be busy preparing the evening meal. Together, Nisha and he would try to figure out how to use the mirror. It would be better than racking his brains by himself. A small smile came to his face involuntarily as he thought of Nisha. It was good to have found his friend, even though she didn't remember who he was. It made him feel a little less alone in this strange environment.

Perhaps it was the smile that roused the older guard's suspicion, but his giant hand clamped down on Anand's shoulder. 'I'm due for a break right now. I'll take you to the servants' quarters myself. You might get lost and wander all over the mansion.'

Anand tried to protest, but it was no use. The guard marched him to the servants' area and sternly supervised him as he scrubbed his face, changed his tunic, and donned a fresh turban. Anand barely managed to stuff his old turban, with the mirror wrapped in it, into a jubba pocket before he was sent off to the dining hall, where Haider Ali's guests — just a handful of noblemen — had already gathered for a light repast. Among them Anand recognized the two men who had tried to persuade Haider Ali to take over the kingdom earlier. His thoughts in a whirl, he made for an empty punkah station. Why was the chief minister meeting with these people now?

Covertly, as he pulled the punkah, Anand watched Haider Ali. There was a new expression, hard and resolute, on his face, and sharp lines ran from his nose to the corners of his mouth. The chief minister had changed — whether it was because of the rejection by his old friend, or because of Kasim's influence, Anand wasn't sure. But with a sinking heart he knew that things were moving fast towards a catastrophe.

A line of servants entered, bearing covered dishes and pitchers. Behind them, to Anand's surprise, came Nisha. She was dressed in a beautiful blue silk ghaghra that fell in rich folds to her feet and a matching choli. A spangled veil covered her face, and gold bangles shone on her wrists. Why was she here? Anand wondered. He had learned enough of the customs of the nawab's court to know that women usually did not appear in front of male guests. As he watched, Nisha took the first dish and served each of the guests a few kababs. Then she took goblets of frothing lassi from a servant's tray and carefully set the chilled buttermilk drinks in front of the men. The noblemen exchanged glances, their faces mirroring their amazement at this unusual occurrence, but Haider Ali, who had obviously instructed her in this, nodded in approval.

'This, as you know, is my dear niece, the only heir to my fortune,' he said to the nobles. 'I have asked her to come out from the zenana quarters and serve you today because you are as close to me as my own brothers.'

'It is a great honour,' a nobleman said, bowing.

'We will look upon her as upon our own daughters,' another one declared.

'We will uphold the honour of your house as though it were our own honour,' said a third. He bit resolutely into a kabab, then added. 'We have eaten your salt. Now any insult to you – or your niece – is an insult to each one of us.'

Haider Ali nodded, looking satisfied. The talk moved to other issues – the best Arabian horse dealers, the unusually hot weather and lack of rain, the singers who would be coming to the festival tomorrow night – but Anand could see that an important decision had been reached. Nisha's appearance had forged the final link in a chain. Now all the noblemen present here were committed to supporting Haider Ali, whatever his plans may be.

Did those plans include taking over the realm tomorrow night, once Kasim had wreaked havoc on the royal family?

When the nobles were done eating, Haider Ali invited them to join him in listening to a sarod player who had travelled all the way from Delhi to be at the festival.

'It will relax us all after this hard day of deliberation,' he said. 'Would you like to listen, too, Paribanou?'

'If it pleases you, respected Uncle, may I walk awhile in the garden instead?' she said. 'I have been in my room all day, and would dearly like some fresh evening air.'

Haider Ali nodded gracious permission and led the company out of the dining room. Nisha, who brought up the rear, gave Anand a brief, meaningful stare through her veil before she followed them through the door. Craning his neck, Anand saw her turning into the passageway to the right. He waited until the servants came in to clear the dishes. In the commotion that followed, he slipped down the same passage.

sixteen

What the Mirror Showed

Haider Ali's garden was cool and peaceful, with shady gulmohur trees
spreading their leafy arms over beds of deep red roses and fragrant
queen-of-the night shrubs. But Anand had no time to appreciate the
fish-headed fountain or the paved paths that meandered through a
herb patch filled with coriander and mint plants, for Nisha was
beckoning urgently to him from behind a lush honeysuckle creeper
that filled a corner of the garden. As soon as he came close, she
grabbed his arm and pulled him into a small space between the
creeper and the wall.

'There! Now we'll be safe,' she said. 'No one ever comes into
this corner of the garden. Did you find the mirror?'

He nodded, took out the turban from his pocket and
unwrapped it.

'But it's so small!' she said, her voice disappointed. 'Will it work?'

'I don't know,' Anand said. 'We'll have to try. Be careful! The
broken edges are very sharp.'

Together, they bent over the sliver, looking into it. But all they
could see were bits of their faces framed by the sky, which was a
sunset pink by now.

'I think you're supposed to do something special,' Nisha said. 'You used it before, didn't you?' she added, a bit accusingly. 'Don't you know what to do?'

Trying to recall what exactly he'd done in the ruins, Anand gripped the edges gingerly and lifted the mirror to the horizon. But when he looked, all he could see was the reflection of his eyes. The mirror would not let him see through it.

'Let me look,' Nisha said, lunging impatiently for the fragment. Then she dropped it with a cry. 'Ow! It cut me!' Indeed, a bead of blood bloomed on her fingertip.

Anand was more concerned with the state of the mirror. He kneeled and picked up the sliver and laid it on his turban. 'That's no way to treat an object of power!' he said angrily. 'Besides, what if it had broken again?'

Nisha set her mouth stubbornly, ready for an argument. As the chief minister's niece, she wasn't used to having people criticize her. Then her eyes widened.

'Look!' she exclaimed. 'It's grown bigger.'

Anand looked down at the mirror. Indeed, it had. It was a little wider than his palm now.

'The side that my blood touched – it grew!' Nisha whispered, her eyes wide. Bending, she gently touched her finger to the other three sides of the mirror, leaving a dot of blood on each.

Under their amazed eyes, the mirror began to expand. Slowly, but steadily it grew until it was the size of Anand's two hands placed side by side. Nisha picked it up, her mouth open in wonder. It was certainly large enough for them to look through now! But when Anand and Nisha peered into it again, they still only saw their reflections.

'It's no use!' Nisha said, handing it back to Anand desolately, after they had tried everything they could think of – including turning the mirror upside down. 'If there's a trick to using the mirror, we don't know what it is.' She looked at the darkening sky. 'I'm going to have to go in – Layla Bibi must be having a fit, wondering where I've disappeared to this time. I'm surprised she hasn't come looking for me yet.' She shook leaves and grass from her expensive silk skirt and grimaced at a mud stain. 'Goodbye for now,' she said, trying to sound hopeful. 'Maybe we'll figure out something else by tomorrow.'

Anand's body crumpled with the day's accumulated tiredness. By tomorrow, they both knew, it would be too late. To get this far and have to give up! *O mirror!* he thought, shutting his eyes in despair. *Why won't you help us!*

He must have been really tired, because the mirror seemed very heavy all of a sudden – too heavy for him to hold on to. It slipped from his hand and tumbled to the earth – except this time it fell face down. And when Anand picked it up, holding it back-to-front, he could see something through the silvered backing. It looked like a street, with newly-lit lamps wavering on both sides. Large mansions bordered it, their gates guarded by turbaned men, each wearing his master's colours. The scene extended a long way, clear and detailed as a miniature Mughal painting.

'Nisha!' he called, and when she ran back, pointed out the scene to her.

'Ya Allah!' she exclaimed. 'Why, that's the street outside these garden walls! That's the mansubdar's house. And that pink building belongs to Munir Khan, whose crybaby of a daughter comes to play with me sometimes. Why, by angling the mirror we can look right into the houses, through their walls. Oh, look, a cook's apprentice in the mansubdar's kitchen is stealing a piece of fried chicken, hiding it in his jubba while no one is looking!'

They turned to each other in jubilation.

'You learned how to use the mirror!' Nisha cried. 'That was really clever of you! How did you do it?'

A pleasant warmth spread through Anand at the compliment. There weren't many people who thought well of him in this strange world. But then, being an honest person, he said, 'It was by chance – though it makes sense now.' He thought he could feel the mirror throbbing again under his hands, but he continued. 'If from a different world, you had to look into the mirror to see what was here – '

'Then when you're in the same world, you need to look out through it,' Nisha finished. 'You were very lucky, to drop the mirror the way you did!'

The mirror was hot in Anand's hands now. He looked down at it wonderingly. 'Maybe it wasn't just luck,' he said. 'Just before it fell from my hands, I asked the mirror to help us – '

'You mean it heard you and responded?' Nisha asked, intrigued. 'Oh, I want to try this!' She took the mirror from Anand's hand. He waited for her to remark on its hotness, but she did not seem to notice it. 'Mirror,' she said. 'Please show us the magic conch we are searching for.'

Nothing happened. Nisha glanced at Anand. 'Maybe I wasn't polite enough for an object of power,' she whispered to him. Bowing, she intoned, 'Respected mirror-sahib, would you kindly show us the way to the conch? We would be forever grateful for your benefaction.'

Nothing again. After a moment a disappointed Nisha handed the mirror back to Anand. 'I still think it was chance,' she said. 'Maybe we can find the conch anyway, by pointing the mirror in different directions – '

A strange thought had just occurred to Anand. *It couldn't be*! he thought to himself. To Nisha he said, 'Let me try something,' he said. Holding the mirror, he repeated Nisha's request in his head. This time, the mirror began to throb. When he raised it, it seemed to pull his hands westward, where the sky was still red, the way a magnet might be pulled toward a lode of iron. Through the mirror's backing, they could see a huge golden dome.

'May the saints bless us!' he heard Nisha whisper. 'That's the nawab's palace! If the conch is indeed there, how will we ever get to it?'

'Lady Paribanou!' shouted an exasperated and familiar voice. 'Are you out there in the garden? By the Prophet Muhammed, that child will drive me to an early grave!'

'What are we going to do?' Anand whispered.

'I'm going to have to go right now, before Layla Bibi finds you with me,' Nisha whispered back. 'Wait for me outside the back gate

156

tomorrow morning before the muezzin sounds the call for the second prayer – I'll try to get away somehow. We'll have to go to the nawab's palace. There's no other way.'

'Paribanou!' Layla Bibi shouted again, her voice rising dangerously. 'I know you're out there. Come in right now! Or else I'll come and get you. And when I do, you'll get a spanking, just the way you used to when you were little.'

Nisha grinned. 'She won't really come out here. She's afraid of insects – crickets especially. But she will give me a spanking if I delay any longer. And her palm – it's made of iron!' She made her voice sweet as sugar and called back. 'I'm coming right away, Layla Bibi. I'm sorry! I got carried away watching the sunset. It was so beautiful!'

'But how will we get into the nawab's palace?' Anand whispered. 'They don't just let people in there randomly, I'm sure –'

Nisha sighed. 'I wish my uncle and the nawab hadn't had that fight. Then I could have paid the begum a respectful visit, as I've done often before, and looked around quietly while I was there.' Then her face brightened. 'Wait, I know just what we'll do!' she said, clapping her hands. 'No, I mustn't say anything about it right now – that will bring us bad luck. Just be there on time tomorrow!' She ran off into the gathering darkness, leaving Anand afire with curiosity.

After the sounds of Layla Bibi's bitter reprimands had disappeared into the mansion, Anand re-wrapped the mirror in his turban – it no longer fitted in his pocket – and crept through the garden to the kitchen. There he managed to blend in with a group of cook's apprentices who were leaving the house. Luckily for him, the apprentices were given the leftovers from the evening's meal. Anand wrapped as much as he could in a banana leaf. Once out of sight of the chief minister's mansion, he wolfed it down under a streetlamp. Never before had hard chapatis and cold kabab-bits tasted so delicious!

After the meal, he drank water from a roadside spigot, and then trudged along until he found the tree-lined compound of a mosque. Though he longed for his pallet, he didn't dare return to the punkah boys' quarters for fear of being apprehended by Latif. He gathered a pile of leaves and dry grass in the shadows of a large tamarind tree and lay down, hoping that no one – man, animal or spirit – would find him. With one hand he kept tight hold of the wrapped mirror, feeling its sharp outlines through his turban-cloth. A jumble of thoughts knocked around in his head. *The mirror responded to me! Every time I called on it – from the time in the tunnel when Kasim was about to catch me until today – it helped me. Could that be my special gift, then, to speak to objects of power and have them listen?*

The moon had travelled halfway across the sky, and the night watchman had made his second round, banging his iron-tipped stick on the stones of the road, and shouting 'Hoshiar!' before Anand fell into an exhausted sleep. The last thought in his mind was, *If I can communicate with objects of power, why can't I make contact with the conch?*

⚶⊚⚶

Anand woke to the strident cawing of crows. His clothes were rumpled and dusty, and his bones ached from having slept on the ground, but he forgot all his discomforts as his startled eyes flew to the sky, where the sun hung hot and yellow already. Oh no! He had overslept! The muezzin must have sounded the second prayer call long before now. He should have been at Haider Ali's back gate, waiting for Nisha, hours ago. Without even waiting to wash his face at the cistern beside the mosque, he grabbed the mirror, still wrapped in the turban, and ran to the chief minister's mansion. His stomach churned with hunger. He hoped Nisha would remember to bring him some breakfast. But most of all, he longed to hear what her plan was.

Outside the chief minister's back gate, the road was filled with commotion. There were vendors trying to sell their wares and servants hurrying to and fro on errands. There were legless beggars and holy men chanting prayers, hoping for alms. Anand stood in a corner, trying hard to look as though he was there on important official business. He watched the gates for Nisha, but she was nowhere to be seen. Worries gnawed at him. What if she had been there already to search for him, and had gone back to her room because she couldn't find him? Would she get a chance to come out again? Had he ruined her plans by oversleeping? Or – perhaps this was worse – had she gone off on her own, without him?

It was crowded near the gate, much of the space taken up by a donkey-cart filled with ripe watermelons. People had to squeeze by Anand, and several of them yelled at him to get out of the way. But he hung on stubbornly, not wanting to move to a spot where he couldn't see the gate. A boy – a messenger, Anand guessed, from his turban and the matching red tunic on which a rolled parchment was embroidered – shoved him as he strode by, making him stumble.

'Hey, watch where you're going!' Anand shouted angrily. 'You almost made me fall into the ditch.'

'It was your fault for blocking my way!' the messenger boy retorted. 'And so what if you'd fallen into the ditch? Your clothes are so dirty already, it would have made no difference.'

Though Anand was generally a peaceful person, he bristled at the boy's tone. Hands fisted, he advanced on the messenger-boy, who shook his staff at him threateningly. 'Move aside! I've an important message – for the shahzada, none else – and you'd better not delay me unless you'd like a bump on your head.'

Then, unexpectedly, he winked at Anand.

Taken aback, Anand stared into the messenger boy's face. Could it be? The boy flashed him a familiar grin, then hurried off into the crowd. Anand followed, trying to be unobtrusive in case anyone was watching them.

The messenger boy took several turns until he reached the animal market, filled with the squawking of chickens and the bleating of goats. 'Best place to talk without being overheard,' he explained to Anand when the latter caught up with him.

'Nisha? Is that you?'

The boy drew himself up to his full height. 'The Lady Paribanou, you mean!'

'Yes, yes, of course,' Anand stammered. 'I'm sorry I overslept!'

'You should be! I've been hanging around the gate for over an hour now, terrified that one of the guards would recognize me.'

'Your clothes! Where … ?'

'I gave the girl who cleans my room a gold coin to get me her brother's uniform – he's one of my uncle's messenger boys.' Nisha grinned proudly. 'I did a good job with getting all my hair under that turban, didn't I? Did I fool you, at least for a little while?'

'You did,' Anand admitted. 'You're a good actress!'

'We'll see how good I am when we get to the shahzada's palace.'

'You weren't joking, then, about having to deliver a message to the shahzada?'

'I have a message for him right here,' Nisha said, delving into the pouch she was carrying and coming up with a sealed parchment. 'From the Lady Paribanou, sealed with her special seal. Let's see if it does the trick and gets us in to see him.'

⁂

Outside the imposing marble palace, the nawab's guards examined the seal and seemed convinced that it was genuine. But they were not inclined to let a mere messenger boy in to see the prince.

'If we did that with every messenger that brought letters to the royal family, Their Majesties would be receiving messengers only, from morning till night,' one said.

'And look at your companion! His clothes are filthy, and he stinks, too!' another guard said. 'The shahzada would have our heads if we sent that one up to his room!'

The guards guffawed. Nisha's nostrils flared in anger, and she was about to make a retort. Anand quickly put his hand on her arm in warning. *The insult doesn't matter*, he told her silently. *What's important is to find the conch.* He didn't know if she could feel his thoughts, but after a moment she let out a breath and said, politely enough, 'I'm sorry, I cannot give you the letter. The lady Paribanou would have *my* head if I did so. Don't you see what she has written across the top, just above the seal? *To be handed to the shahzada alone by my personal messenger.* And if I go back without delivering it, you can be sure the chief minister will hear of the incident – and of the people who prevented me from delivering it.'

The guards glanced at each other uncertainly. Clearly, they did not want the chief minister's wrath to descend on them. Finally one of them gestured to Nisha with reluctance. 'Very well, boy. I'll take you to the prince's quarters. From there, one of his personal guards will escort you to the shahzada. This one, though – ' here he pointed at Anand – 'will have to wait for you here.'

Nisha wasn't pleased, but she had to accept the decision. With an apologetic grimace at Anand, she allowed herself to be led down a hallway by the guard. Anand squatted under a palm tree next to the gate, wondering what would happen next. He could hear the guards talking excitedly about the coming night's festivities.

'The elephants will be leading the parade,' one said. 'I hear they've been specially decorated with beads and jewels for the occasion.'

'Do you know that there will be dancing bears, and fireworks, and even a magician?' added another.

'Singers have come from as far as Ispahan,' a third said.

'What I'm interested in is the food! Special halvaikars have been hired, and they've been cooking sweetmeats since yesterday. You can smell it all the way across the palace compound! They say the palace servants will be allowed to eat all they want after the guests finish their meal.'

Hungrily, Anand wondered what kinds of sweets the cooks were making. Nisha had been too preoccupied to bring him any food, and his stomach was complaining bitterly. He remembered how his mother used to make the best rasogollahs. On his birthday she'd wake him with a kiss and a bowl of the sweet white balls floating in syrup. Even after they'd grown poor, she would somehow save up enough money to make a few for his birthday, because she knew how much he liked them. He thought of that faraway time with a sigh.

His reverie was broken by a guard calling to him.

'Hey! Boy!' he yelled. 'The shahzada wants to see you!' He glanced at Anand's rumpled clothes suspiciously, obviously wondering what the prince would want with a street urchin. Nevertheless, he led him down a labyrinth of sumptuous corridors, their walls covered with tapestries and their floors with Kashmiri rugs. Finally, he knocked on a door.

'Who is it that dares disturb the most glorious shahzada?' cried a stentorian voice from within. Anand guessed it belonged to the shahzada's personal attendant.

'Noble Ahmed Miah, it is I, Rasul the gatekeeper,' the guard replied, his voice quavering. 'I have brought the boy the shahzada wished to speak with.'

The door swung open. The guard bowed to a very large man standing there. He wore loose pants just as the other servants did, but his upper body was covered only by a vest made of chain mail. In his hand was a wicked-looking curved scimitar. The man stared impassively at Anand, then nodded silently to him to follow him. His heart beating with nervousness, Anand followed Ahmed, noting how the attendant's huge muscles gleamed and rippled as he moved.

They walked down yet another corridor, this one decorated even more lavishly with tapestries of battle scenes stitched in gold and silver thread. Ahmed opened a door decorated with ivory carvings and murmured something.

'Send him in, send him in,' the shahzada's voice was high and impatient. 'And Ahmed, see that we're not disturbed by anyone until I finish speaking to these-uh-boys.'

Entering the room, Anand noticed the shahzada sitting on a high divan piled with cushions, while Nisha, still in her messenger-boy uniform, sat on a thick carpet on the floor. Not sure what he should do, he remained standing near the door.

As soon as Ahmed had performed his salaams and backed out of the room, the shahzada jumped off the divan. 'Help me push this to the door,' he said to the others. 'My door doesn't have a lock, because my mother is afraid that otherwise an assassin or a kidnapper may trap me in here! As a result I never get any privacy. People are always coming in to check on me – especially when I've specifically asked them not to.'

Anand glanced at the prince with a new sympathy. For the first time he realized that being a prince had its disadvantages. Panting and puffing, the three of them managed to push the heavy divan against the door, blocking it. 'There!' the shahzada said in satisfaction. 'Now I can listen to your stories in peace.' He turned to Nisha and stared at her with some interest. 'I can't believe you dressed up as a boy and walked through the public streets on your own to come here, Paribanou!' he said. 'Didn't it feel strange to be without your veil, having people stare at you? Weren't you scared that someone would recognize you?'

'I was scared,' Nisha admitted. 'But I soon realized that people don't pay as much attention to a messenger boy as they would to the chief minister's niece! But enough about me! This is the boy I was telling you about – '

'This one?' The shahzada wrinkled his elegant nose in distaste. 'But he looks like an ordinary servant boy – and not a very clean one, at that.'

Nisha's eyes flashed in annoyance. 'And I look like a messenger boy! But I'm not one, am I? Things are not always what they seem, Mahabet. An intelligent person like you should know that already.'

A smile appeared on the shahzada's lips at the compliment, the irony of which he missed. He puffed out his chest. 'Yes, of course, I know that,' he said. Then he scowled at Nisha. 'But you should be addressing me as Your Majesty! Only someone descended from a royal family is allowed to use my name.'

Nisha rolled her eyes in exasperation but remained silent. She knew as well as Anand did that they needed the shahzada's help and could not afford to displease him.

Turning to Anand, the shahzada asked, 'Have you really come from another world in search of a powerful magical conch? And are you really a great sorcerer in that world?'

Anand swallowed, taken aback. Nisha had obviously been embroidering the truth! 'Uh – I wouldn't exactly call myself a great sorcerer – ' he started to say. But Nisha interrupted him.

'Like all great people, he is humble. But what's really important is that in his magic mirror he has seen that the conch is somewhere in your palace.'

'A magic mirror!' the shahzada exclaimed. 'Show it to me!'

Anand felt a sense of foreboding, but he knew he would have to show the mirror to the shahzada if they were to gain his cooperation. Reluctantly, he started opening the bundle, but Nisha interrupted him.

'Anand hasn't had breakfast yet, and I wasn't able to bring him any food. Can you please give him something to eat? And maybe you could loan him a set of your clothes as well? That way, we'll rouse less suspicion when you take us into the vaults.'

The shahzada didn't look too pleased about sharing his clothes with Anand, even if he was a great sorcerer in another world. But he went to a cupboard and took out a pair of loose pants and a simple tunic, and led Anand to the bathing area. Thankfully, Anand washed his face and hands in a silver basin, scrubbing himself with rose-scented soap. When he changed into the new clothes and stepped out, Nisha clapped her hands. 'That's good!' she said. 'Now you look like a young nobleman, Anand. If anyone asks, Mahabet – I mean His Supreme Majesty – you can say you're one of his friends, come to pay him a visit.'

The shahzada led Anand to a corner of his room, and waved negligently at a table piled with fruits, stacks of rolled-out bread and sweets of many kinds. 'They always bring me too much food,' he said. 'Eat what you want.'

'But hurry!' Nisha added. 'We need to start searching as soon as possible.'

Anand had a very satisfying meal of mangoes and bananas, sweet laddus, and thick, soft naan bread that melted in his mouth. He washed it all down with a glass of pomegranate juice, which was as delicious as he had imagined, seeing it in his vision in the forest.

As soon as he'd finished, the shahzada extended an impatient hand. 'The mirror – I want to see it now!'

Knowing he had no choice, Anand unwrapped the turban and handed it to him. 'Be careful! The edges can cut your fingers,' he warned.

The shahzada turned it over in his hands and peered into it, both front and back. 'It's just a broken mirror,' he said in annoyance, tossing it back at Anand so suddenly that Anand had to lunge forward to catch it in his turban-cloth. 'Paribanou, are you trying to make a fool out of me?' His nostrils flared with anger. 'Perhaps I should call Ahmed and have you both taken away – '

Anand's heart quailed as he remembered the fierce-looking

Ahmed, but Nisha stood up and placed her hands on her hips. 'Stop threatening us, Mahabet, as though we were your servants!' she said. 'If we were taken away, you'd lose the chance to be part of a great adventure – the only adventure you'll probably ever have in your boring royal life. Is that what you want? If so, go ahead and call Ahmed right now.'

The shahzada looked dumbfounded. Anand guessed that no one had ever dared to speak to him quite like this. He glared at Nisha, but she scowled back at him, undaunted. After a moment he lowered his head. 'No,' he admitted reluctantly. 'I don't want you to go. I-uh-I like having you here, Paribanou.'

His reluctant admission seemed to have appeased Nisha. 'The mirror only works when Anand asks it to,' she explained in a friendlier voice. 'That's because he's a great magician, and respectful, besides. That's something you could learn from him, Mahabet – respect. I saw how you threw the mirror at him. You'd better not do that again! You don't want to anger an object of power. You never know what might happen. Didn't I tell you how it repelled the evil magician Kasim when he tried to enter this world?'

The shahzada stole a fearful look at the mirror. 'You shouldn't be telling me what to do,' he began, though less belligerently than before. 'I'm the royal heir, after all – '

'Not for long, if Kasim has his way!' Nisha retorted. 'Let's not waste any more time arguing. Anand, are you ready?'

While the two of them were bickering, Anand had been focusing on the mirror, asking it silently for guidance, waiting until it grew hot in his hands once again. Now he pointed it to the northwest corner of the room. 'It's telling me to go in this direction,' he said.

'I could have told you that!' Mahabet said dismissively. 'That's where the royal treasury is – all twenty-four chambers of it.'

Anand exchanged a troubled look with Nisha. Twenty-four chambers! It would be impossible to search so many rooms in such a short time. Their only hope was the mirror.

The shahzada led them down a corridor past several sets of guards who looked at them questioningly but did not dare to stop the prince. But when they came to the gates of the treasury, they found its massive doors chained and locked. Four guards stood on either side of the gates, carrying muskets.

'Open the doors at once,' Mahabet commanded. 'I wish to go into the vaults and choose some jewels to wear at the festival tonight.'

'Your Majesty,' the chief of the guards bowed and said, 'Please forgive us. We do not have the ability to open these gates. There are two sets of keys for these locks. The chief treasurer keeps one set, and the begum keeps the other.'

Anand and Nisha stared at each other. This was a problem they hadn't anticipated.

'Do something, sorcerer,' hissed the shahzada. 'Don't you know how to open locks?'

The mirror was hot and throbbing in Anand's hands as though it was trying to communicate something to him. He closed his eyes, squeezing them in his effort to understand. An image appeared against his eyelids.

On an impulse, he said to the prince, 'Order the guards to leave us for a little while. We need to be alone.' When the guards had retreated to a bend in the passage, he pressed the edge of his finger to one side of the mirror, letting the sharp edge cut it a little. When the blood came, he touched it to all four sides of the mirror, then waited. But the mirror did not grow.

'Let me try!' Nisha said. She, too, allowed a corner of the mirror to prick her finger. But her blood didn't make the mirror grow either.

'But I saw an image,' Anand said, confused. 'A finger against the mirror edge, then blood, and the mirror expanding – '

'I think each person's blood only works once,' Nisha said. 'We have to use someone new.' She turned and stared at the prince. 'Mahabet, we need your help.'

'Oh no!' the shahzada said, shrinking back against the wall. 'I couldn't. I feel faint when I see blood – especially my own.'

'Mahabet!' Nisha said in exasperation. 'Don't be such a baby!'

'Please help us,' Anand said. 'If we don't find the conch in time, your whole family will be destroyed by Kasim.'

'That means your own parents,' Nisha said. 'And yourself, of course. Do you think what Kasim's going to do to you will hurt less than one little cut on your finger?'

The shahzada squinched shut his eyes and reluctantly held out his index finger, which trembled a little. 'When the time comes, will you tell everyone how brave and unselfish I was?' he asked.

Nisha hid a smile. 'Indeed I will, Mahabet. I think all this time I've judged you wrongly, thinking that you were a spoilt brat and a bully – '

The shahzada opened one eye to see if she was making fun of him, then closed it again promptly. 'Don't delay!' he ordered Anand. 'The waiting is killing me.' He took in a deep breath, held it and scrunched up his face.

Anand pressed an edge of the mirror gently against the shahzada's finger. When a drop of blood appeared, he touched it to the mirror's sides and set it down on the ground.

'It's growing!' the shahzada said, his voice squeaky with excitement.

'Hush! The guards will hear you,' Nisha said. 'Of course it's growing! But why did you set it down on the floor, Anand?'

'I don't know,' Anand replied. 'I'm just following the images I saw inside my head.'

The mirror was now as long as Anand's forearm and equally wide. As the children stared down into it, its shining surface began to undulate and grow transparent. But instead of seeing the floor through it, they could now see into a different room. The room was filled with chests, boxes and iron safes mounted on the wall.

'Why, that's one of the underground treasury chambers. I didn't realize it lay beneath this passage,' the shahzada said.

'Are we supposed to step through the mirror, the way you did before?' Nisha asked.

Anand nodded. 'I think so. I'll go first, if you like.' He wondered if the experience would be the same as last time, when he had travelled down a black glass tunnel. But scarcely had he stood on top of the mirror when the surface seemed to melt under his feet. He fell through it, landing with a rather hard thump on a pile of gold coins. He managed to roll out of the way just in time before Nisha came through.

'Amazing!' Nisha said, grinning from ear to ear. 'I couldn't believe how the ground just opened up under my feet! I must say I hadn't quite believed you before, but now I do!'

'Does this mean you also believe that you are really Nisha and not Paribanou?' Anand asked hopefully. But there was no time for Nisha to answer because at that moment the shahzada came through the mirror.

'Ow!' yelled Mahabet as he fell on the coins. 'Ow! You should have warned me that this was going to happen!'

Nisha tried to stifle her laughter but failed. 'What's the matter? Did Your Majesty bruise the royal behind?'

Mahabet glowered at her.

'Now, Nisha!' Anand admonished her. 'Mahabet has been most helpful to us. He's part of our team now. You mustn't make fun of him.'

'I'm sorry!' Nisha said to the shahzada. 'It's just that you looked so surprised when you landed on the ground.' She reached toward him and helped him up. 'Forgive me?'

Mahabet gave an ungracious sniff, but he looked pacified.

'Now what?' Nisha asked.

Acting on instinct, Anand raised his arms up, calling silently to the mirror. He wasn't totally surprised when it fell through the ceiling, landing gently in his hands. The ceiling above them returned to its original state of solid stone. When he raised the mirror up, looking through the backing, he felt it pulling him forward.

'The conch isn't in this room,' he said. 'But don't worry. I think the mirror is taking us where it is.'

'Can I hold it? Can I?' the shahzada asked eagerly.

Anand mentally consulted the mirror. It did not seem to have any objections, so he handed it over to Mahabet, warning him to be careful. But he need not have worried. This time Mahabet held up the mirror reverentially, with an awed smile on his face. The mirror led them past several vaults until they reached a small alcove at the end of a corridor. It looked as though no one had been in this part of the treasury for a long time. Cobwebs hung from the wall, and the chests stored here were old and covered in dust. But Nisha gave a cry and ran forward, brushing the cobwebs aside with her hands. 'I recognize this place! I saw it in my dream. And this – I'm sure this is the chest where I saw the conch!'

The three of them bent over the chest, which was full of expensive tableware – ruby studded goblets, embossed silver bowls and plates made of gold – and started to empty it. They had almost reached the bottom when Anand saw a gleam of white. He thrust his hand in among some gold spoons and felt the dear, familiar shape of the conch against his fingers. His heart filled with gladness and triumph – but also with hurt. *Why did you make it so hard for me to find you?* He asked the conch in his head. *Why didn't you call me and tell me where to look? How much time I wasted searching for you! How many dangers I had to face! We could have been together all this time.*

Do you think I liked being stuffed in the bottom of a chest full of spoons? the conch replied in its unmistakable voice. *I'd have preferred to be with you, too. But in this world my powers were limited. Also, there were other reasons. You'll find them out soon enough.*

Anand couldn't hold on to his anger any longer. He was just too thankful to have found the conch again. *I'm glad we're together finally,* he said. The conch didn't speak, but a warmth radiated from it and filled Anand's whole body.

'Is that it? Did you find it?' Nisha cried. 'Let me see it!' Her face grew rapt with attention as she held the conch in both her hands, gently stroking it with her thumb. There was a remembering look on her face, but she didn't say anything.

'Why, it's tiny!' Mahabet said, craning his neck over Nisha's shoulder to take a look. But he seemed more interested in the mirror, which he was cradling in his arms. 'How clever of this mirror to lead us to it!' he said as he polished its surface with a corner of his tunic. 'We'd never have found it otherwise.'

Anand smiled to himself. The shahzada was falling in love with the mirror just as Anand had with the conch. Objects of power tended to have that effect on people. But they didn't have the luxury of enjoying such emotions now. It must be almost evening. All too soon it would be time for the festival – and for facing Kasim and his jinn. His stomach clenched at the thought. But at least now he had the conch with him!

I'll have to run over to the hathi-khana and show you to Abhaydatta and plan a strategy with him, he told the conch as he hid it in one of his inside pockets.

That will not happen, the conch said.

Why not? Anand asked, puzzled. But the conch didn't explain further.

'We need to get out of here quickly,' Nisha said. 'I must get home and get dressed for tonight. Allah knows what kind of trouble is waiting for me back there! Layla Bibi is probably going to chain me to my bed from tomorrow.'

'The mirror's pulling me up this staircase and toward this wall,' Mahabet said. He walked up the stairs and placed the mirror waist-high against the stone at a certain spot. Immediately Anand could see through it.

'There's a garden outside,' he said.

'That's the Gulabi Bagh, where my father likes to spend his evenings enjoying the roses that he's had imported from all over the world,' Mahabet said, looking. 'We must be at the very edge of the building here.'

'I think the mirror is telling us that we can go out this way,' Nisha said. Sure enough, when she placed her hands against the mirror, they disappeared into the wall. 'It's made a tunnel for us here!' she exclaimed.

'I told you it was a special mirror,' Mahabet said proudly.

They climbed through the tunnel into the garden, where they parted. Nisha ran off to the chief minister's mansion to face Layla Bibi's wrath. Mahabet, who had taken possession of the mirror when it came floating through the wall behind them, went to his rooms. He invited Anand to come with him.

'I can give you one of my formal outfits, and you can go to the festival as my guest. I'll tell my mother you're the son of one of the nobles who has come into the city to see the festival. So many people have arrived recently – she won't suspect anything.'

Anand was tempted. It would be good to rest for a while in Mahabet's cool room, to eat with him and ride to the festival in a royal palanquin. But then he shook his head. 'I must meet Abhaydatta. He'll be so glad to see the conch. And the mirror, too. He'll be amazed to learn in how many ways it can be used. But most importantly, he'll tell me how to deal with Kasim this evening.'

'Abhaydatta?'

'You'll have to meet him. He looks like an old, illiterate elephant-keeper, but he's a master magician – though in this world for some reason he is unable to use his powers.' A thought struck Anand suddenly. 'Maybe now that I've found the conch, his powers will be restored! Goodbye for now – I'll have to hurry if I'm to make it all the way to the hathi-khana before the elephants are taken out for the parade.'

'You can't go running through the streets in the clothes I gave you,' Mahabet pointed out. 'They're too expensive. Someone wearing clothes like that should be riding a horse, with attendants following him. You might make people suspicious – '

'But there's no time to go back to your quarters and change,' Anand said. 'I'll have to take a chance.'

Mahabet tugged at his finger. 'Take this, then,' he said. 'It's my signet ring, with my father's seal on it. All the higher officials will recognize it. If you do get into trouble, maybe it will help you.'

'Thank you,' Anand said gratefully, slipping the ring onto his finger. 'I'll return it to you tonight.'

'Uh, also – ' Mahabet fidgeted awkwardly as he spoke. 'I think you should leave the mirror with me – it'll be safer in my room.'

'I don't know,' Anand began. He was uncomfortable at the thought of parting with the mirror. What if he needed it suddenly? Also, he wasn't quite sure he could trust Mahabet with such a powerful magical object.

'Please!' Mahabet continued, a look of entreaty on his proud face. 'It'll slow you down if you have to carry it to the hathi-khana because it's so big now. I'll take good care of it, I promise. I'll hide it where no one would even think of looking.'

Anand considered the matter. Without Mahabet's help, they would never have recovered the conch – and he could see that the mirror meant a lot to the shahzada. He felt a surge of sympathy for the lonely boy. *Let him keep it for now. Soon enough, when we leave, he'll have to give it up.* 'But you must promise not to use it,' he said to Mahabet sternly. 'Objects of power can be dangerous if handled by someone who doesn't know what he's doing.'

Mahabet lowered his eyes meekly. 'You are right,' he said.

But as Anand hurried towards the hathi-khana, he realized that the prince had not given him his promise.

seventeen

The Magic Show

Outside, the roads were bustling with people who, dressed in their colourful best, were already making their way to the maidan, the large field near the palace where the festival was to be held. Although seats were reserved for the nobility, commoners would have to scramble to find a good place from which to see the show. Because the hathi-khana was at the opposite end of the palace complex from the maidan, Anand had a hard time pushing against the streams of families that carried bulky baskets of food and rugs to sit on while they waited for the show to start. Several of them informed him he was going in the wrong direction, and one man even good-naturedly turned Anand around and pointed out the way to the maidan.

His pace was further slowed by the fact that the major roads, cordoned off for the elephant parade, were guarded by mounted soldiers to make sure pedestrians would not enter them. Several times Anand had to take a detour that cost him precious minutes he could ill afford. Finally, when he was only a few minutes away from the hathi-khana, he found that the road leading to its entrance had been closed off completely. In the distance he could see the elephants being lined up in readiness for the parade. Was that Abhaydatta, leading Nisha's elephant to its place in the line? In desperation Anand ducked under the rope and dashed down the road. But before he had gone a few paces, he found his way blocked by two horsemen.

'You can't go down this road, young sir,' one of them said, speaking more politely than Anand expected. 'The elephant parade is about to begin.'

Ah, it was because of the shahzada's clothes, of course! They made the soldier think he was noble-born. 'Even otherwise, a young nobleman should not be wandering the streets alone today,' he added. 'There are too many strangers in the city – some of them dangerous. Please tell us which noble house you belong to. One of us will escort you back there.'

Anand stared at him, momentarily at a loss for words.

The second soldier frowned. 'Perhaps he doesn't belong to a noble house at all,' he said to his companion. 'Look, he has no jewels, and no shoes! Have you ever seen a courtier's son running around the city barefoot? I think he stole the clothes he's wearing – and he's up to some mischief. I say we throw him in the lock-up until after the festival.'

His companion nodded. 'You're right. We *have* been instructed to deal sternly with troublemakers. Nothing must ruin the festival!'

The second soldier reached down and grabbed Anand roughly by the shoulder. 'Off to the lock-up with you. And on the way there you can tell us where you stole these expensive clothes.'

'Wait!' Anand said as the man dragged him along. 'You're right – I'm not a courtier's son, but I do belong to a noble house. I'm one of the shahzada's attendants, and I'm supposed to take a message to the mahout who handles his elephant. See, here's his signet ring that he gave me to carry.'

The soldiers peered at the ring. 'The shahzada's attendant?' One said, still suspicious. 'Why aren't you wearing the uniform of the royal house, then?' When Anand had no answer, he said, 'I think he's telling us another lie. Why, that ring he showed us could belong to anyone. Maybe he stole that, too.' He grabbed Anand by the collar this time. 'No more talk, you rascal, or you'll get the thrashing you deserve.'

'Stop!' Anand said with as much authority as he could muster. 'Take me to the commandant of your unit. Surely he will recognize the shahzada's ring.' Remembering how Nisha had dealt with the guards at the nawab's palace, he added, 'I'm carrying a very important message, and if it isn't delivered, the shahzada will have the heads of those who stopped me.'

The soldiers whispered uncertainly between themselves. Then one of them lifted Anand onto his horse and rode off to find the commandant. In the distance, a trumpet sounded, and drums began to roll. The parade was beginning.

'Let me go!' Anand entreated. 'I've to get to the mahout before the parade starts. Or else it'll be too late.' But the soldier would not listen.

By the time they found the commandant, the parade was under way. In the distance, Anand could see the horses, decorated with silk ribbons and bells, prancing along the road. Behind them, the elephants, painted and bejewelled, moved majestically down the cordoned avenue. Anand waited in an agony of impatience while the commandant examined the ring and finally declared that it did indeed look genuine.

'It's too late!' Anand burst out. 'I'll never be able to catch up to the elephants now.'

'I'm sorry,' the commandant declared. 'There's nothing I can do.' He turned away to attend to other business.

By this time, the elephants had already passed them, and the crowd was yelling and clapping at the knife-jugglers who followed. Anand slumped down on the back of the horse. Not only would he be unable to speak to Abhaydatta now, he doubted that he'd manage to push past this huge crowd and get to the maidan on time. Most certainly he wouldn't be able to find himself a spot close enough to the royal pavilion to protect the nawab and his family in any way.

Oh conch! He cried inside his head as he slipped a hand inside his jubba to touch it. *I should have paid attention to what you said and stayed with Mahabet. But I had to try and see Abhaydatta! I just had to! Surely you understand that.*

It seemed to him that the conch had grown heavier, though it did not seem any larger than before. A warm pulsing seemed to be coming from it. Following a vague instinct, he took his hand, his fingers still tingling from touching the conch, and placed it lightly on the arm of the soldier who had brought him to the commander.

'Please help me,' he said.

To his surprise, the soldier nodded. 'You were telling us the truth all the time, but we didn't believe you. It's only right that I should try to aid you now.' He manoeuvered his horse along a less crowded back road and then cut across an alley to another part of the cordoned-off avenue. 'The parade will be arriving here in a few minutes,' he said. 'You won't have much time, but you should be able to shout out your message to the mahout. Here, I'll help you stand up on my horse so the mahout can see you.'

Anand stood up, balancing precariously on the saddle, and tried to see what was going on. There were the horsemen, marching proudly. After them came the elephants, garlanded with bright flowers. Matangi was leading them! And there, behind four or five other elephants and their mahouts, was Abhaydatta, riding Nisha's elephant. Anand tried to catch his eye, but he was busy adjusting the elephant's headdress and did not see him.

Matangi saw Anand, though. She trumpeted in pleasure, then ambled over to the edge of the road, despite her mahout's shouts, and nudged his face gently with her trunk. Anand gave her a quick hug. 'You look so pretty, Matangi!' he whispered. 'But you'd better keep moving. I don't want you to get in trouble. I'll come and see you later.'

Then Abhaydatta was abreast of him. 'We found it!' Anand shouted. Fumbling in his pocket, he held up the conch. It was so heavy now that he had to use both hands to hold it securely. A great smile broke over Abhaydatta's face. He raised his hands to his forehead in salutation. Anand held his breath, waiting for something special to happen. Maybe a ray of light would shoot out from the conch and restore the master healer's powers? But as far as he could see, nothing spectacular occurred.

'Tell me what I'm supposed to do tonight,' he cried.

'You will have to decide that yourself, Anand, depending on what happens. When the time comes, I think you will know what to do.'

'But can't you help ...?'

Abhaydatta's elephant had travelled past Anand by now, and he had to strain to catch the healer's answer.

'I still don't have any powers. I asked the conch not to restore them as yet, for that would have taken some of its energy. It needs to conserve itself for tonight. And Anand, remember to watch the sky, because ...' The rest of his words were drowned out by the beating of drums. Anand stared after him anxiously. The outcome of the evening, it seemed, rested on him and the conch. He remembered again the metallic, grating voice of the jinn, devoid of mercy, and did not feel equal to the challenge.

Oh conch! He thought. *What are we going to do?*

I don't know, came the unsettling reply. *I've never faced a jinn before. Furthermore, this is a strange world! My powers feel suffocated here. You must get me as close to the royal family as possible. Perhaps that will help.*

'Now that you have delivered your message, I must return to my duties,' the soldier said, setting Anand down on the ground.

'Wait! Can't you get me a little closer to the royal pavilion?' Anand asked.

'I'm sorry,' the soldier replied. 'I've been gone from my regiment too long already. They'll be needing me.' He wheeled his horse away, leaving Anand to fight his way through the crowd.

By the time Anand arrived at the edge of the maidan, he was tired and sweaty. From where he stood, he could see that the field was chock-full of people. He tried to manoeuver his way past them and get closer to the royal pavilion, but it was like trying to push through a brick wall, and ultimately, with a whispered apology to the conch, he had to abandon his efforts. Looking around, he saw a grove of large tamarind trees over to one side. Men had already filled their lower branches hoping to get a good look at the festivities, but there were still some space on the higher, thinner limbs. With some effort, Anand clambered up on one of them. He was not really comfortable in a tree, but he thanked his stars that, when he'd been in the village, Ramu had taught him to climb one. He clung to the branch uneasily with one hand while he held onto his pocket – with the increasingly heavy conch in it – with the other. He hoped fervently that the branch would not give way beneath their combined weight.

His perch did give him an unobstructed view of the pavilion, though. He could see the nawab being carried in an open palanquin from the palace to the pavilion. Dressed in a spectacular kurta made of stiff gold cloth that shone in the light of the setting sun, he slowly climbed the stairs – the pavilion was about two storeyes high – and ascended the throne while people cheered. He was followed by a group of favoured courtiers, who seated themselves on low stools that were placed on either side of the throne. Anand checked to see if Haider Ali was among them, but he was nowhere to be seen.

The shahzada followed next and took his seat on a carpet piled with cushions. He was accompanied by the sons of several noblemen, all of them dressed in elaborate formal costumes that sparkled with jewels. Unlike other times, though, the shahzada's shoulders did not slump with boredom. In fact, he examined the crowd with alert attention – probably looking for him, Anand guessed. From time to time he whispered something into the ears of the boy sitting next to him. This surprised Anand. Until now he had seen the shahzada display only contempt or indifference for his companions. Perhaps he was changing. Objects of power sometimes had a positive effect on the humans that came in contact with them. Hadn't the conch transformed him, Anand, from a timid boy who lived in the Kolkata slums and felt sorry for himself to someone who was ready to dedicate his life to helping others?

The back portion of the pavilion was draped with silk curtains. That must be where ladies of the zenana were seated. Anand wondered if Nisha was peering through the curtains, searching the crowd for him, worried by the fact that she couldn't see him anywhere. He wished there was a way to reassure her that he was, indeed, present. That he would fight Kasim to the utmost of his ability, though he wasn't certain that that would be enough.

The parade had reached the cleared area in front of the pavilion. The riders made their horses rear up in unison, their headdresses bobbing, to salute the nawab. The elephants kneeled down and raised their trunks and trumpeted. Then Matangi came forward and, taking a flower garland that her mahout gave her, threw it up so that it landed near the nawab's feet. As though that were a sign, jugglers leaped onto a stage that had been constructed directly in front of the pavilion and performed their best tricks. Women were tied onto spinning wheels while blindfolded men threw knives at them, making the crowd gasp with fear and amazement. A man balanced himself on a rolling barrel while he juggled twenty sharp-edged scimitars at a time.

Then came the acrobats, triple somersaulting through the air, forming human pyramids that were ten-men high. They were followed by a snake charmer who put his head inside a python's mouth; a contortionist who literally tied himself into a knot; and a strong man who broke links off an iron chain with his teeth and swallowed them whole. The crowd cheered wildly at these feats and praised the nawab for allowing them to witness such marvels.

Next came troupes of singers and musicians, and poets from all over the country whose offerings were translated into Urdu by the court scribe and declaimed loudly through a horn so that everyone present could hear them. They were rewarded with purses of coins thrown to them by the nawab's attendants. Finally, dancers whose unusual costumes indicated that they had travelled from many distant corners of India to participate in the festival presented themselves onstage.

Dusk had fallen by now, and hundreds of flaming torches lighted up the maidan. Servants sprayed the air with brass pichkaris filled with rosewater. A cool, moist breeze carried the fragrance through the crowd, rousing appreciative murmurs. Remembering what Abhaydatta had said, Anand looked up at the sky. But it was a deep and innocent blue, inhabited only by a stately full moon, so he gave his attention to a group of dancers that whirled and jumped dexterously in spite of the enormous painted masks they wore.

When the dances had ended, Anand noticed two men stepping

up onto the platform. Squinting his eyes through air hazy with torch-smoke, he could make out that the taller one was Haider Ali. Unlike the other courtiers who were festively attired, he was dressed in a severely-cut gray kurta more appropriate for a battlefield than a celebration. By contrast the shorter man wore an enormous turban that sparkled with sequins and a many-coloured robe that fell shimmering to his feet. He walked with a swagger, and his arms were hidden in his billowing sleeves, so Anand could not see if he carried anything. It was Kasim! And his many-coloured robe, from what Abhaydatta had said earlier, indicated that his power was at its fullest.

Haider Ali performed a low kornish and extended his hand toward Kasim, obviously presenting him to the nawab. Anand longed to hear what he was saying. If he could, it might help him prepare for what Kasim was planning. But after what Abhaydatta had said about the importance of the conch conserving its powers, he could not ask the conch to help him.

The winds had grown stronger now. A gust blew grit into his face, making him blink. An idea came suddenly into his mind. Probably, in this world, which had its own magical rules, it would not work. On the other hand, had he not been able to see through the wall in the emerald room when he had needed to?

Closing his eyes, he willed himself to remember what he had heard on a high platform on a tree-tower in a different lifetime. He wished he could have had Raj-bhanu – the old Raj-bhanu, laughing and confident – to help him. He would have been so much better at this. But Anand was on his own, and the only help he would get had to come from inside him. *You can, you can,* he told himself. As though in reply, the words rose haltingly to his lips.

From east and west, south and north,
Marut, wind spirit, I call you forth
From sky and earth, far and near,
Bring me the news I need to hear.

The wind picked up in strength. There was a yellow cast to it now. As it blew through the trees, the tamarind leaves rustled and whispered. Anand focused all his attention on the sounds. Slowly, he began to catch words among the whispers. Soon he was able to distinguish the voices of different speakers. It seemed to him as he squinted through the yellow haze that his eyesight was growing clearer as well.

'Most glorious Nawab Najib, Saviour of the destitute,' Haider Ali was saying, 'on this joyous occasion I would like to present to you a very special person who has travelled great distances to be here. He is a renowned magician and if you wish, he can perform for the pleasure of the company assembled here. I am sure you will be amazed at his powers.'

Najib extended a friendly hand towards the chief minister. 'I have been wondering where you were all this time, Haider,' he said. 'Anyone you bring with you is most welcome at this court.'

Haider Ali bowed stiffly but did not take the nawab's hand.

'Come, Haider, why so formal? Are you still angry at our difference of opinion the other day?' the nawab said, smiling. 'Surely an old friend like you will not hold it against me? I am heartily sorry if I offended you. You took me by surprise with your most generous offer, and I replied too hastily! I have, in fact, been trying to persuade the begum to change her mind. But we will discuss all this later, in private. Meanwhile, come, sit at this stool on my right. I have saved it for you.'

Anand could see that Haider Ali was taken aback by Najib's graciousness and especially by the apology. Nawabs rarely apologized in public! He hesitated for a moment, but the nawab still held out his hand, so he bowed over it and took the seat the nawab had offered him.

'Kasim!' the chief minister called to the magician. From so far away Anand could not tell for certain, but he thought he saw the chief minister shake his head. He was signalling to Kasim that he should not do anything to harm the nawab! Anand's shoulders relaxed as he took a deep breath. It seemed as though the problem that had worried him so deeply was about to resolve itself. And it took no more magic than a bit of human kindness and humility, and a remembrance of friendship!

Kasim gave a flourishing bow in response. He brought his hands out from the long sleeves of his alkhalla and raised them high. 'Your Highnesses!' he said. 'I am most delighted to have been invited here. I will give you a show the likes of which you have not seen in your lifetime.' He clapped his hands and a wand appeared in each hand, a white wand in his right, and a black in his left. He waved the wand in his right hand and fireworks shot up into the sky from it and burst into sparkling flowers high above the head of the crowd. Kasim waved his right hand again, and a flock of golden birds appeared around his head, singing sweetly as they circled him. The crowd yelled their admiration at these feats. With another wave he made a basket of ripe lychees materialize before the throne. He offered them to the nawab, who tasted one and pronounced it to be exceedingly sweet. Another wave of the wand and sweetmeats dropped from the sky into the crowd. At this, people went wild, cheering and clapping as though they would never stop.

'And now,' Kasim said softly, so that only the people in the royal pavilion – and Anand – heard him, 'a special item designed especially for the pleasure of my patron the renowned Haider Ali al Dauleh, Pillar of the World, esteemed chief minister of the realm – and soon-to-be nawab.' The courtiers exchanged uneasy looks, not sure they had heard correctly. But before anyone could ask what he meant, Kasim pointed the wand in his left hand, the black wand, at the sky.

'No!' cried Haider Ali. 'I don't want you to do this!'

'It's too late now, esteemed minister sahib,' Kasim responded with a mocking laugh. Anand looked up and saw – he hadn't realized when it had happened – the sky was black with what appeared to be thunderclouds. But as he watched the clouds shifted and took on a giant form that covered the sky, looming over the crowd. It had no face, only two holes where the eyes should have been. They were an electric blue – the colour Anand had seen emanating from the pit in the ruins. Anand could feel malevolence radiating from them. The black giant lifted his hand. There was a sound like grating metal – Anand recognized it as the jinn's laughter. Then a bolt of lightning shot from his hand directly towards the royal pavilion.

Before the shocked Anand could react, the bolt hit the throne with a crack so loud that it sounded as though the world itself was breaking apart. The throne was reduced to a charred, smoking mass. Another bolt exploded the staircase leading from the pavilion to the ground. At the same time, the silks behind the throne burst into flames. Pandemonium reigned as courtiers screamed and threw themselves off the pavilion in order to save their lives, several of them breaking an arm or a leg in the process. Behind the silk curtains, the women of the palace were screaming as well. Was Nisha trapped in there? Anand hoped there was a second staircase behind the curtains down which she might escape. His heart tight with foreboding, he squinted through the smoke at the remains of the throne. Was the nawab dead? Was Haider Ali, who had been sitting next to the nawab dead, too? For now that the chief minister no longer supported Kasim's plan, Anand suspected that Kasim wanted him out of his way. But the smoke was too thick for him to see for certain.

Then Anand's eyes were caught by a movement at the other end of the pavilion. The shahzada had managed to reach the edge of the pavilion and stood there clutching a silk cushion to his chest. The flames were very close to him now. *Jump, Mahabet!* Anand shouted, though he knew the boy couldn't hear him. But Mahabet was frozen with fear as he looked down on the huge drop to the ground. Then a figure darted from the smoke and took the shahzada's hand. It was the boy he'd been talking to earlier. Together the two boys jumped off the pavilion, arms and legs flailing. From where he was on the tree, Anand sent them a wish for a safe landing as they disappeared from his sight.

The burning pavilion, emptied of people, began to collapse. But wait, who were those two men struggling to their feet, coughing? Anand recognized the chief minister's stalwart frame, bent as he supported the nawab, who looked like he might collapse at any moment. Their clothes were torn and sooty, and there was blood on their faces, but they were alive! Haider Ali must have managed to pull the nawab from the throne just before it was destroyed by lightning. But they were trapped now. Najib was too frail to survive a fall to the ground – and they both knew it.

'Looks like this is the end for me, old friend,' Anand heard him say to Haider Ali.

Haider Ali bowed his head. 'It is all my fault. I should never have listened to that accursed magician. I deserve the worst of punishments – '

'Whatever mistake you made in the past,' Najib said gently, 'you have made up for it by saving my life with your quick actions just now. And now you must jump – you have a chance of surviving, even if you do break a limb.'

Haider Ali shook his head firmly. 'I will stay with you until the end,' he said.

'Well then, Haider, I think it is time for us to ask Allah's pardon for all our sins,' the nawab said as the flames swept closer. He lowered himself heavily to his knees to pray.

There was another loud crack. A thunderbolt hit an enclosed area of the maidan where the horses and elephants had been gathered for the final parade that would end the evening's festivities, setting the fencing on fire. Crazed with fear at being surrounded by flames, the animals burst out of the enclosure, the horses trampling people under their sharp hooves, the elephants catching men and women in their trunks and flinging them through the air. People were screaming and stampeding in every direction, crushing each other underfoot as they tried to escape with their lives. Anand thought he saw Abhaydatta on Matangi's back, trying to calm her as she pivoted her head violently from side to side.

'Hai Allah!' someone near Anand cried out in a voice of despair. 'It is the end of the world!'

The words brought Anand back to his senses. He could not afford to panic! If there was any possibility at all of saving the people around him, it lay in his hands. *Conch!* he cried. *Help us!*

For a moment the conch did not respond. When it did speak, its voice was so muffled and weak that Anand was racked with anxiety. *Hold me up high, Anand. We are too far away – it will take all my effort – but I will do what I can.*

Gripping the branch between his knees, Anand raised the conch as high as he could with both hands. It pulsed heavily in his palms.

A thin cobweb of mist seemed to stream from its tail. The mist sped through the maidan, dividing as it went, and wherever it went, it seemed to dispense coolness and calm. People stopped their blind running and tried to help the injured, and the animals grew quiet. When the mist reached the pavilion, the fire began to die down. However, Anand could see that the mist was taking a heavy toll on the conch's powers. With each passing moment it grew lighter, and its pulsing was weaker. Anand wasn't sure how long it could keep up what it was doing.

Taking this opportunity, Abhaydatta rushed Matangi to the sagging platform, where Najib and Haider Ali still clung to one of the planks.

'Your Highness, let go and allow yourself to fall. Matangi will catch you,' he yelled.

Najib hesitated. Anand could tell that he didn't believe the elephant would be able to do what the mahout promised. But finally, having no other choice, he did as instructed. He need not have worried. Matangi grabbed him in her trunk as though he were no heavier than a bunch of bananas and seated him on her back. Haider Ali, seeing that the nawab was safe for the moment, jumped off the pavilion. Anand could no longer see him.

The horrifying crackle of thunder filled the sky again. Anand's eyes flew upward, and automatically he clutched the conch tight to his chest. The jinn had grown larger than ever, and his electric-blue eyes glowed more ominously. 'Who is it that dares set his will against Ifrit, mightiest of jinns? Who is it that has grown tired of his life and wishes to gamble with death?' he boomed. Anand was afraid that his words might start another stampede of terror. But it seemed that ordinary people did not have the ability to hear him, for the men on Anand's tree clapped their hands to their ears and cried that this was the worst lightning storm they had experienced in their lives. It seemed as though no one except Anand could see the jinn, either.

'Speak, coward,' the jinn roared, 'before I destroy every single man, woman and child in this kingdom!'

Anand did not doubt that the jinn would indeed do as he threatened. Passing a tongue over his dry lips, he whispered, 'It is I,

Anand, healer from the Silver Valley.' He was hoping that the jinn might not hear him, but he was not so lucky.

'You, puny boy?' came the jinn's booming voice. 'What gives you the audacity to battle Ifrit's magic, which he learned thousands of years ago among the pyramids of Mishar? And where have you hidden yourself? What strange ability do you possess that keeps me from seeing you?'

Anand was surprised to learn this. Was Abhaydatta chanting protective sutras to conceal him? He feared the old healer would not be able to keep it up for long, especially as he was now responsible for the nawab's safety as well. Nor could he count on the conch – it felt light and fragile in his hands, drained of the power it had gathered with such difficulty. It was no match for the jinn's forces. No matter what happened to him, he wanted it to be safe. He clasped it close and felt it throb weakly in response.

'Ah, petrified into silence, I see!' The jinn's laugh was like a million iron chains being dragged across a dungeon floor. 'Dumbness will not save you, fool. Get ready to pay for your impudence as I burn the entire maidan to ashes. And don't think you can escape me! I might not be able to see you, but in a moment my Searcher will smell you out.'

Even before he finished speaking, innumerable arrows of fire began to rain down from the sky. The field was filled with cries of fear as men and women ran back and forth in a frenzy, trying vainly to find cover. The ones unlucky enough to be hit directly by arrows burst into flame. Their screams of agony could be heard across the entire maidan.

Conch, I know you have exerted yourself to your limit, but you must help these unfortunate beings, Anand cried.

We, came the reply, so faint that it worried Anand. *You must help, too. I cannot do it on my own. The very air in this world saps my powers.*

Looking up, Anand could see a dark shape flying low above the heads of the crowd, flapping its black wings like a giant bat. The Searcher! It let out a monstrous shriek as it passed over Anand. At the sound, a fist of terror clutched Anand's heart and his body trembled· as though in the grip of a malarial fever. Perhaps the Searcher could sense his fear, for it doubled back and passed over him again, shrieking even louder, its face an empty blackness under its hood. Immediately a shower of fire-arrows appeared over Anand's head. The jinn had discovered him! The tamarind tree next to him began to burn as arrows hit it. *Jump down, Anand!* his instincts screamed. *Run from here as fast as you can!* He bit down on his lip to stop himself. If he ran away – even if somehow he managed to escape the jinn – it would mean a horrible death for many, many others: the crowd on the field, the nawab's family, Raj-bhanu, Nisha and Abhaydatta. He couldn't live with that on his conscience.

I don't know what to do, he cried to the conch. *But instruct me – I'll do it or I'll die trying.*

Good, said the conch, its voice sounding stronger. It began to pulse again. *Hold me up and blow into me with all of your life-breath. Keep blowing until I tell you to stop. Put your entire attention into the blowing. And no matter what happens, this time, for the Great Power's sake, don't let go of me!*

Anand gritted his teeth resolutely. *I won't,* he vowed.

A crack of lightning hit the tree on which he sat. The branch next to him broke off and tumbled down, and some other branches caught fire. *I'm going to die,* he thought, *but not without a fight.* For the second time in his life, he put the conch to his lips, squeezed his eyes shut, and blew.

He had expected to hear a huge roar, the way he had the last time while battling Surabhanu in the Himalayas, but he heard nothing. Yet something was happening – because it felt as though every last bit of breath was being sucked from him into the conch. Gasping, he filled his chest with air once more and, remembering what the conch had said, put all other thoughts out of his mind. Vaguely he heard Abhaydatta in the Silver Valley saying, *sharpen your awareness until it is keener than the keenest knife.* This time, amazingly, he knew how to do it! With all the power of this new, sharp awareness, he blew into the conch again and again.

The conch began to vibrate. Fast, then faster, so that it jerked his eyes open, then so fast that its speed was beyond computation.

The vibration shook Anand's whole body, but this time he was prepared and held fast. Wherever this vibration spread, he could see the air warping slightly, the way desert air warps to form a mirage. And like desert air, this, too, was creating a mirage – or was it an alternate reality? Inside the field of the vibration was a total emptiness: no colour, no form, no life. Whatever it touched as it sped toward the sky – leaf, bird, star – they all disappeared. The vibration aimed itself at the jinn's dark form. Anand watched in amazement as it reached his feet, which began to dissolve into nothingness.

The jinn gave an enraged cry. 'Ill-fated boy, you dare to try your tricks on me? You think your puny disappearance spell can harm me? I who endured four centuries of hellfire when Bismillah cast me down? I, now stronger than ever before, having eaten the life-spirits of one hundred men? I will turn your own magic against you and make you vanish forever. Then you will know the true extent of the power of Ifrit.'

The jinn curled his fingers into claws and pointed them at the vibration. A huge shock went through Anand as though an invisible hammer had struck him. The pain, profound, intense, twisting itself inside him, made him cry out. He could feel the vibration changing direction, the conch's energy being forced to recoil upon itself. A weight like that of a gigantic iron blanket was descending on him. The branch on which he sat began to bend under its pressure. A few more seconds and it would crush both the conch and him.

With a resounding crack, the branch broke, and Anand fell to the ground. His breath was knocked out of him, and his right shoulder throbbed brutally. Still, he held on to the conch with grim resoluteness. The pressure was almost unbearable now. Any moment now his lungs would burst. But remembering what the conch had said, he held it to his mouth and blew weakly into it. It was clear that he was going to die, but strangely, the prospect no longer filled him with terror. *Until my last life-breath, I am yours,* he said to the conch in his head.

This time when he blew, he heard a sound. It took his dazed brain a moment to understand that it was the conch – but instead of producing the roar that had swept Surabhanu into the centre of the earth, it was speaking. It spoke softly, but Anand sensed that the resonance of its words spread across the entire sky. Vaguely, he was aware of the fact that the reverse-vibrations had stopped and the pressure had lifted.

'Truly your power is great, Ifrit, enough to destroy this boy many times over, for though one day he will be a great sorcerer, his abilities have not yet unfurled themselves. Fortunately for him, he is not alone. I, Devadatta, Gift of the Gods, am joined to him by his life-breath and his love. Even so you might have defeated us, for in this realm my powers were greatly weakened. But when Anand resolved to give up his life in our battle against you, his courage wrought a deep change upon the energies of Bismillah's world, which had been set by him to repel all outside powers. Now they have tuned themselves to our need, so that the spell that Anand and I had unleashed together can grow to its full potential. And jinn, it is no ordinary disappearance spell!' The conch's voice grew vast and echoed in Anand's ears like the ocean. 'By the power invested in me to rid the world of evil, I commit you now to the Great Void.'

The jinn's form shuddered. 'The Great Void!' he whispered.

'Yes, another name for which is Death-in-Life, where you will wander, suffering what you have made others suffer, until you have repented at last for all the harm you have done. For you, I am afraid, that will take a very long time.'

Instinctively, Anand sat up and, with the last of his strength, pointed the conch at the jinn and blew into it once more. The vibrations began again, but this time they shot upward so fast that they made him dizzy. Looking up, he saw the jinn's form begin to disappear as though he were being pulled into the heart of an invisible tornado. The jinn's mouth opened into a ragged circle of electric-blue, and an inhuman cry came from it. Anand could see him straining with all his might to pull away. But in a moment he had been sucked into the Void. All that remained above the maidan was a colourless space, terrifying in its frozen emptiness. It sent a chill through Anand's entire being. The last thought in his mind before he pitched forward in a faint was, *Will the sky ever come back?*

eighteen

The Nawab Makes a Proposal

Waking, Anand found himself in an unfamiliar room with a low ceiling and small windows set in its crooked stone walls. He was lying on a straw pallet on the floor, and when he tried to turn his head to see more, every muscle in his aching body protested, making him cry out.

He heard footsteps outside, and Nisha ran in. She was dressed once more in women's clothing, but her long veil was thrown back from her face. She was followed by Mahabet, who proudly sported a bandage on his left arm.

'Anand! I'm so thankful you're conscious again! Abhaydatta – this is his room you're in, by the way – told us that we mustn't try to wake you. He said you'd faced a huge danger, and that this was your mind's way of trying to recover. So I didn't do anything except apply a poultice on your lips and hands.'

At her words, Anand looked at his hands. They were bandaged all the way up to his wrists.

'They were badly blistered,' Nisha explained. 'The blast of power from the conch must have done it – '

Anand tried to sit up, but he was too weak and fell back. 'The conch,' he said anxiously. 'Where is it? Is it safe?'

Nisha nodded. 'Abhaydatta has it. He found it underneath you when he picked you up. You were clutching it so tightly that he had to use a charm to open your fist.'

'A charm? Did he recover his powers, then?'

'He did. They came back to him when he held your hand with the conch inside it. Ah, I think those are his footsteps – '

'Anand!' the old healer said, smiling as he entered. Though he was still dressed in his old mahout's clothing, he looked different. There was, Anand thought, a calm majesty in his gait. 'I thought you might be up! How do you feel?'

Anand made a face. 'Like one of the elephants used me as a football!'

The healer touched his head lightly. 'Nisha has already prepared a potion to remove all your aches. Now that you're awake, she can bring it for you.'

'Right away,' said Nisha as she hurried out.

'I'll help you, Paribanou,' said Mahabet, following her.

'She remembers everything?' Anand asked. 'Did you – ?'

'I think it was mostly the conch's doing,' Abhaydatta said. 'Just being around it has helped us all. Raj-bhanu has recovered, too, though that took more time and some effort on my part.'

'How long have I been lying here?'

'Two days and two nights,' Abhaydatta said. 'Nisha and the shahzada have been here whenever they could get away. They have some important things to tell you – '

Anand's head buzzed with weakness and excitement. But there was something even more important that he needed to ask. 'The conch – is it all right?'

A shadow passed over Abhaydatta's face. 'It is all right, but not the same as it was before. Even for an object of such power as it holds, destroying the jinn took an enormous effort. I was not sure either it – or you – would survive the ordeal.' He took a velvet bundle from his pocket. 'But you can see for yourself.'

Eagerly, Anand unwrapped the bundle, then stared in shock. It was the conch, yes, but what a change had come over it! Where before its colour had been pure white, like a newly blossomed jasmine flower, it was now stained with brown, as though it had been put through a furnace. Worst of all, a crack ran halfway down its length.

'Oh conch, conch,' he murmured, holding it to his face, his eyes brimming with tears.

'I'll go and check on that potion,' Abhaydatta said. Tactfully, he pulled the door closed behind him as he left the room.

Anand couldn't stop himself from crying as he looked at the conch. Thankfulness mingled with regret in his heart. *You succeeded, conch,* whispered. *You destroyed the jinn. Without you, none of us would have survived. But what a price you had to pay for it!* He held it as gently as he could and stroked the crack with his index finger. *You used to be perfect, but now —*

That's just what a conch needs to hear, after going through the battle of its life!

The conch's familiar, indignant tone made Anand smile through his tears. He pressed his cheek to it, then pulled back, afraid he might injure it further.

Please! It's not as though I'm an invalid, the conch said. *I won't break just because you're pressing your face against me. On the other hand, maybe you* should *stop. You're making me all wet.*

Anand couldn't help laughing as he wiped the conch with his shirt, then wrapped it in velvet again and tucked it into his pocket. The conch's physical structure might have been affected by the battle with the jinn, but its spirit appeared to be intact.

Nisha burst into the room with a glass, followed by Mahabet, who carried a covered basket. 'Drink this,' she ordered. 'And don't you dare make a face! In the Silver Valley the potion-master used to sweeten it with fresh honeysuckle stamens, but I couldn't find any here. And it's not as smooth as I'd like it to be, because I didn't have the proper grinding stones.'

Anand downed the bitter, lumpy mix and felt a warmth spread throughout him. Already some of the aches were leaving his body. Nisha opened up his bandages and pronounced that the blisters were healing well. Gently, she spread some more poultice on his hands and face.

'You're good at this!' Anand complimented her. 'The potion master will be so proud when you tell him everything you did.'

A shadow flitted over Nisha's face at his remark, though Anand couldn't understand why.

'She is indeed wonderful! You don't know this, but she saved my life twice,' Mahabet said as he placed the basket he was carrying on the bed and uncovered it. Inside was a wonderful meal of buttered chapatis, pulao rice with pistachios, and pieces of chicken grilled on the tandoor until they were a delicious golden-red. 'My father had Zafar send this down for you from the royal kitchens,' he explained. 'My father wants to thank you as soon as you're well enough to meet him. You're a hero, Anand – at least to those of us who know what really happened at the festival!'

Anand smiled. He, Anand, a hero? It was kind of Mahabet to say that! It struck him that the shahzada had changed from the sullen, spoiled boy he had been just a few days back. But the tantalizing smell from the basket kept him from thinking too much. He dug in with ravenous relish. 'I'm going to miss Zafar Miah's cooking when I go back to the Silver Valley!' he said to Mahabet. 'But tell me how Nisha saved your life.'

'Paribanou is the one who helped me jump from the pavilion when I was too frightened to do it on my own – ' Mahabet began enthusiastically.

'That boy sitting next to you – that was Nisha?'

'Yes! She came back to my quarters right after you left. She was afraid that Layla Bibi and her uncle would be so angry with her that they wouldn't let her come to the festival. So I gave her a set of clothes, a festive turban and some jewels and told everyone she was a visiting nobleman's son. Was I glad about that when things started going wrong!' He gave Nisha a grateful smile. 'Even the most terrifying events are easier to bear when you have a friend with you.'

Nisha looked down at her hands. Anand thought she blushed.

From the way in which Mahabet was looking at Nisha, and from the way he'd been following her around, it seemed to Anand that she was fast becoming more than a friend to him. And she didn't seem to dislike it. Would this cause a problem, he wondered worriedly, when it was time for them to return to their own world? But he only said, 'Yes, friends are truly a gift from God. Now tell me, how did she save your life a second time?'

'It was after the jinn disappeared from the sky. We were huddled on the ground near the pavilion. I'd hurt my foot when I jumped – though now it's cured, thanks to Paribanou's poultices – and we were trying to stay out of the way of the panicky crowd. But Kasim saw us. He was crazed with anger because all his plans had failed. He pulled a dagger from his belt and vowed that he would kill me with his own hands. He rushed at me and grabbed me around the throat before I knew what was happening. He would have stabbed me right then, if Paribanou hadn't jumped on him from behind.'

'I bit him,' Nisha said proudly. 'And clawed at his eyes.'

'He was so infuriated, he forgot about me and turned to attack her – '

'I shouted at Mahabet to run, but he wouldn't – '

'How could I leave you?' Mahabet said simply.

'I saw Mahabet pick up a cushion – it was the cushion he'd been carrying earlier when we jumped – and hobble back toward Kasim. I thought, that's brave of him, but what can he do with a *cushion*?'

'I yelled at Kasim, calling him the son of a pig. Paribanou's turban had come off in the scuffle, and I shouted that he was a coward, attacking girls because he didn't dare fight with men. That made him turn toward me.'

'He rushed forward,' Nisha added, 'his knife held high. It was a horrible looking knife, with a forked tip like a snake's tongue. I thought, *that's the end of Mahabet, for certain*, and started to cry. Mahabet held the cushion to his chest. I thought, *that's no use, that'll never stop Kasim!* But then something amazing happened! When Kasim's hand reached the cushion, it was pulled into it – and the rest of Kasim's body followed.'

'He gave the most horrifying shriek as he disappeared. I think my eardrums are permanently injured!' Mahabet grinned, then added, 'You must be wondering what happened.'

Anand nodded, though already he could guess the answer.

'It was the mirror! Mahabet had hidden it between the cushion and its cover. Wasn't that clever of him?' Nisha said breathlessly.

'I'm sorry!' Mahabet lowered his eyes. 'I know you told me not to use it. I was going to leave it in my room, but I was scared, and its presence was so comforting – '

Anand knew what he meant. His hand went to the pocket with the conch in it. 'It did save your life and rid us of Kasim, so I can't be too upset! I wonder which world the mirror sent him to – '

'I don't care,' Nisha said with a shudder. 'As long as I don't have to face him ever again. His face – it was so full of hate – it was horrible! But Anand, now it's your turn to tell us how you and the conch destroyed the jinn.'

Anand described the incident as best as he could – though much of what had happened was already blurry in his mind, and other parts, such as the bit about the conch saying he would be a great sorcerer, he omitted out of modesty. He mentioned that the conch had a name, but he didn't say what it was. He knew that true-names – especially those of objects of power – held deep magic in them and should not be invoked lightly. Several times in his story, he paused. It all seemed so unbelievable now, as he lay on the pallet, his stomach comfortably full, his friends around him, and sunshine lighting up the window.

Halfway through the telling, Abhaydatta came and sat on a corner of the bed, listening intently.

'You called up the Great Void!' he said in an incredulous voice. 'I have not known such a thing to happen in my lifetime, though I have read of it in the Books of Wisdom. It is extremely dangerous. By doing so, for a moment you tore the fabric of the universe. You are extremely lucky that you were not pulled into the Void along with the jinn.'

'I didn't do anything,' Anand said. 'It was the conch.'

'The conch and you became one when your breath entered it. Your willingness to sacrifice your life gave it the extra power it needed to destroy the jinn. I am amazed that it revealed its name. Objects of power very rarely do this, though clearly its name added power to its spell. It must trust you very much indeed to do so in your hearing! You must not let anyone know this name, for it will give him or her power over the conch. But now, if you are up to it, the nawab and chief minister would like to see you.'

'I'm ready!' Anand said. Nisha's potion, along with the large and excellent lunch he had consumed, made him feel like a new person. The nawab had sent a chestful of fine clothes for him. Quickly he washed and changed into a fine kurta with matching pants. Outside, royal palanquins waited to carry each of them to the nawab's private audience chamber.

Just before he got into his palanquin, Anand asked Abhaydatta the question that had been in his mind ever since he awoke. 'Now that our work here is done, when do we leave for the Silver Valley?' As he spoke the name, a longing came over him to be in that magical place again, to hear the chants of the healers at dawn and to walk under the flowering parijat trees.

'We leave tonight,' Abhaydatta said.

Mahabet drew in his breath. 'So soon?'

'Can't we wait a few days?' Nisha asked.

Abhaydatta gave her a sharp glance from under his bushy eyebrows. 'Important work awaits us elsewhere,' he said. 'We must stop in the village of Sona Dighi and help those who have been harmed by the jinn before we can go home. But I will discuss the details of our leaving later. The nawab awaits us now.'

⁂

The private audience chamber, with its marble friezes and mosaic tiles laid out in a lotus design, was a beautiful room, small enough to create a sense of intimacy. On a raised dais, the nawab sat on a silver throne decorated with carved peacocks. Next to him on an elegant silver stool sat Haider Ali. Anand walked over a carpet so thick and soft that his entire foot sank into it with each step and bowed to them both, a deep kornish for the nawab and a slightly lesser bow for the chief minister.

'Is this not the punkah boy who returned my snuffbox to me last week in court?' Najib asked Haider. With a smile, he added, 'It seems that, in just a few days, he has learned the customs of our court well!' Turning to Anand he said, 'My son informs me that you are the one that saved us from the dreadful firestorm conjured up by the magician who tricked my friend Haider into inviting him to the festival.'

Anand nodded. It was close enough to the truth, and less complicated. He suspected that Abhaydatta had instructed Mahabet as to what he should say to his father. It would be far more disturbing if the nawab learned about the jinn and the devastation that Kasim had planned to wreak on his entire family.

'I do not know how you did it, but I thank you most sincerely!' Najib took a thick strand of pearls from his neck and gave it to Anand. 'Please accept this as a token of my gratitude. You will be rewarded with a chestful of gold as well. Never again in your life will you have to pull a punkah!'

Anand thanked him, though he knew the gold would be of no use to him after tonight.

'And you, my child,' the nawab said, taking Nisha's hand. 'My son tells me that you saved his life twice. He cannot stop talking about how brave you were, risking your own life in order to stop the magician from stabbing him. Indeed, you were most heroic!'

'Your Highness!' Nisha spoke demurely from under her veil. 'Mahabet is too kind. It was he who, in spite of his injury, came back to rescue me. He is the one who – uh – frightened the magician away.'

'I am glad to hear that,' the nawab said. 'Earlier, Mahabet, I must confess that I was concerned about whether you would make a good ruler, but now I have no qualms about leaving my kingdom in your care!' He took off another necklace and gave it to his son, who stood up, tall and proud, to receive his father's gift.

Turning back to Nisha, the nawab said, 'My dear Paribanou, I didn't know what to offer you as a reward, but ultimately, after consulting with your uncle, I have decided to offer you the title of future Begum of Bengal.' Seeing Nisha's confused expression, he laughed. 'That means you and Mahabet are to be engaged!'

Anand exchanged a glance with Abhaydatta. This was an unexpected complication! Nisha stared at the nawab, too taken aback to thank him. 'But didn't the begum have other plans?' she asked.

'Not any longer,' Najib said. 'Mahabet has flatly refused to marry anyone else! It is clear that you have won his heart!'

Nisha lowered her head, blushing. 'I humbly thank Your Royal Highness,' she said, performing a deep kornish to him and then one to the chief minister, who rose from his seat and embraced her, his severe expression transformed by a smile. 'My child!' he started, but was then too overcome by emotion to say more.

'I am delighted to be welcoming you – and my old friend Haider – into our family,' the nawab said. He removed the most valuable of his necklaces, made of gold and rubies, and placed it around Nisha's neck. 'I don't want to waste any time. We can have a public celebration in a month's time, but Haider and I have decided that we will hold a small engagement tomorrow, which the court astrologer assures us is an auspicious date.' He raised his hand to dismiss them, and turning to Haider, began discussing details of the ceremony.

❧❀◉❀❧

When they came out of the audience chamber, Mahabet told the others that he must leave them for a while. 'Ahmed will be waiting in my quarters with the tailor – I am to be fitted for my engagement outfit,' he told them. 'It would be ungracious to keep them waiting.'

Remembering how rudely the prince spoke to his attendants earlier, Anand hid his smile. He was glad Mahabet had undergone such a positive change. He suspected that, in addition to the mirror, Nisha, too, had something to do with this improvement! But it worried him as well. How would Mahabet handle Nisha's absence, once she was gone?

'We leave at midnight,' Abhaydatta told Mahabet, 'For that is the hour when magical journeys may be made with the least amount of harm to the environment. You must bring the mirror at that time to the far end of the Alley of Tailors, where Anand came into this world. It is there that we must use the mirror to reverse that journey and return to the ruins.'

'Will you take the mirror with you?' Mahabet asked the healer anxiously.

'I don't know. The mirror, as an object of power, will make its own decision. Nisha, you must find a way to get there by midnight, too.'

Mahabet gave Nisha a distraught glance. 'Why does Paribanou have to go with you? Don't make her go! She belongs to this world – she belongs with me!' He took her hand. 'Don't leave! You're the only friend I've ever had.'

'I would never force her to return to the Silver Valley against her will,' Abhaydatta said. 'Nisha, my child, tell us what you want: to develop your powers as herb-mistress and healer, or rule this land as a begum?'

'I – I don't know!' Nisha stammered. 'It's a hard choice. Give me a moment to think.' She paced up and down, clasping and unclasping her hands, while Anand held his breath. Finally she said, avoiding his eyes, 'I choose to stay. Not because I wish to be begum, or to rule a kingdom, but because Mahabet wants me to stay. You have each other, as well as the Brotherhood and the conch. Mahabet has no one but me.'

His face bright, Mahabet put his arm around her shoulders. 'Thank you, dearest Paribanou! Never in my life will I do anything to make you regret this choice. Shall I call your palanquin so that you may go home and prepare for tomorrow? I am sure Layla Bibi will be most excited to hear about our coming engagement!'

Nisha gently disengaged herself and turned to Anand and Abhaydatta. She took their hands in hers. 'I hope you understand,' she said. 'I will remember you always, and with love.'

Abhaydatta shook his head sadly. 'That will not be possible. Before I leave tonight, I must alter the memories of all who have known us at the nawab's court. None of you will remember us once we are gone.'

Nisha looked startled, as though she hadn't considered that possibility.

'I am sorry that you will not be coming with us, but certainly I understand your choice,' Abhaydatta said. He kissed Nisha on her forehead. 'Goodbye. May the Great Power bless you. Anand, say your goodbyes to Nisha.'

'Goodbye,' Anand said mechanically. He couldn't believe that Nisha, who had been with him since the beginning of his adventures, was leaving them. The company of the conch would not be the same without her.

Nisha gave him a regretful glance. She drew in her breath, as though she was going to tell him something important. But she only said, 'The Great Power bless you both,' and climbed into the waiting palanquin.

Anand stood staring at the palanquins as they receded in the distance. To never see Nisha again! To return to the Brotherhood without her! The anticipation he'd felt earlier at the thought of going home had turned to ashes in his mouth. It was only the presence of the conch – he slipped his hand into his pocket and held it tightly – that stopped him from running after Nisha's palanquin.

nineteen

The Bonfire of Holika

Once they got back to his rooms, Abhaydatta made Anand lie down.
'You must rest,' he said. 'Your body has not recovered fully yet. We must make it as strong as possible before it undergoes the shock of time travel tonight. I will send Raj-bhanu with a potion to help you sleep.'

Anand drank the potion that Raj-bhanu, recovered and smiling now, brought to Anand. Though this potion was sweet, he wished he could exchange it for the bitter, lumpy one Nisha had made for him in the morning. Raj-bhanu, excited about returning, kept up a steady stream of talk about how wonderful it would be to be back in the valley, but Anand answered in monosyllables, pretending to be sleepy so that Raj-bhanu would leave him alone. But of course when he was alone, sleep wouldn't come to him – only sadness.

In the evening four of the nawab's servants, accompanied by armed guards, brought Anand a sealed chest from the treasury. 'From His Royal Highness Najib, Shah-en-shah of Bengal,' they intoned as they set it down in Abhaydatta's room. When they had left, Abhaydatta asked Anand to open it. The chest was filled to the brim with gold mohurs, each coin carrying the stamp of Najib's face on it.

'Why, there's a veritable ransom in there!' Raj-bhanu exclaimed in wonder. But Anand turned away without interest. The gold couldn't change the desolation he felt within. 'Do what you want with it,' he said to Abhaydatta.

'Are you certain?' asked Abhaydatta. 'I can transport it, with the help of the mirror, to the Silver Valley, and have it kept safe for you. Even a healer might find a chest full of gold useful at certain times.'

Anand shook his head firmly. 'Give it to someone in need,' he said.

Abhaydatta stared at him in admiration. 'It is not every young man – even in the Brotherhood – who can give away such a treasure. Anand, truly you have the qualities of a great magician, one who is a leader of wizards. Very well, I know exactly what to do with it. Raj-bhanu, come, we must find Matangi! Anand, you stay here and keep an eye on that chest.'

When he was alone, Anand took off his pearl necklace and laid it on top of the chest, then closed the lid. Beautiful though it was, the necklace only made him sadder. He didn't want to keep anything that would remind him of Nisha.

Raj-bhanu returned with a cart on which they loaded the chest. Covering it with dirty bed sheets so the guards would think they were going to do their washing, the two of them pushed the cart through the fortress gates to the lake. On the far side, Abhaydatta was waiting with Matangi. She had dug a deep hole in the soft mud with her tusks. They lowered the chest into the hole. Then Matangi helped them cover it up again. On the mud, Abhaydatta placed a number of stones laid in a particular design. 'They will mark the spot, and also protect the treasure,' he explained to Anand.

But Anand wasn't listening. His heart was too heavy for him to care about what happened to the gold. Pressing his face to Matangi's sides, he wept the tears he had kept in all this time. *I'll miss you! I'll miss you!* he said silently, though it wasn't clear to whom he was saying it. Matangi blew on his hair gently, trying to comfort him. When he had wept all he could, she lifted him onto her back one last time and gave him a ride to the hathi-khana. When the guards at the gateway ordered Anand to get down from the royal elephant, she stomped her foot and advanced on them menacingly, tusks raised, until they abandoned their posts and fled into the guardhouse.

⁂

Anand, Abhaydatta and Raj-bhanu waited in the shadows of the Alley of Tailors. Around them, the city slept. Above, the moon seemed to be in mourning behind her veil of clouds. From a distant tower, the ringing of a gong indicated that it was midnight. It was a lonely sound. Where was Mahabet? *Perhaps he won't come and we'll all have to just remain here*, Anand thought. His heart couldn't help leaping at the thought, though he felt guilty immediately afterwards.

As you should! The conch said in a stern tone. But it ruined the effect by giving a small chuckle.

How can you laugh when I'm so sad? Anand asked angrily. *And how is it you're so cheerful? Aren't you going to miss Nisha, too?*

No, declared the conch.

But she's one of the company of the conch! How can you be so heartless?

Because I'm a conch! Conches don't have hearts!

Furious, Anand decided he wasn't going to talk to the conch for a very long time.

Just then, he saw a movement at the other end of the alleyway. A moment later, Mahabet appeared, wrapped in a cloak. He carried a cushion. Anand guessed that the mirror was hidden inside it. 'Sorry I'm late,' he said. His voice sounded funny, as though he'd been crying, and when the moon came out from behind a cloud, his face looked swollen. The shahzada was afraid of losing the mirror, Anand thought with a twinge of sympathy. Angry though he was with the conch at the moment, he knew how unhappy he would be if he were separated from it.

'I thank you for bringing the mirror, shahzada,' Abhaydatta said. 'Please place it on the ground here – we have little time.'

'Are you going to take it with you?' Mahabet asked anxiously.

'It isn't I who will make that decision,' Abhaydatta explained

❘ 203 ❘

patiently to him again. 'It is the mirror. But until we step through it, we won't know whether it decides to come with us, or stay with you. You must prepare yourself for either of these outcomes.'

Mahabet took out the mirror and placed it on the ground, stroking it gently and whispering to it. He glanced back at the shadowed walls of the alley. Just then one of the shadows detached itself from a wall and advanced toward them. Anand saw that it was another cloaked figure. He stiffened. Beside him, Abhaydatta gripped his staff and Raj-bhanu made a protective gesture with his hands. Then they saw that it was Nisha.

Seeing her upset Anand further. She should not have come to bid them farewell again! It made the pain of leaving her harder for him. He turned his face from her deliberately and asked Abhaydatta, 'Who is to step through the mirror first?'

'I will go first,' Abhaydatta said, 'to make sure all is safe at the other end.' Then he looked at Nisha gravely. 'What brings you here, child?'

'I'm coming with you,' Nisha blurted out. She looked at his face uncertainly. 'If you'll have me, that is.'

'What made you change your mind?' a curious Raj-bhanu asked.

'When I got back to my unc ... Haider Ali's house, Layla Bibi started getting me ready for the engagement. She put a coffer full of jewels on the bed and asked me to choose the ones I wanted to wear for the ceremony. I sat staring at them. I couldn't choose. None of them mattered to me, though I could see how valuable they were. An emptiness came over me. It was then I realized that, much as I've enjoyed my life here, I don't really belong in this world. My true place is in the Silver Valley, because only there can I become who I was meant to be. It's also where' – here she threw Anand a shy glance – 'my closest friends are, the ones who have been through the roughest times with me. I explained it to Mahabet. He understands.'

Wiping at his eyes, Mahabet nodded. 'I could see that Pariba – Nisha wouldn't be happy here, without all of you. And I do want her to be happy – even if it means that I must lose her.'

'You have learned something very important about love,' Abhaydatta said to him. 'I commend you.' To Nisha he said, 'Of course you may come with us, child. You are one of the company of the conch, after all. But we must all wait a few minutes. I need to work an additional memory charm so that tomorrow no one will wonder where the chief minister's niece has gone.'

'Please,' Mahabet said in a small voice. 'Can you please not change my memory? Knowing all of you is the best thing that has ever happened to me. I would so much like to remember all of you –' He glanced at Nisha, then glanced down.

Abhaydatta considered his request for a long moment. 'I will do as you say,' he finally said. 'For I sense that these memories will give you strength during the upcoming trials of your life, and teach you to love more deeply. There is a further reason that I sense vaguely, though I cannot tell what it is. It is hidden still in the mists of time.'

'Thank you!' Mahabet said fervently.

'But in return you must promise never to mention us – or the events that occurred while we were here – to anyone,' Abhaydatta said.

Mahabet held up his right hand, 'By Allah, I promise.'

Abhaydatta walked a little way apart to work the forgetting charm, and Raj-bhanu accompanied him. Nisha was having a last whispered conversation with Mahabet. From the emphatic way in which she punctuated the air with her forefinger as she spoke, Anand guessed she was giving him advice.

Inside his pocket, Anand could feel the conch's amusement, tangible as heat.

You knew all the time that she was coming, didn't you? he asked accusingly.

Only after she made up her mind.

You could have told me. It would have saved me a lot of heartache.

The conch gave a theatrical sigh. *You humans! Always wanting to know everything ahead of time. Where's the drama, then? Where's the adventure? Besides, you know I'm not supposed to tell you things that you're capable of finding out by yourself. How else will you grow?*

Oh, very well, Anand said grumpily. But he couldn't remain grumpy at a time like this. Nisha was walking toward him, biting her lip nervously, not sure of how he would react.

He gave her hand a squeeze. 'I'm very glad you changed your mind! The Silver Valley wouldn't have been the same without you. And Mahabet, thank you for letting her go.'

Mahabet nodded, but he continued to look forlorn.

Anand wanted to do something to cheer up the shahzada. But what?

Then he knew. He closed his eyes to focus better and knelt to touch the mirror.

Mirror, he asked silently, *Will you stay with Mahabet? He will be so lonely when we are gone.*

The mirror's response – though not formulated into words like the conch's – came to him clearly. *Yes, O wizard, I will keep him company. Over the years, as he grows in wisdom, I will teach him how I may be used to help his people. But this much you can tell him now: if he ever needs you, he may do so by concentrating on your image and looking into me. And if you should ever need him, think of me, the Mirror of Fire and Dreaming, and he will see your reflection here.*

Anand's eyes flew open in amazed gratitude as he realized that the mirror had given him its name. *The Mirror of Fire and Dreaming!* he thought. I wonder what other magical powers it has! But why did it call me *wizard* when I am only an apprentice?

He rose to find Abhaydatta observing him intently. 'You communicated with the mirror, didn't you?' the healer asked.

Anand nodded, then said to Mahabet. 'The mirror has decided to stay with you.'

'Truly?' Mahabet's face lit up and he, too, knelt. 'Thank you, mirror-sahib!' he said, touching it reverently.

'We must not delay any longer,' Abhaydatta said. 'The midnight hour is almost over. I will open the gateway. Nisha will follow me. Then Anand, and finally, Raj-bhanu, who knows the appropriate closing chants.'

He spread his arms wide and began to sing in a language that Anand didn't know, though the words sounded ancient. The mirror glowed and flashed in response and sent out a shaft of silver light. Stepping onto the mirror, Abhaydatta was enveloped in that light. He was gone. Nisha waved goodbye to Mahabet and stepped up in his place. She, too, disappeared.

Quickly, Anand told Mahabet what the mirror had communicated to him. 'So, you see, this need not be a final farewell,' he concluded, then stepped on the mirror. His entire body tingled as the silver light flashed over him and through him.

This time, he felt himself not falling but floating along a rainbow arc through a space that seemed to be filled with the softest clouds. How long he travelled like this, he had no idea. Time as he knew it had no meaning between worlds. He thought he slept. When his eyes opened, he found himself in the red dust of the ruins, in the same room at the edge of the palace where he had hidden in such fear when Kasim had chased him. His three companions were around him. Raj-bhanu was singing – in that same unknown language again – as he drew his hands together in a closing gesture.

Anand glanced past the half-broken wall to where, just a few moments ago, the Alley of Tailors had stood with its cramped row of shops. He tried to match other parts of the ruin to the bustling city he had been living in. There, where a marble column leaned precariously, wasn't that where the chief minister's mansion had stood? And that frieze – didn't that belong to the zenana balcony in the court? But the memories of that distant time were already fading from his mind. All he knew for certain was that he was surrounded by shal trees and thigh-high weeds, with crickets chirping in the bushes, and foxes howling in distant groves. He shivered in the cold wind that had started blowing, for while the others wore the clothes they had on when they left the Brotherhood, he was dressed, once again, in the patched half-pants that Ramu had loaned him. How could it be so chilly here when in Najib's world it had been midsummer? In moving to a different world, had they moved to a different season as well? If so, how much time had passed since Anand had stepped through the mirror in the ruin?

'Come,' Abhaydatta said, 'We must get to Tara's hut before dawn. There we must decide how best to help the villagers, which was our original reason for leaving the Silver Valley.'

Stumbling in the dark, stubbing their toes against stones from the ruins, they made their slow way through the forest without even a glowlight from Abhaydatta's staff to aid them in finding their way. The old healer had said that they must save all their magic for the work that awaited them tomorrow. And even otherwise, magic was never meant to be used for a healer's personal convenience.

Dawn was almost breaking when they knocked on the door to the wise-woman's hut, thankful that it stood away from the rest of the village. They knocked many times, and Abhaydatta had to call her name before she opened it, peering nervously through a crack. Her face looked very thin, and Anand could see that her white hair was more unkempt than before, and her eyes moved wildly over their faces as though she didn't recognize them. She started to close the door, but Abhaydatta wedged his staff into the crack and said something to her in a soothing murmur. A shudder went through her. She let out a deep breath, stood back, and did not stop them from entering.

It was dark inside, and damp and chilly. Windows hung askew on hinges, as though someone had tried to tear them off. The firepit where the wise-woman formulated her spells looked as though it had not been used in a while. There was no wood, but Raj-bhanu chanted briefly and clapped his hands, and golden flames rose from the cold, sooty stones. Tara gazed at the fire for a while, holding out her hands to its warmth. She seemed more herself now. She listened attentively as Abhaydatta told her about Kasim and the jinn, and how they had been defeated. She did not smile – she looked as though she might have forgotten how to – but she gave a great sigh of relief. From the bottom of an earthenware pot she gathered a handful of puffed rice – it was all she had, she said apologetically – and gave them to her guests with a bit of jaggery and a cup of brackish water.

Things were bad in the village, she told them in broken sentences as they chewed on the stale food. Last summer there had been a drought, then a famine. The winter had brought them more troubles. The fields were so hard and barren that no crops would grow. In their desperation, people even ate the seed grain that they always saved for planting. Their situation was more difficult because most of the men were sick in their spirit. The few that were well went away to the cities to find work and did not return. Those who were left – women and children, mostly, or the very old – foraged in the woods and around the lake as best as they could, but food grew harder and harder to find, and the lake was almost dry. Many fell ill; many were on the brink of starvation. Some had died. And she had been able to do nothing to help her people.

'My rain chants failed. My medicines could not help the sick. It was as though Kasim put a curse on us all when he went into that other world,' she said, weeping and rocking. 'When the babies began to die, the villagers turned against me. One night they tried to tear down my hut. Some even tried to stone me. I had to run into the forest to save myself. But I knew without my presence worse things would happen to them, so I came back secretly, and have hidden myself in here ever since.'

Abhaydatta held her hands in his until she grew quiet. 'You are not alone any more, sister,' he said. 'Together we will devise a plan to make this village as it once was. But first, the young ones must sleep.'

'All I have are a few torn blankets,' Tara said. 'I gave the rest to the villagers months ago.' She showed them an alcove thinly lined with straw. 'I will send prayers – ineffective though they may be – for your good sleep,' she told them. To Abhaydatta she bowed and said, 'Master, I am sorry that there can be no rest for you yet.'

'No matter,' Abhaydatta told her. 'Soon for me there will be only resting. Tonight we must prepare.'

Anand was troubled by the old healer's words. He wanted to ask the conch, what does he mean, *soon for me there will be only resting?* But he was too tired. Shivering a little under the threadbare blanket, he curled his fingers around the conch and thought he felt a current of warmth envelop him. As he drifted into sleep, he could hear the rise and fall of the two voices in the next room, conversing, and later, singing in languages that he did not understand yet, though somewhere inside him he knew that he would learn them – and many more – one day.

～�•☙✦☙•～

Anand awoke to the smell of food. Rubbing his eyes, he made his way to the firepit, where Abhaydatta was stirring a pot while Tara set out shal leaves to serve as plates. 'Khichuri,' he told the hungry boy. 'Wash up and wake the others quickly. It is noon already, and much must be done before sunset.' They all ate the lentil stew, which tasted delicious.

'Where did you get the ingredients?' Anand asked, for in addition to the usual rice and lentils, the khichuri had many fresh vegetables in it, and was delicately spiced. The old healer smiled but made no answer. As soon as lunch was over, he sent Nisha and Anand to the forest to gather as much wood as possible. He and Raj-bhanu, he told them, would go to the village and invite everyone to join them for a feast that night. 'For today is the festival of Holi. We have no colours to play with, nor are the villagers in a mood for such jollity. But I think they would all like to eat and warm themselves at the bonfire of Holika.'

Anand did not ask him where they would get so much food. It would arrive from the same place the khichuri came from, he guessed!

By evening Anand and Nisha had gathered a large pile of wood and, with Tara's help, set up a bonfire in the field next to her hut. In a corner, they stacked bundles of twigs, tied with vines, for use during the ceremony. They lit a few torches and stuck them with some effort into the hard earth. Then they set out lines of shal leaves, on which the villagers were to eat, along the ground.

'It is time to bring food for our guests,' Tara said to them. 'Go into my hut and see what you can find there.'

Inside Tara's hut, they discovered four small, covered earthen pots sitting by the firepit, each smelling delicious. Neither Anand nor Nisha was surprised by the appearance of the pots, though they did wonder that there weren't more of them. They carried the pots to the bonfire area, where straggling groups of villagers had already begun arriving. Anand was shocked at their gaunt faces and ragged clothes, the bones that jutted from their emaciated bodies, their dreary, hopeless stares. Among them he saw Ramu and his grandmother. He waved to the boy, who had been so friendly to him before, and called his name, but Ramu scowled and looked away. Worst to behold were the men whose spirits had been stolen. They walked aimlessly behind the others, slack-jawed and vacant eyed. Their hair was matted and their clothes filthy and torn. Often, they wandered off toward the woods and had to be led back to the group.

The villagers looked anxiously at the pots of food – they could all see how small they were. A whispering began. Then a resentful voice cried out that they had known that neither the strangers nor the wise-woman could be trusted. As though that were a signal, the villagers began to shout insults, and many of them stooped to pick up stones. But Abhaydatta stood in front of them unafraid. He greeted them all courteously and asked them to sit, and something in his voice made them drop the stones and obey him. Then, without further delay, he gestured to Anand, Nisha and Raj-bhanu to help him serve the dinner. Tara was already filling earthen cups with water. As she placed a cup in front of each villager, some of them muttered at her, but others were ashamed and looked away.

The children walked behind the two healers, each of them carrying a pot. From his pot, Abhaydatta ladled out steaming rice. Raj-bhanu's pot held fried fish, and when he placed these next to the rice, a sigh of anticipation rose from the crowd. Anand discovered that there was a vegetable curry in his pot, while Nisha's was full of milk-sweets. At first he wasn't sure how much to serve – the pot was not very large, and the villagers were many. But Abhaydatta did not seem worried about running out, so he, too, began to dish out generous portions. The pot, he noticed, always remained halfway full, no matter how much he took out of it.

When the villagers had eaten, an old man – perhaps he was the village headman – spoke in a grudging voice. 'We thank you for feeding us, strangers. It is the first full meal any of us have had in months. But now tell us what you want from us. For no one, we've learned, does anything for another except when he wants something in return.'

'I am sorry that you should think so, elder,' Abhaydatta replied, his crisp, hard voice rising into the night. 'A man of your years should remember better and counsel your people more carefully. Has not your wise-woman, Tara, served you all her life? What has she ever asked for in return? Is she not here, even today, in spite of what you have done to her? It is for the sake of her love that you have all been fed.'

The villagers lowered their eyes, abashed, and the elder was silent.

'I do not wish to chide you,' Abhaydatta said in a kinder voice. 'You have suffered greatly, and often suffering will turn a person bitter and suspicious. But now your sufferings are coming to an end. It is the festival of Holi, a time of good cheer, and that is why we have invited you here tonight. Let us all listen, once more, to the story of Holika. After the tale is told, we will circle the bonfire together and invite good luck back into our lives.'

Tara started then. In her husky voice, she told them the story of Prince Prahlad, who was a great devotee of God although he was born into a family of demons. Furious at his devotion, Prahlad's father, the demon-king, ordered the child to be killed. He was dropped into a pit of poisonous snakes; archers shot at him with their arrows; he was thrown in front of a mad elephant. Nothing could harm him, for his faith was firm and his mind centred on God. Finally, his aunt Holika, the demon-king's sister, formulated a plan.

'Light the greatest bonfire that ever was,' she cried. 'I will hold Prahlad in my lap and sit in it. As you know, I have a special power: no fire can harm me. This way, Prahlad will burn to death, and we will be rid of him.'

'The king did as she asked,' Tara told the villagers, who were listening in spellbound silence. 'But when the fire was lit, with Prahlad and Holika sitting atop the woodpile, God protected Prahlad, and it was Holika that burned to ashes. Soon after that, the demon-king was killed by God, who appeared in the form of a great beast, half lion and half human. Prahlad became the new king and ruled his people peacefully for many years. It is to celebrate his victory over evil that we light the bonfire of Holika each year.'

Now Abhaydatta beckoned the villagers forward, one at a time, and gave them bundles of twigs to carry as they circled the fire, where Tara was leading them in a chant, calling for all good things to come to them. Anand noticed that when a man who had lost his spirit came up to him, the old healer touched him on the chest and spoke softly into his ear. Then the man would draw himself up a little straighter and look around him in surprise, as though he were waking out of a long sleep.

'Do you know what he's saying?' Anand whispered to Raj-bhanu.

'He is reminding them of who they are. He is reaching into them to pull out their true-names, the ones that even they did not know of. Neither Kasim nor the jinn could touch those names. By speaking his true-name in each man's ear, Abhaydatta has begun their healing, though the process will take many days to complete.'

The chant grew louder as the people threw the twigs – which symbolized all their troubles – into the fire. It blazed up in a huge wall. The villagers clapped their hands as they walked, and though their movements were still weak, they seemed lighter than before, as though a burden had been lifted from them. 'Jai Hari, Jai Hari,' they sang. 'Victory to the Great One who removes all our miseries.' Compassion rose in Anand as he watched their worn faces, alight for the first time with hope, and from deep in his heart, he wished them well.

'Come,' said Raj-bhanu, 'we must join them, too, and chant the blessing mantra for them.'

They slipped into the circle. Anand was concerned that he would not know the mantra Raj-bhanu had mentioned. But when Raj-bhanu started singing it softly, he found the words rising inside him, spontaneous as breath.

Sarve bhavantu sukhinah
Sarve santu niramayah

Sarve bhadrani pashyantu
Ma kashchit dukhha bhag bhavet.

May all beings be happy
May all beings be healed
May all behold only what is good
May no one experience sorrow.

Now Abhaydatta's voice took up the blessing, and Tara's. There were other voices, too, singing from far away. Anand could not see them, nor did he know who they were, but he could sense their care surrounding the entire village, holding it as a mother does a child. The conch began to sing as well, its voice like the stars, and as it did, music welled up in Anand. He felt himself melting. For a moment, he had no arms and legs, no separate body. All around him, outside and inside, there was only the music, another word for which was love.

twenty

The Return

When the bonfire grew low, the villagers left, many of them stopping to thank Abhaydatta and bowing to Tara, or touching her feet to show respect.

'Let's eat now!' Abhaydatta told his companions. Pleasantly exhausted, they sat on the porch of the wise-woman's hut to have their dinner. There was just enough food left in each pot to fill their stomachs, and it was delicious! When they were done, Abhaydatta took the pots and dropped them into the bonfire. Anand could hear the earthenware breaking as it fell.

'Why did you do that?' Nisha cried in dismay. 'Those were valuable magic pots! Tara Ma could have used them to feed the villagers again and again!'

'He acted rightly,' the wise-woman said. 'It would not be good for them to become dependent on me. Now that they have been healed and blessed, they must fight the battle of life on their own.'

'But they're so poor — they have nothing with which to start over!' Anand said.

Abhaydatta smiled but said nothing. Just then a small figure darted out from behind a tree.

'Ramu!' Anand cried. 'What are you doing here?'

'I came to apologize,' Ramu said.

'For what?' Anand asked in surprise.

'Earlier in the evening you said hello. But I didn't talk to you because I was angry with you. After you disappeared in the ruins, Kasim was so furious that he ordered us all to follow him to the pit. I ran and hid, but the other men couldn't disobey him. I think he used his mind-power on them. I heard a great explosion a little while after that. I was too afraid to move for a while, but finally I crept to the pit. Kasim had disappeared – just like you had – and the men had become like the others. Their eyes were empty and they couldn't tell me what happened. All I could find was a heap of broken chains at the bottom of the hole, as though a huge animal had burst from them. It was so difficult to bring the men back to the village! They didn't know who they were, or who I was, and they kept wandering off in the wrong direction. It was even harder to face the mothers and wives when we returned – empty-handed, of course, for Kasim had not paid anyone. Then, and later, when the food was all gone, I blamed you for all our troubles. When my grandmother had to sell our buffalo, I cursed you. But tonight I saw how you and your friends helped us, how much you cared for us. I realized that Kasim would have harmed us just as much even if you hadn't been there. Maybe more. It was good he followed you wherever you'd gone. That's why I'm sorry.'

Anand threw an arm around the boy's shoulders. 'Don't apologize, Ramu! I understand. I'm sorry you had so many troubles. I worried about you when I was in – ' He broke off, knowing he could not mention the world of Najib, or his journey through the magic mirror, to the boy. 'I want to thank you for teaching me to climb trees. It came in very handy!' he finished.

'I can teach you many other things,' Ramu said eagerly. 'I'll teach you how to go up the coconut trees – they're the hardest, because their barks are so rough and there's nothing to hold on to. I'll teach your friends too, if they want. We can do it tomorrow morning – '

That sounded like fun, Anand thought. He started to agree, but Abhaydatta stood up.

'Unfortunately, we have to leave tonight,' the healer said. When Ramu's face fell, he patted his shoulder. 'There's something very important we have to do before leaving, and for that I need the help of a brave and clever fellow like you. But it will require you to come into the forest with us and Tara Ma.'

Ramu swallowed nervously and looked as though he was about to refuse. But finally he said, 'I'll come.'

They followed the path that the labourers used to take into the forest. It was overgrown with moss and almost invisible. But tonight there was a full moon, and it shone down on them through the shal trees, enabling them to move without too much difficulty. When they reached the ruins, Abhaydatta steered them away from the building to a large field where the ground dipped like a bowl. It was filled with weeds and shrubs, but Anand recognized it. 'The lake!' he whispered.

Abhaydatta nodded. Briskly, he walked to the far edge of the field and began pulling up weeds. They all helped him – Anand with growing excitement as he realized what they were doing. Soon he could see, embedded into the ground by the passing of centuries, a group of stones set in a certain formation.

'Look well,' Abhaydatta said to Tara Ma and Ramu. 'Under the stones lies a chest from olden times. It is filled with gold coins and' – he sent Anand an amused glance – 'a pearl necklace.'

Anand wasn't really surprised that the healer knew about the necklace.

'The treasure Kasim had been searching for all this time!' Ramu breathed.

Abhaydatta smiled but did not correct him.

'Can the two of you guide the villagers back here tomorrow? Will you remember the way?' he asked. When Ramu and Tara Ma nodded, he warned them, 'It may not be as easy as it seems. Some ancient magic still lingers in the forest – and it might try to trick you. But if you persist, you will succeed. Bring shovels and picks, and baskets to carry the coins. Tara Ma will help them decide how the money can best be used to improve the life of the villagers. I know you will need to buy seeds and fertilizer. Perhaps Ramu – and others like him who were forced to sell their cattle – can buy them back. Maybe you can build a better school, where all children, rich or poor, can study for free. Perhaps you can hire people to train you in new methods of agriculture – '

'Two villages away they're using tractors and machines to pump water from the ground,' Ramu said excitedly, 'so that even when the rains fail, their crops don't die. And they have an air-conditioned storage building, so produce won't rot – '

'I am sure you will make good choices,' Abhaydatta said to them. To Tara Ma he added, 'Keep the necklace carefully. It will bring luck to the village.' He bowed to her. 'Now we must be gone.'

The wise-woman clasped each of their hands in hers. 'I do not have the words to thank you for what you have done,' she said. 'But I know you require no thanks, for you have chosen the path of service, and what you do is its own reward.' To Anand, she whispered, 'I am fortunate to have known you! One day your name will be entered in the Books of Wisdom, though I will not be alive to see it.'

Then she took Ramu's hand, and together they walked back to the village.

᠅

When only the healers were left alone in the field that smelled faintly of fennel and wild mustard, Abhaydatta said, 'Anand, you may now request the conch to take us home.'

'Home!' said Nisha.

'I can't wait!' said Raj-bhanu.

Excitement swept over Anand as he held the conch high and made the request, but he was nervous as well. What if he couldn't hold on to the conch again this time? What if he lost it – and his companions?

Don't worry, the conch said. *I've figured out your limitations! This time I'll hold you. Just put out your palm, and ask the others to touch me.*

Anand explained the conch's instructions and braced himself for the spinning, which began as soon as their hands were touching. But this time it was as though he were encased within a bubble. He was aware of a chaos of movement around him, but it could not touch him. Then once again his eyes closed – in trance or sleep, he wasn't sure which – and when they opened, he found himself, with his companions, on the icy mountainside outside the secret entrance to the Silver Valley. He shivered a little, recalling the last time he was here, exhausted from having battled Surabhanu, afraid that Nisha and Abhaydatta – caught in his animal form – were dying. He remembered the test the elders had set him before they would allow him to enter, a test so difficult that he had almost given up.

But this time it was different. As soon as Abhaydatta struck the flat stone in front of the peaks with his staff, the peak split open with a great rumble. There was the crystal doorway Anand remembered so well! Through it, he could see the road that ribboned its way into the valley, lined with silver trees blooming with the fragrant parijat flowers. Apprentices in their sun-yellow tunics played music, while a white-robed man – Somdatta, the chief healer himself – stepped out onto the snow, embraced Abhaydatta, and, bowing formally to the others, welcomed them back.

⚜

Anand sat balanced on the edge of the chair in Somdatta's simple sitting room, his palms sweating, his mouth dry. The chief healer had him sent a messenger during the feast that had been held to celebrate the return of the conch, saying that he wanted to see him – alone – in his hut as soon as possible. The messenger, a healer Anand did not know, had waited patiently while Anand forced down his dessert. The rice pudding with raisins that was usually his favourite seemed to stick in his throat. He did not even have a chance to tell Nisha where he was going. When he gathered his courage to ask the messenger what the chief healer wanted, the man had given an enigmatic smile.

'He will tell you himself,' he had replied. 'Be patient.' But

Anand didn't need to be patient. He knew exactly why he had been sent for. To be punished.

The entire community had turned out to applaud as Abhaydatta and his companions had walked from the entrance to the Silver Valley to the Hall of the Thousand Pillars. There, Anand had returned the conch to its shrine and joined in the chants of blessing and the songs of joy. In all the commotion of celebration, he had forgotten how many rules he'd broken when he'd left the valley, but they came back to him in full force now as he waited for Somdatta to appear.

First, he had left secretly, and without the chief healer's permission. In fact, if he were to be honest, he had flagrantly disobeyed Somdatta, who had asked him to wait for the council's decision. Second, he had taken Nisha with him – thus causing another apprentice to break the rules – and in the process had endangered her life. Third and most important, he had taken the conch away from its home, away from the Brotherhood, who drew upon its power to do their healing. Who knew how much harm had been done – in the valley and in the world – because of his thoughtless act?

He wondered how he would be punished. He had never seen anyone being punished in the valley the way children were punished in schools in the outer world. No apprentice was made to stand in the corner, balancing books on the palm of his hand, or made to wear a dunce cap, or caned on the backs of his legs. No one was cuffed on the head the way Haru, Anand's employer in Kolkata, used to hit him when he got angry. Even the minor penalties his mother had given him when he irritated her – not speaking to him for a few hours, or making him clean the floor or wash the dishes – seemed out of place in the valley.

But then, he'd never seen the other apprentices do anything that deserved a reprimand.

How was it that they were all so good?

The answer came to him, cold as an icicle forming along his spine.

Because the bad ones like you are sent away.

He couldn't imagine his life away from the valley, separated from Abhaydatta and Nisha – and especially from the conch. No. He *could* imagine it. It would be like the Great Void, that emptiness worse than death. At the thought, he couldn't stop his tears, though the last thing he wanted was to have the chief healer see him cry.

Somdatta chose that moment to enter the room. His deep-set eyes observed Anand, who sat with his face lowered, for a long, silent moment. Then he said, in his usual kind voice, 'What's wrong, Anand?'

'I know you have to send me away.' Anand tried to control his voice, which shook dangerously. 'And you're right. I must be sent away so that no one else ever does the terrible thing I did.'

'And what terrible thing was that?' Somdatta asked mildly.

Anand looked up suspiciously. Was the chief healer playing some kind of cruel game with him? 'I took the conch from you for my own selfish purpose. I caused great trouble to the Brotherhood. I – '

'My boy, the conch can never be taken anywhere unless it wishes to go. This was true even when Surabhanu stole it earlier. At that time, it allowed itself to be taken to teach us a lesson, for the Brotherhood had grown lax and complacent. This time, I suspect, it did it for love – and because, ultimately, your purpose was not a selfish one.'

'But my punishment – ?'

'You've already sentenced yourself, and suffered the consequences in your mind. There is no necessity for me to cause you further pain. I will ask you for a promise, though.'

Anand looked up, still apprehensive. Was the chief healer going to ask him to give up his duties related to the conch?

'Don't disappear like that again, without a single word to any of the healers! When we awoke in the morning to find the conch gone – and the two of you as well – it gave us a bad turn.' Somdatta patted his head. 'See these new gray hairs? You can personally take credit for every single one of them!'

Anand lay down on his pallet in the sleeping hall with a thankful sigh. It had been a long day, swinging him up and down like the Ferris wheels he used to ride at the Paush fairs in Kolkata. How happy he felt to be back, even though he knew he'd have a hard time making up the many lessons he'd missed! He was grateful that his hallmates, though their eyes were filled with curiosity, did not question him about his absence, for he wasn't sure if he was allowed to speak about his adventures. *I must ask Abhaydatta tomorrow*, he thought with a yawn. Meanwhile, he was exhausted, and ready for a good night's sleep.

It was hard, though, for some reason, to get comfortable. He kept turning restlessly from side to side. He felt cold, but then the covers seemed too warm. Why, he'd slept better than this on the bare ground in Najib's world! He missed the conch – he'd grown used to having it in his pocket, to touching it whenever he needed courage or comfort. His pillow felt hard and lumpy, as though it were filled with nuggets of lead. In irritation, he picked it up and shook it, and stared as a pouch fell out from the pillow-cover. With trembling fingers, he opened it. Inside was the strand of pearls that Abhaydatta had given him, the pearls that he had tried so desperately to find.

Where did you come from? he thought in amazement – and some annoyance. *You certainly weren't here earlier, when I was searching for you! I must have looked in my bed twenty times. I even stripped it down, took the cover off the pillow, and checked under the mattress. Did one of the other apprentices hide you as a prank?*

They did not. I chose to absent myself.

Anand stared. The words had appeared in his head, though he certainly had not thought them. Was the strand of pearls communicating with him?

Tentatively he asked, *But why? Why did you make me go through so much trouble?*

You had grown careless. You were supposed to check me every day, were you not?

True, he said, a bit ashamed.

You needed to be shaken up a bit. Besides, had you taken me, all tarnished, to Somdatta, he would have sent a team of senior healers to help Abhaydatta. But I knew the healer wanted you.

He did? Me? But why? I know so little, compared to ...

Humans! the strand said in some exasperation. *Blind as baby mice, that's what you are!* And though Anand asked what it meant, it would say no more.

≈⊙⊙∽

Early next morning Anand went to the Hall of Seeing, hoping to catch Abhaydatta alone. He was lucky. The master healer was busy polishing the walls with a soft cloth, but when Anand handed him the pearls and reported the previous night's conversation, he stopped and let the cloth fall from his hand.

'The pearls spoke to you?'

'Not like the conch does, but yes, the words did appear inside my head.'

'This makes it the third object of power you have communicated with.' Abhaydatta paced up and down the Hall of Seeing as he spoke, stroking his beard. He did not seem his usual calm self. 'Until now I wondered if it might be a coincidence – but not any more!'

Anand stared after the healer, not sure if he had broken some unknown rule. 'Should I not have talked to it?' he asked uncertainly.

'No, no! I am just amazed that you were able to do so. It is most unusual.'

'But surely you must have spoken to the pearls,' Anand said. 'They belong to you, after all.'

Abhaydatta smiled ruefully. 'O, I've spoken to them often – not that objects of power belong to anyone! If anything, it is we who belong to them! I know how to use the pearls, and they've helped me many times. But they've never spoken back to me. Nor did the mirror, though I asked it many silent questions while we were together in the nawab's world. Nor has the conch, though like all the Brotherhood, I am tied to it by the deepest of ties.' He paused and gave Anand an almost wistful look. 'It appears you have a rare and precious talent, one that every healer in the Brotherhood would love to possess.'

❘ 223 ❘

Anand's eyes widened. 'You mean ...?'

Abhaydatta nodded. 'None of us here in the Silver Valley has this gift, nor has it appeared in the last seven generations, though in the Books of Wisdom I have read about wizards of past times who could communicate with any object of power, no matter how far away it was. For the moment you will have to develop this power on your own – it is not something that any of us can help you with. Later we will consult the Silent One ...'

'Who is he?'

'A hermit who lives much higher up in the mountains, and appears only when we need his advice. He will tell us where you must go for further training.'

'Go?' Anand asked in distress. 'You mean I have to go away from the Silver Valley? From Nisha? And from you?'

'Do not trouble yourself – it will not happen right away. There are many skills you need to learn first.' Here the healer allowed himself a smile that deepened the wrinkles at the corners of his eyes. 'From what I've heard from your teachers, some of them might take you quite a while. Go now, and attend to your duties.'

As Anand turned to leave, the healer added, 'And child, remember this: I will always be with you and Nisha, even when I seem to be gone.'

⋘⋙

Though he was hungry, Anand decided to skip breakfast and visit the conch instead. He had so much news to share, and so many questions to ask! More importantly, he longed to hold the conch in his hands. It seemed as though he had not done so in a long while, though he knew that it was only yesterday that he placed it in its shrine. This time – when everyone was gathered in the dining hall – would be his only chance to speak to it or touch it, for otherwise the Crystal Hall was never empty. The conch's magnetic presence drew both apprentices and healers to spend as much time with it as they could. Anand understood their need, but it made him a little jealous.

So! said the conch as Anand approached the shrine. *Found something you thought you'd lost, did you?*

Anand shook his head in amused exasperation. *I came to tell you about that, but it seems like you know already! How is it you always know everything?*

Not quite everything, the conch said modestly. *Just everything that's worth knowing. Like the fact that you've discovered some special abilities.*

Yes! Objects of power seem to – ahem – like me. You'd better watch out – you might face some competition soon!

Oh, really? said the conch. It did not appear unduly perturbed.

Footsteps sounded outside. Breakfast was over. Anand knew he had only a few more minutes of privacy. *May I hold you?* he asked shyly, afraid the conch was going to tease him, but it only said, *You may.*

When he touched the crack that ran along its shell and marred the conch's beauty, Anand couldn't help feeling a deep sense of loss. *Can't you heal yourself?* he asked in anguish. *Maybe we could do it together, you and I ...*

Thank you, the conch said, its voice serious. *I appreciate your care. Repairing the crack is not difficult, now that I am back in my own world. I could do it this instant, if I wished. But it is important that it remain.*

But why? You were so beautiful, so perfect before ...

Sometimes vulnerability inspires love more than perfection does. Seeing my cracked body might make healers understand how every significant victory requires a sacrifice. It might make them fight harder to protect what I stand for, which is at once immensely strong – and immensely fragile. And Anand, what I stand for is more important than me. You, especially, need to learn this.

Anand nodded, but inside his mind he thought, mutinously, that nothing was ever going to be more important to him than the conch. There was something else, though, that he needed to ask. *During the bonfire, when we sang the blessing, everything – everyone – seemed to melt together. It was so beautiful. Did you feel that? What was it?*

That was Life as it really is. I feel it all the time, though few humans ever do. But perhaps you may grow to be one of them.

Anand heard voices at the entrance to the hall. He had only a moment longer. Hastily he put the conch back in its shrine. *Will I really have to go away from the Silver Valley to develop my gift?* he asked. *Do you think Nisha will be allowed to go with me? And what did Abhaydatta mean when he said he'd be with me even when he seemed to be gone?*

Anand thought he felt a wisp of sadness rise from the conch at the last question. But he must have imagined it, for the very next moment it was scolding him roundly. *There you go again – wanting to know everything before its time! Haven't I told you that you must wait and discover these things by yourself? How else …*

I know, I know – how else will I grow! Anand couldn't resist giving the conch an impudent grin. From the corner of his eye, he saw a group of healers entering the hall with their meditation mats. There was time for just one more question.

The mirror of fire and dreaming – it called me wizard. Does that mean I'm going to be a great magician in the future? The kind whose name is written into the Books of Wisdom?

Not if you don't pass your examinations! the conch made its voice stern. *Isn't it today that Ravidatta is going to test the first level apprentices on the Making spells? The last time he gave your class peacock feathers and asked them to turn the feathers into live birds, didn't yours end up as an ant-eater?*

In the distance, a gong rang, calling all apprentices to their lessons. With a last laughing wave at the conch, Anand ran to find his classmates. He was so delighted to be back in the Silver Valley that even the thought of Ravidatta's convoluted Making spells could not dampen his spirits. The blue sky, smiling back at him, was filled with clouds as frothy as the buttermilk he had drunk in Paribanou's room. He could almost read what the clouds said, he was sure he could! They promised him many more adventures as exciting as the one he'd recently had.

Filled with elation, Anand ran and ran, his body so light that he thought he would fly right into that wondrous, waiting future.